A MILLIONAIRE AT SIXTEEN

A MILLIONAIRE AT SIXTEEN

OLIVER OPTIC

TO
MY FRIEND AND CO-LABORER IN OUR VINEYARD
Nathan Bangs Williams
THIS VOLUME IS VERY CORDIALLY INSCRIBED
WITH MY KINDEST REGARDS

Originally published in 1898.

Published by Wildside Press.
Visit us online at wildsidepress.com.

PREFACE

A Millionaire at Sixteen is the second volume of the "All-Over-the-World" series; and while the book may be read independently of the first, it is the continuation of the adventures of Louis Belgrave, who was presented to the reader in the preceding story. Possibly some of my numerous friends may have accused me, after reading the first volume, with being unnecessarily liberal to my hero, in supplying him with "the missing million," even augmented to nearly half as much more, so that he is actually a millionaire and a half; but the present story will assure such critics that even this vast sum was necessary in carrying out the purpose of the writer. But no one need tremble for his moral safety, for he will find that the young man in his moneyed abundance is well guarded by his "guardian-mother," and by his prudent and conservative trustee.

The magnificent steam-yacht, the purchase of which required the figure at which the fortune of the hero was placed, was not obtained for sporting and pleasure uses; for Louis Belgrave has no taste for racing, and is utterly opposed to betting, or anything that can be construed as such. He had acquired a relish for yachting, though he was extremely modest in his desire in regard to the character and cost of his craft. The exigency of the story demanded such a steamer as he was persuaded by his accomplished nautical friend to purchase. This was the only excuse he could find for such a degree of extravagance; but happily his income enables him to stand the expense of sailing such a steamer. He was actuated by the very highest of motives in consenting to buy the yacht, and, in fact, it seemed to him to be his duty to do so. His mother, whom he almost worships, is borne away from him over the ocean, and the steamer seemed to him and his advisers the only means by which he could recover her, and restore her to her friends. With such an object in view, money was hardly to be considered.

The writer still holds to his belief set forth in the preceding volume that exciting incidents do not corrupt or mislead the minds and hearts of young people, and he still keeps his hero above reproach morally; and his magnificent venture is intended to promote his education, to make him a wise and good man. He has no vices, and under the system of his nautical friend, he is not likely to acquire any.

William T. Adams.
Dorchester, Mass., March 5, 1892.

CHAPTER 1
INTRODUCING SIR LOUIS BELGRAVE

"Buy a yacht!" exclaimed Squire Moses Scarburn, a gentleman whose avoirdupois exceeded two hundred pounds, honest weight, as he shook his fat sides with wholesome laughter. "Why not buy an elephant?"

"I am not in want of an elephant just now," replied Louis Belgrave, of whose worldly goods and chattels the stout gentleman was the trustee.

"A yacht is a very expensive plaything, my little joker," added the trustee.

"So is an elephant; besides an elephant is clumsy, and a yacht is not. I can't say that I have the least desire to see the elephant."

"I should as soon have thought of your proposing to buy an elephant as a yacht," continued Squire Scarburn, a shade more seriously.

"An elephant may be a luxury to some people, like the nabobs of India; but my fancy does not lead me in that direction."

"You could put a howdah on his back and ride him all over the State, to the wonder and admiration of great crowds of small boys," said the squire, chuckling as he did habitually, sometimes even when discussing serious subjects.

"I don't care to make any such sensation as the huge beast would produce. He would frighten horses and children, and I might be mulcted in heavy damages, which would not please you any more than it would me," replied the millionaire of sixteen; for such he was, with an income of seventy thousand dollars a year, which was a frightful revenue for a young fellow of his age, to say nothing of a surplus, as the trustee called it, of a hundred thousand or more for any extraordinary expenditure.

His mother was a most excellent woman, rather timid by nature, and made more so by the circumstances which had surrounded her recently. The greatest fear of her present existence was that her beloved son, her only child, would be ruined by his million, though the trustee insisted that there was not the slightest danger of such a calamity.

Though Squire Scarburn held the purse strings, Louis's mother was his legal guardian, and the trustee could refuse to advance money for anything she did not approve. Mrs. Belgrave held the key to the situation; but she was the most indulgent of mothers, and her son had a great influence over her, not only because he was one of the most considerate, devoted, and reasonable young men in the world, but for other reasons which appear in the past history of the family; and practically the young gentleman was his own master.

"Well, Sir Louis Belgrave, an elephant may be expensive in the direction you indicate, and perhaps an elephant is not precisely the beast to carry a young knight-errant about the country. Possibly a mule would be more appropriate and less expensive," continued Squire Scarburn, intensely amused at the picture he was painting at the expense of Louis. "Suppose you buy a mule; and then you will want a donkey for Felix McGavonty, for I conclude you intend to make him your squire."

"Not a bit of it, Uncle Moses," as the two boys mentioned usually called him, for both were his *protégés*; "I want you for my Sancho Panza. Nothing less than a justice of the peace and a man of some weight in the community shall be my squire. Oh, I desire to carry out your brilliant idea in a respectable manner!"

"I certainly have the weight; but don't you think I am a little too stout for an errant squire, though I should do very well for office practice? I weigh over two hundred pounds," replied Uncle Moses, greatly amused at the fancy of his ward; and he enjoyed it none the less because the jest was at his own expense.

"You are not a pound too heavy!" exclaimed Louis. "The fatter you are the more ridiculous the whole thing will be; and I know that is what you are driving at. If you weighed five hundred pounds I should like you all the better for my squire."

"I fear I should not be spry enough for you, Sir Louis, and I must decline the situation in favor of Felix. I shall have no serious objection to the expense of a mule for you and a donkey for Felix. That would not exhaust your income of seventy thousand for this year."

"I don't believe it would, sir. Why, the other day you were making fun of me because you could not see how I was to spend even half of my income! The fact of it is, Uncle Moses, you have invested the million and more too well, five and six per cent; and you are going to make it hard work for me to get away with what is coming to me every twelvemonth."

"The misfortune is, Sir Louis, that you and your mother are not accustomed to this plethora of income, and you have not yet got a fair hold on the seventy thousand a year. You don't exactly know which way to turn to make a big hole in your revenue. But I have no doubt you will improve in good time," chuckled the trustee.

"I have no idea of being whipped out by an income, however large it may be," replied Louis, still in the best of humor, in spite of the heavy burden imposed upon him by Fate and his grandfather of spending his income. "I have projects and schemes in my head, Uncle Moses, that would make you dizzy if I should mention them; and as I wish you to have a level head I will not say anything at all about them yet a while."

"A million dollars, more or less, is a sufficiently large fortune for any American citizen to possess," continued the trustee, smoothing down his fat face for the first time in a full hour, as though he intended to say something more serious.

"I should say that a man with a million ought to escape starvation, if his money is as well invested as you have placed mine," replied Louis.

"No levity, my little joker, for I was about to say something very serious," added the squire.

"Are you about to propose the fat man in the Dime Museum for my squire?"

"I have done with that subject for the present, though I don't know how soon you may compel me to resume it. I am, unhappily for you, Louis, the sole trustee of all your property."

"Unhappily! Why, the fact that you are my trustee is the one thing under the sun that saves me from the necessity of committing suicide by over-eating!" exclaimed the young millionaire. "I might have had some old hunks for a trustee, who wouldn't do a single thing to help me spend my bulky income. In that case I should rather not have any million."

"You keep flying off at a tangent so that I can't ventilate my views in regard to big fortunes," said Uncle Moses, trying to look serious. "I dare say you have forgotten my introduction to this subject."

"No, sir, I have not; you observed that a man with a million was just as well off as a rich man."

"I did not put the remark in just that form; but that is the substance of what I said. Compared with some men in this country, Louis, you are a poor boy with only a million. But you need not starve, and you need not go about the streets in ragged garments, if you are only economical."

"I have already learned to live within my means, and so has my mother; so I think we shall contrive to get along without any absolute suffering. On seventy thousand a year we ought to be fairly comfortable. But I wonder how those poor people who have only twenty or thirty thousand a year contrive to get along. Do they go hungry and out at the elbows?"

"I suppose they do, metaphorically at least. They have to live on their fat as I do."

"They don't all have it to live on."

"They grub along somehow; and you who have enough to keep you out of the almshouse ought to be kind and charitable when you meet a poor fellow with only twenty thousand a year. But we wander. A million is enough for you; and in view of the fact that you are confronting some difficulty in spending even half of your income, my responsibility as trustee is becoming very serious."

"I am sorry for you, my dear trustee, and I am sure I shall make your duties come easier upon you by and by; but I hope this heavy burden will not cause you to lose any of your flesh," laughed Louis.

"I am willing to sacrifice half of my fat in any good cause, such as saving you from the disaster of becoming a double millionaire, or even worse than that. Buy a yacht? Certainly! Purchase half a dozen of them rather than have your fortune increased. That would compel me to make additional investments for you, and I should be overworked," said the good man, puffing as though he were already suffering from his financial exertions.

"I don't want a high-flyer yacht like the Blanche. I have my own ideas of yachting; and I am afraid I shall not be able to do a great deal in getting rid of the income; but I will exert myself in that direction."

"That's right, Sir Louis; do the best you can for me," added Uncle Moses, fanning himself with a newspaper, as though wrestling with the young man's income had unduly heated his corpulent frame.

"I am afraid I am not competent to scatter a very large income; but I will do the best I can. I was not brought up to that occupation."

"I suppose you have your eye on a yacht that will suit you?"

"No, sir; not my eye, but my mind is on one. I was talking with a gentleman at the hotel to-day about yachting, and he did me the honor to say that I had the right ideas on the subject."

"What are your ideas, Sir Louis?"

"I do not desire an expensive yacht; an ordinary schooner that will not cost over five thousand dollars, with not over six men, will satisfy me. I want to go from port to port, and enjoy myself in a quiet way, and take my mother with me."

"That sounds very sensible for a young knight-errant," added the squire.

"You insist upon setting me down as a sort of Don Quixote who wants to be tilting at windmills and wine-sacks all the time; but I don't believe I am that sort of a fellow at all," said Louis seriously.

"I think you are fond of adventures, like the average boy, wherever you find him, if he has any life in him. Now that you have plenty of money you can gratify your tastes, whatever they may prove to be, for heretofore you have had no chance to spread yourself."

"I have had all the excitement I needed, and I have never ceased to enjoy my studies, especially French and German."

"Now, Sir Louis, my boy, I am not an old woman, or a man without any vertebral stiffening. You have always been a good boy; you have faithfully attended to all your duties, and have not been in the least inclined to be a spendthrift. For these reasons I have full confidence in you. But I solemnly warn you, little joker, that if you get to running too fast, if you are in danger of spoiling yourself or letting others spoil you, I shall shut down upon you like an avalanche in money matters, even if I am compelled to invest your unexpended income."

"That's fair, Uncle Moses; but Don Quixote was a cheap sort of knight-errant, and if I imitate him, I am not likely to follow the career of the Prodigal Son."

"I am willing to pay all reasonable bills approved by your mother, who is your legal guardian. What would be reasonable for a young fellow with seventy thousand a year would not be at all reasonable for one with only ten thousand; so that I shall be liberal with you. Though you inherit your grandfather's money, you are to a considerable extent the architect of your own fortune, for you unearthed the missing million."

"I think I understand you perfectly, Uncle Moses."

"I should think you might; but understand, above all things, that I have not the remotest idea of permitting myself in any degree to contribute to your ruin or injury by giving you too much money, though you shall have all you can use in a reasonable manner, your mother and myself to be judges of what is proper. As you are aware, I have over a hundred thousand dollars surplus, which can be used for any extraordinary expenditure needed at the beginning of your career?"

"What could I possibly want with that?" asked Louis rather blankly.

"If you desire to live in a brownstone front on the Fifth Avenue, near your good friend Mr. Woolridge, I should consider that within your means," replied the trustee with a pleasant smile.

"Whew!" exclaimed the young millionaire. "I don't want anything of that sort. It would be putting me into a cage, like a monkey."

"Prefer adventures, Sir Louis," added the squire with one of his jelly-like laughs.

"I shall be satisfied for the present with a cheap yacht, of good size, handsomely fixed up, with my mother's parlor on board of her. I have bigger ideas behind this one, but I will not lift the curtain yet. If you don't want to lecture me any more now, I will go and see Mr. Frinks Fobbington at the hotel; and he is the gentleman who talks yacht with me."

"Nothing more now, Sir Louis," replied Uncle Moses. "But when you get ready to buy the vessel, I shall want my friend Captain Ringgold to see her."

Louis left the office, and soon reached the hotel.

CHAPTER 2
SOMETHING ABOUT THE BELGRAVE FAMILY

Sir Louis Belgrave, as Squire Scarburn insisted upon calling the millionaire hero, had never been dubbed a knight in the nineteenth century, for chivalry is an obsolete institution. He was a very enterprising young man, and he had already done some "big things." There was no king or queen, no legion of honor, no National Academy, to honor him with a title or give him a bit of ribbon, and Uncle Moses had conferred the former upon him.

The title was a mere pleasantry, and did not amount to a "hill of beans" in a republican country. It was rather derisive than otherwise; yet it seemed to please the worthy trustee, and simply expressed his idea that the boy was fond of adventure.

Peter Belgrave was the paternal grandfather of Louis. He had married the daughter of Hans Von Blonk, and through her had come into possession of an immense tract of land, which had been the old Dutchman's farm. This territory became very valuable, and even before the owner of it died it was largely covered with houses, mostly occupied by residents of New York City, and received the name of Von Blonk Park, because Dutch names were fashionable at that time.

Peter was a shrewd man, and sold his land at high prices. Almost in spite of himself he accumulated about two millions of dollars, which he invested. He had only one child, Paul Belgrave, the father of Louis. When the War of the Rebellion broke out, this boy was filled with patriotism, and soon went into the army.

Peter's patriotism did not amount to much, for he believed the war would be the utter ruin of the country, and that the Confederate Army would soon be in New York City. His property was his only solicitude, for he was satisfied in his own mind that the work of confiscation would soon begin in the metropolis. He turned all his large fortune into gold, and stored it for a time in a safe deposit institution. Then he built a brick vault for it under the old-fashioned chimney in the cellar of his ancient mansion. It took him six months to move the money to his house.

His wife had died before the departure of his son, and the old man lived alone in the old house. He had been a mason in his younger days, and he had the skill to build the vault without assistance from any one. While the war was still raging, and his son was far away, Peter dropped dead of apoplexy. He had been entirely secret in all his precautions for the safety of his money, and had no confidant. His secret went down to the grave with him, and there it remained for nearly twenty years.

Paul Belgrave was severely wounded in one of his battles, was sent home and discharged. He was a partial invalid for years, but he married Maud Nashwood, the daughter of his guardian, who was the belle of the county. He continued to live in the ancient mansion, and he never gave up the search for the missing million; but he died without having obtained the slightest clew to the lost treasure.

Mrs. Belgrave was a beautiful woman at thirty-three, and many sought the hand of the fair widow. About two years after the death of her husband there came to the Park a good-looking man by the name of Wade Farrongate. He met the widow in society and church. He was a noted connoisseur in horses, attended all the races, took part in them, and was a marvellous jockey. He trained horses for the course, managed pools, and held the stakes of the betters.

He was a handsome man, and several of the ladies he met would have been glad to join their fortunes to those of the brilliant horseman. But Mr. Farrongate would look at no one but the fair widow; and though she was a member of the church, active in all good works, she could not resist the good-looking horse-trainer. He married her, and all went well with them for a couple of years.

From the beginning Farrongate seemed to take a dislike to Louis Belgrave, though the boy tried to be pleasant, and used every means within his reach, for his mother's sake, to conciliate him; but he would not be conciliated.

Louis overheard a conversation between Farrongate and his mother, and ascertained that the jockey proposed to return to England, where he was born and had lived most of his life, taking his wife and her son with him. At another time he listened to a conference between the horse-trainer and an old citizen of the Park, in which Farrongate manifested a strong desire to learn all the particulars relating to the missing fortune of Peter Belgrave.

Louis was satisfied that Farrongate had married his mother from mercenary motives. Her deceased husband had made a will in which he left all he had, wherever it might be found, to Louis, his only child. He gave to his wife, while she remained his widow, the use of the old house with the half an acre of ground on which it was built, together with a couple of new houses he had erected and rented, and also made her the guardian of their son. In case the boy should die before he became of age, all the property was to go to the wife. Squire Moses Scarburn was appointed executor and trustee under the will.

Louis was treated very roughly by his stepfather, in spite of the youth's efforts to conciliate him. The jockey abused him, resorting at last even to blows. The high-spirited young fellow rebelled. He was entirely satisfied in his own mind that Farrongate was wicked enough to put him out of the way, so that his mother could inherit the property, including the missing million, which hardly any person believed would ever be recovered. Louis was inclined to believe that the jockey had some exclusive information in regard to the lost treasure.

When Louis could no longer endure his lot at home, he made a confidant of Squire Scarburn, telling him all he had overheard in regard to the jockey's plans. Farrongate admitted to his wife that his real name was John Scoble, and that he was a deserter from the British army. He pretended that some strong reasons compelled him to leave the country of his adoption, and return to his native land.

Farrongate had induced his wife to believe that he sincerely wished to live a good and true life. The poor woman was so infatuated with her husband, who had always treated her very kindly, however it was with her son, that she finally consented to go with him, and take Louis with her. But after all he had heard from the lips of his stepfather, her son would not submit to be taken to England, for he was sure that the plan of going was a conspiracy against his health and happiness, if not against his very life.

The boy rebelled, though he said not a word at home. He was not infatuated with the jockey, as his mother was, and was confident that he was concerned in some villainy on this side of the ocean, which made it necessary for him to quit the country. Mrs. Farrongate and her son were to leave the Park by a late train, and go on board of a steamer that sailed at five o'clock in the morning; but their destination was concealed from Louis.

The stepson had reason to believe that the occasion for going abroad was to be created at the races the next day, and he made it his business to ascertain the nature of this excuse. On the day Mrs. Farrongate was to leave her home to take the steamer, Louis had a quarrel with his stepfather, and in defence of himself and his mother actually knocked him down with a cane. Then he fled from the house, and the next day went to the races. At the close of the day Farrongate decamped without warning, taking with him all the money in his hands belonging to the pools or held as stakes.

Louis went to the pier where the steamer lay late in the evening, with a newspaper extra announcing the robbery in his pocket, and found his mother there. With the aid of the extra he was able to prove to her that her husband was a thief and a swindler, and she consented to abandon him, returning to the Park with Louis's friend, Felix McGavonty. The stepson remained in New York to watch the movements of the swindler.

The jockey went on board of the steamer in disguise, carrying a little valise in his hand. Louis contrived to obtain possession of the valise, which was found to contain all the money the jockey had stolen, and all he had obtained in other ways. With the aid of a sporting nabob, reformed by the hero, all the stolen money was returned to its owners.

Farrongate was arrested as a deserter on his arrival in England, and sent to his regiment. For two years Louis and his mother were not disturbed by him; but when the deserter was discharged, he inherited a sum of money from an uncle in India. Purchasing a vessel, he sailed for New York, and is coming up the harbor when he is discovered by the stepson, who is on board of the nabob's yacht, on a pleasure excursion with his mother. Louis is captured by the jockey, but effects his escape. This exciting event is concealed from his mother, who is in constant dread that her husband will return; though she has repudiated him and taken the name of her first husband. Farrongate and his schooner disappear after this event, and Louis and his mother are at peace.

The boy, who had been a firm believer that the missing million would be found, applies himself with energy to the task of finding it. In the end he is successful, and becomes a millionaire at sixteen. Squire Scarburn invested the money for him; and the young man finds himself in the enjoyment of an income of seventy thousand dollars a year, besides a surplus of a hundred thousand dollars, for the million proved to be much more than that sum. A fine house was to be erected on the site of the old one for the young man and his mother.

Mr. Woolridge, the nabob, abandons the race-course in order to save his young son from its influences, and takes to yachting. Louis and his mother were often his guests on board of the Blanche, and in this manner the young millionaire acquires a taste for the sea and sailing. He now desired to have a yacht of his own, though his ideas of yachting were quite peculiar.

CHAPTER 3
INTRODUCING ANOTHER MILLIONAIRE

MR. FRINKS FOBBINGTON WAS not over twenty-five years old, was well dressed in seemly black, and used the English language as though he was liberally educated. The only inconsistency Louis noticed about him was that his hands were hard, rough, and discolored, as though he used them in some manual labor, to which, however, he did not object.

The hotel at Von Blonk Park was a very respectable establishment, usually filled with boarders engaged in business in New York, distant less than half an hour's ride. Mr. Fobbington appeared to be a guest there, and had taken considerable trouble to make the acquaintance of Louis Belgrave; but he seemed to be a stranger, and there was no one to introduce him.

Professor Seveignien was a boarder at the hotel. Louis had taken lessons of him two years, though he had now discontinued them; but he and his instructor were still warm friends, and his pupil occasionally called upon him. While waiting to see him on the piazza one day, Mr. Fobbington spoke to him. He was very polite, and the young millionaire endeavored to make himself agreeable.

Of course they talked about the weather in due form, as an introduction to more inviting topics. Then the stranger thought the Park was a beautiful place, and as Louis was a native of the delightful resort, as few of its present inhabitants were, he was duly appreciative of the compliment; but by this time the resident of the town could not help seeing that the stranger had some object in view, and he began to wonder what he was driving at.

"I sat within hearing of you last evening, Mr. Belgrave, when you were in conversation with Professor Seveignien," said Mr. Fobbington, apparently coming a little nearer to the subject.

"Are you acquainted with the professor, sir?" asked Louis.

"No, sir; not at all, I regret to say, for he is a very attractive person." Mr. Fobbington had inquired about him of the clerk.

"But we were speaking in French," added Louis, looking with interest into the face of the stranger.

"Precisely so," replied Mr. Fobbington, with an expressive smile.

"I always talk French with the professor for the sake of practice."

"It requires a great deal of practice to enable one to speak French fluently," said the stranger, using that language. "I was very much surprised to observe how well you spoke it. You handle it better than I do, though I have lived a year in Paris."

Louis suggested that he had lived there long enough to acquire the art of complimenting. Mr. Fobbington had made a long reach into the good-will of Louis by speaking French to him, for the young man was a very enthusiastic student of the language. Still using it the accomplished gentleman from Louis knew not where, though he thought his companion must be an Englishman, for his English was even better than his French, came still nearer the subject he was clearly trying to introduce.

"You were talking with the professor about yachting," continued Mr. Fobbington. "I was exceedingly pleased with your views on that subject, especially as they fully conform to my own."

"I am happy to meet a gentleman whose views agree with mine."

"More than that, Mr. Belgrave, I have had no little experience in carrying out those views," added the stranger, with a gush of enthusiasm.

"Indeed?"

"I am an Englishman, an Oxford graduate as you would say in America, and it was my good or evil fortune to inherit an estate which yields a large income. Of course I have to look about me to find the means to spend this income," Mr. Fobbington proceeded, laughing heartily at the gigantic witticism he had perpetrated, though Louis thought Uncle Moses had exhausted that fountain. "Well, I had some trouble about it, for I am not a fast man. In fact, I never had any wild oats to sow."

"You are fortunate," added the embryo yachtsman.

"I don't even drink wine or beer; and which way should a poor fellow with ten thousand pounds a year turn to get rid of his income?"

Mr. Fobbington laughed heartily again; but Louis had just come from a banquet of precisely this sort of humor.

"You said you had had some experience in carrying out the views we hold in common," suggested the Park millionaire.

"Exactly so. My friends, when they found I had a taste for the sea, recommended me to purchase a yacht that would cost from ten to twenty thousand pounds. I had been on a yacht cruise to the Mediterranean, and on another to Norway; but I did not like the style of the thing, or rather there was too much style about it," Mr. Fobbington explained.

"That's just the idea—too much style," added Louis, who was beginning to find his new friend a man after his own heart.

"In fact, I thought my two excursions would have been more enjoyable if they had been made in an ordinary sort of vessel. There was too much varnish, too much discipline, and everything was too nice and precise for a free-and-easy time."

"Just my own opinion," said Louis, with growing enthusiasm.

"Badly as I wished to spend my income, I did not desire a yacht like the Daydream, which was the name of my friend's craft. To cut the story short, I bought a nice schooner that had been used for a packet. She was a good vessel, and she was built in America."

"Built in America!" exclaimed Louis, who thought it very strange that an English gentleman should cruise in an American-built vessel; but he was not posted in navigation laws, and he made no objection.

"That is what her papers show," added the stranger. "But I am wearying you with this long story."

"Not at all; I am very much interested in it. You seem to have abandoned your schooner, and come to the United States to see the country."

"Not at all, my dear fellow, for I came over here in her. She is at anchor at a place they call Southfield. But I have changed my plans," continued Mr. Fobbington, looking inquiringly into the face of his companion, as if to ascertain what impression his narrative had made.

"Then you have become tired of yachting in accordance with your views and mine?" Louis inquired.

"Far from it; but I am going around the world, and I find it would take me about three years to do it in the Oxford," replied the British millionaire. "I cannot give so much time to it."

"Then time is more valuable to you than money, is it?"

"Not exactly that, Mr. Belgrave," replied Mr. Fobbington, looking intently at the floor of the piazza as though he were in doubt whether it was advisable to explain his position. "Money is no object to me, as I have already hinted. But I am going to be frank with you, my friend, though you may laugh at me for it."

"If you say anything that is funny I shall be apt to laugh, but not otherwise."

"Whether you laugh or not I shall tell you what is in my mind; for I must say, candidly, that I have a purpose in view," continued the yachtsman, his brow knitting as though he was engaged in doing some very heavy thinking at that moment.

"I certainly do not wish you to reveal your private affairs to me."

"But I shall do so none the less, for I begin to believe that we shall yet be strong friends. My case is like that of a lobster: I have a lady in my head."

"Which is quite as proper in your case as in that of the lobster," replied Louis, refraining from even a smile that might hurt the feelings of his new friend.

"She is the daughter of Sir William Lambold; and Ethel thinks her life of me. I have received a letter from her since I came to America," Mr. Fobbington proceeded, drawing an envelope from his pocket, and pressing it to his lips. "She says she cannot endure the separation for three long years. That is the reason I have changed my plans."

"I should say that was reason enough," added Louis very seriously.

"I see, Mr. Belgrave; you are in love yourself!" exclaimed the owner of the Oxford. "You can understand me."

"I can understand you, though not for the reason you suggest," answered Louis, laughing heartily, and with a blush on his handsome face. "Perhaps you may not believe it, but I am only sixteen years old, though I am rather large for my age."

"I should have said you were twenty, at least; but you might be in love for all that."

"Hardly, at sixteen," said Louis, shaking his head.

"Boys in the States are frightfully precocious; and some of them are married at that age."

"Not one in a million; and I am not inclined to take even the first steps at that age. Then you are going back to England by a steamer, Mr. Fobbington, in order to meet the lady the sooner," suggested Louis.

"Not a bit of it. I should be the laughing-stock of all my friends if I did that, and backed out of my journey around the world. No; I shall get rid of the Oxford, go by rail to San Francisco, and then by steamer to Yokohama. In that way I shall be at home in less than six months, and my friends cannot ridicule me."

The embryo yachtsman thought they might ridicule him; but he began to see that his agreeable companion had an axe to grind, and thought it best to be a little more reserved.

"You will surely save time, though you will not have the pleasure of yachting in strange climes," added Louis indifferently. "I have an idea that I shall go around the world in my yacht when I have one. I would not miss the South Sea Islands in any event."

"It has occurred to me that there would not be much pleasure in yachting it around Cape Horn, or even through the Straits of Magellan. To come to the point, I have been considering whether to burn the Oxford or sink her in deep water."

"It would be a pity to burn or sink her; you could do better than that by giving her away," suggested Louis, laughing at the apparent desperation of the British millionaire.

"Give her away!" exclaimed he, springing to his feet as though the new idea overwhelmed him. "By the great and moist Neptune I never thought of that! Isn't it strange how stupid a fellow can be when he gets into a difficult situation?"

"It seems to me that presenting her to some friend would be a more comfortable way of getting rid of her than sinking or burning her," said Louis, amused, but not greatly impressed by the conduct of his British prototype.

"You are right, my dear friend; and I am under a thousand obligations to you for solving this knotty problem for me. Now, Mr. Belgrave, would you do me just one additional favor, and then be entitled to my everlasting gratitude?" And Fobbington looked at him with an earnestness which seemed to indicate that he was desperately in need of further assistance in getting rid of the Oxford.

"I should be very glad to do anything I can to aid you," replied Louis.

"I knew you would. Then do me the very great favor to accept the Oxford as my free gift!" exclaimed the owner, grasping both of his new friend's hands, and with a pleading expression on his face.

"Excuse me, but I cannot do that," protested Louis. "You may not be aware of it, but I have an income, and I am distressed to find the means to spend it."

"Poor fellow!" But Fobbington evidently believed that Louis had borrowed this idea from him.

"But after I have looked at her, I may be willing to buy the Oxford."

"Then you shall see her at once," added Mr. Fobbington.

CHAPTER 4
THE PARTY THAT WENT TO SOUTHFIELD

MR. FOBBINGTON WOULD STILL be happy to present the Oxford to his new friend; but confronting the difficulty of spending his income, he sympathized with him, and would not insist upon making the vessel an entirely free gift. They would compromise the matter by making it a sale, a merely nominal sale. Louis must not insist upon paying him too large a price for the craft, and the young millionaire promised not to be very hard upon him in this respect.

"Though it is, of course, a matter of no consequence to me, I should like to ask, out of mere curiosity, at what figure you value the Oxford," said Louis, after they had compromised the principal difficulty of the situation.

"She cost me in Scotland, where I bought her, thirty-one hundred pounds, or about fifteen thousand dollars; but, as a matter of mere form, I am going to sell her to you for ten thousand," replied Mr. Fobbington very graciously. "You must really indulge me in taking off five thousand from what she cost me. I think that will be a fair compromise."

"Perhaps we shall be able to agree after I have seen the vessel," replied Louis, not ready to commit himself; and the compromise price was double what he thought of paying for such a craft as would suit him.

"I hope we shall agree, Mr. Belgrave; but I solemnly assure you that I shall not permit you to pay me the sum she cost me. No, sir! Rather than do that, I will take the schooner out to sea and sink or burn her!" protested the owner of the Oxford very warmly.

"Very well, my friend; I will not insist upon your taking more than ten thousand dollars for the vessel," replied the intending yachtsman, beginning to wonder if his companion was as liberal and disinterested as he assumed to be.

"Now, Mr. Belgrave, when will you look at the Oxford? I trust you will make it as soon as possible. I hoped that you would do me the favor to accept the schooner without paying me anything for her; and then I could have taken the train to-night for San Francisco."

"I am very sorry to delay you even a day; but it was quite impossible for me to lose the opportunity to spend five or ten thousand dollars of my income for a craft that would suit me. You know how it is yourself, and you ought to sympathize with me," added Louis, much amused. "I should like to have my mother see the vessel, for she is to be the companion of my voyages."

"Excellent, my young friend! If there is anything in this world that excites my admiration, it is to see a young man attentive to his mother. Mothers don't grow on every tree; in fact, I don't remember any fellow who ever had more than one mother. I like to see a fellow devoted to his mother, and it is a trait in your character, Mr. Belgrave," rattled the owner of the Oxford.

"I think we can go down to Southfield to-morrow; I will call at the hotel, and let you know at what time," added Louis, rising from his seat.

He took his leave of Mr. Fobbington, and returned to the house of Squire Scarburn, where Mrs. Belgrave was staying during the erection of the new house the trustee was building for her and her son. The unfledged yachtsman could not help thinking of his new acquaintance as he walked to the squire's, but he was not willing to accept him as a friend till he knew more about him. He had a vessel to sell which had answered his purpose as a yacht, and perhaps it would be equally satisfactory to the young millionaire.

It was about tea-time, and he found his mother and the trustee in the parlor. During the meal he told them about the gentleman who owned the Oxford, and they asked him a great many questions. Mrs. Belgrave was willing to see the vessel, and would go with him at ten the next day to Southfield.

"It seems rather singular to me, my son, that you should want a yacht, when you were brought up away from the salt water," said Mrs. Belgrave.

"I never should have thought of such a thing, if we had not been out so many times with Mr. Woolridge and his family," replied Louis.

"Especially his family," suggested Uncle Moses, with a twinkle of the eyes.

"Or a certain member of his family," added the lady.

"That's all nonsense, mother!" exclaimed the young gentleman, with a bright blush on his face.

Mr. Woolridge, the nabob who had invited Louis and his mother to sail in his yacht, had a beautiful daughter of fifteen, who had attracted the attention of the young man. After looking at her as he would have regarded a pretty picture, he had innocently spoken of her with considerable enthusiasm, calling her a sylph. This was before he became a "bloated bondholder," and his mother had been afraid he would get into entangling relations with a maiden whose rich and aristocratic father would show him the door, and thus break his heart as well as that of the sylph.

"I think you were very polite and attentive to Miss Blanche," continued Mrs. Belgrave.

"Wasn't I as polite to Mrs. Woolridge?" demanded Louis, repelling the insinuation with energy.

"If you were not, you ought to have been."

"And I was, mother; besides you are not consistent. You have consented to the purchase of a vessel for me, so that I can sail on my own hook rather than be dependent upon Mr. Woolridge. Why should I do that if I preferred the society of Miss Blanche?"

"I think the defence has the argument," added Uncle Moses. "But perhaps Sir Louis will invite the sylph to sail in his yacht. By the way, what is her name?"

"The young lady's, or the yacht's?"

"I should expect they would both have the same name, if it did not take an act of Congress to alter a vessel's name. The young lady can change hers with less difficulty," twinkled the squire.

"The vessel is called the Oxford now, and one Blanche is enough."

"One among ten thousand—the girl, and not the vessel."

"I don't think I shall change the name of either the young lady or the vessel," added Louis.

"We shall see the vessel to-morrow, and we will drop both her and the sylph for the present," interposed Mrs. Belgrave. "Don't you think it strange we hear nothing more from John Scoble?"

She looked at her son as though she expected him to answer the question. She had an intense dread of the man who had been her husband for two years. Louis had met Scoble face to face a few weeks before, had stunned him with the blow of a stick, and escaped from him; but all this had been concealed from his mother to save her from anxiety and terror.

"I have heard nothing of Scoble lately," replied the son, meaning since he escaped from him; and he thought the subject had better be changed. "I hope you will go down to Southfield with us, Uncle Moses, and see the Oxford."

"I should be very glad to go if I could; but I have an engagement," replied the squire. "Take Captain Ringgold with you if he will go. He knows all about vessels, and I know nothing at all."

"I will go over to his house and see him about it after supper."

Nothing more was said about Scoble, to the great relief of the young man. He wondered what had become of the miscreant and his vessel, which he had named the "Maud" after his wife, doubtless to assist in conciliating her, and thus make easy his approach to the missing million. Mr. Woolridge had employed detectives to watch the schooner and her owner; but one night the vessel disappeared, and nothing more had been heard from her. Louis had studied the ship-news for weeks without being any the wiser for it.

The intending yachtsman hastened to the house of Captain Ringgold as soon as he had finished his supper, and found him at home. The worthy shipmaster had retired from the sea at forty with a competency, not much of it acquired, however, in his profession. He promptly consented to go with Louis on his visit to the Oxford, and to assist him with his knowledge and experience. He asked him some questions about the vessel, and turned up his nose literally at the idea of purchasing such a craft as he described.

"You are behind the times, Louis," said he with emphasis. "You don't want an old tub like the one you tell me about. You ought to have a steam-yacht."

"A steam-yacht!" exclaimed Louis, laughing at the idea of such extravagance. "I ought to be a ten-millionaire to be able to do that."

"You could be reasonable in running a steam-yacht as in anything else. If you are going to keep a yacht, have something first-class."

"I don't want a high-flyer, and I am not up to a steam-yacht," replied Louis, unmoved by the argument.

"I know a first-rate chance for you to get the finest steamer that floats, brand-new, and to be sold at a fair price," Captain Ringgold proceeded. "Colonel Singfield had her built in the very best manner for his own use. She had made her trial trip, and that is all, when the colonel died."

"How much would she cost?" asked the embryo yachtsman rather tamely.

"To settle the estate she can be bought, just as she stands, all ready for sea, inside of a hundred thousand dollars, though she cost a good deal more than that."

"Neither my mother nor Uncle Moses would consent to the purchase of a vessel so expensive as that," said Louis, shaking his head.

"If I could afford it I would buy her, for I should like to command just such a craft," added the captain with enthusiasm.

"It is useless for me to think of buying such a vessel. What is her name? I should like to see her; but I am sure she will not be bought for me."

"She has no name yet. Colonel Singfield wished his daughter to find a name, and then they had not agreed upon it when her father died. You could name her to suit yourself, Louis."

"I must not even think of such a thing as a steam-yacht. It would be a very expensive plaything," persisted Louis.

"All right, Louis; I won't say too much about it. I will go with you to-morrow at the time you say," added Captain Ringgold, as the visitor took his leave.

Louis went to the hotel and made the arrangement for the trip with Mr. Fobbington. On his return to the squire's house, he found that Felix McGavonty, who had been a crony of Louis since both of them wore short clothes, also desired to see the Oxford, and Uncle Moses gave his consent.

At the appointed time the party arrived at the station in Southfield, and Mr. Frinks Fobbington was there to receive them. Louis thought he looked very much disconcerted about something, though he could not imagine why he was so.

"I am glad to see you, Louis," said Frinks, as he took the hand of the young nabob, though he did not gush as he had the day before. "But I did not suppose you were going to bring the whole population of the Park with you."

The unexpected number of the party seemed to be the cause of the dissatisfaction on the part of the owner of the Oxford, though Louis could not understand why this should annoy him. He introduced his mother and the others.

"This is Captain Ringgold," said he, in presenting him. "He is an expert in vessels, and I wanted his opinion of the Oxford."

The party took a carriage and proceeded to a wharf.

CHAPTER 5
THE VICTIM OF A CONSPIRACY

"Where is your vessel, Mr. Fobbington?" asked Louis, after the party had alighted from the carriage at the wharf, at which there was not a single craft of any kind.

"There she is," replied the owner of the Oxford, pointing at a schooner, painted white, at a considerable distance from the shore, with her foresail and mainsail flapping and banging in the fresh breeze.

A boat with two oarsmen was waiting at the wharf for the party, and the Parkites embarked immediately. The Oxford was anchored at a short stay in the middle of a landlocked bay, and the water was smooth, so that the lady was not affected by the motion. The visitors went up the accommodation steps to the deck of the vessel. She presented a neat appearance, though there was nothing gaudy or stylish about her, and Louis and Captain Ringgold proceeded to examine her.

When the boat was hoisted up at the stern-davits, the two sailors went forward, and began to trip the anchor. Without any orders from the owner and captain they then hoisted the jib. Before the party were fully aware what was going on, the schooner was under way, and standing out of the bay.

"What are you about, Mr. Fobbington?" demanded Louis, rushing up to the British millionaire at the wheel.

"Oh, it's all right; I wanted you and your friends to see the vessel under way, for you want to know whether she can sail or not," replied Mr. Fobbington, with what seemed to Louis to be a mocking laugh.

"Why, yes, Louis; we want to see her sail," interposed Captain Ringgold. "I should like to know how she works before I give my opinion of her, though perhaps I had better go into the hold and look at her timbers before we get into rough water."

"I am afraid my mother will be sea-sick," suggested Louis.

Fobbington had laid a course which would carry the schooner close-hauled out of the bay, and he called the two sailors, directing them to show the party into the hold. Captain Ringgold and Felix went with them, but just as they had gone down, Mrs. Belgrave called her son. She said she began to feel sick, and she wanted to return to the shore, for the sea outside looked rough and uninviting to her. Before he could join his companions below, the Oxford was passing out of the bay, and the lady was sick in earnest.

Louis conducted her to the cabin. As he reached the foot of the companion-way, he discovered, seated at the table in the middle of the apartment, John Scoble!

The truth flashed upon him instantly that he was the victim of a conspiracy. Frinks Fobbington was a creature of Scoble, and had lured him on board of the vessel.

By this time Mrs. Belgrave was too sick to notice anything; and with her face partially covered with her handkerchief, she had failed to see the only man in the world into whose presence she dreaded to come. Louis saw a stateroom with an open door, into which he conducted his mother, tenderly supporting her on his arm. He assisted her into a berth, and prepared everything in front of it for her use. Then she begged him to leave her by herself, and she should soon be better, for she was never sea-sick more than a few hours.

Louis went out into the cabin, closing the door behind him. Scoble was no longer there, and had evidently determined to keep out of sight for a time. There was another stateroom in the cabin; but the door was open, and Scoble was not in it. He looked all about this part of the vessel without being able to find him. Near the companion-way was the pantry, the door of which was open. He looked in and saw a door in the bulkhead, through which he concluded the real captain of the schooner had retired, and he did not care to search for him. He was likely to show himself soon enough.

Louis Belgrave did not feel at all like a young millionaire when he found himself in the cabin of the vessel he had proposed to purchase, with his repudiated stepfather in command of her. The sight of his tyrant, as he had come to regard him when they lived together in the old house, was a terrible shock to him. He was disgusted in realizing that he had fallen into a trap, and, what was a hundred times worse, that he had dragged his mother into one.

The young man did not apprehend on the part of Scoble any violence to his guardian-mother, as he sometimes called her, and always regarded her. Though he had practically been her guardian in saving her from the conspiracy of her husband, she was not only his legal guardian, but she had been his guardian angel from his birth to the present moment. Whatever he was morally, intellectually, and spiritually, he owed to her; and no human being, not even Blanche Woolridge, could come between her and himself.

As his mother was in no peril, and wished to be alone, Louis went on deck. The accomplished Mr. Fobbington was still at the wheel, and the two sailors were on the forecastle. The cook appeared to be getting dinner in his galley. He walked the whole length of the vessel, looked into the hold or between-decks, as the space seemed to be to him; but he could find nothing of Captain Ringgold and Felix. They had strangely disappeared.

The stylish owner of the Oxford had changed his garments, laying aside his nobby suit of black for one of blue, daubed with grease, tar, and dirt. Louis was able to understand by this time why the hands of the elegant gentleman he had met at the hotel were so little in keeping with his fastidious appearance in every other respect.

Fobbington's face was still that of the gentleman who spoke French so fluently; but that was all there was left of him outwardly. He looked as good-natured as when Louis met him on the piazza, and he approached him, hoping to ascertain what had become of his two companions.

"*Eh bien?*" (well) "Monsieur Fobbington?" said he, approaching the betrothed of the daughter of Sir William Lambold, baronet.

"*Eh bien,*" replied the wheelman. "But, my dear little bantam, you need not trouble yourself to call me Fobbington any longer, for the name is rather too long for every-day use. My name is simply Wilson Frinks, and Fobbington is only a swell name; but there is not the slightest need of using it here."

"Then you change your name as you do your costume," replied Louis, who thought the fellow, whatever he was, had coolness and impudence enough to fit out any scoundrel for such an enterprise as he was likely to undertake.

"Well, it takes a little time to change my dress; but I can change my name in the twinkling of an eye," replied Frinks, as pleasantly as though they were still on the piazza of the hotel. "If you have a pencil and paper in your pocket, you might amuse yourself by figuring up how much time you could save in a month's voyage by saying Frinks instead of Fobbington, for it takes just three times as long to utter the latter as the former."

"No doubt that would be a very interesting calculation; but I am not in the mood just now to cipher it out," answered Louis, looking about him to obtain more information in regard to the situation.

"I hope you are quite contented and happy on board of the Oxford," added Frinks with a smiling face, which appeared to represent his satisfaction at the success of the scheme he had brought to a termination.

"Perfectly happy, my dear fellow; in fact, I am in a state of ecstasy."

"I am very glad to hear you say so. I took you for a magnificent fellow, and I did not believe you would groan or sulk under any possible change of circumstances. I am always happy, and I am especially so at the present time."

"You have good reason to be happy, for I suppose you are on the way to meet Miss Ethel Lambold," suggested Louis, with something like a smile, though it was a very sickly one.

"Well, hardly, my dear Louis," he replied, chuckling again as though he was still enjoying his victory over the young millionaire. "Do you know, my beloved friend, that I am a man who despises a liar?"

"Indeed! Then of what an amount of self-condemnation you must be capable!" exclaimed Louis, looking sharply at the wheelman. "Why, if his satanic majesty should come on board of the Oxford to look for a liar, I should not know where to hide you."

"Because you are not well enough acquainted with the cabin, hold, and steerage of this vessel," replied Frinks, laughing at his companion's remark. "But if you put me out of sight, he would be sure to take you; and perhaps he would if he saw me."

"No, sir; I think he would agree with me that you are the champion liar of this mundane sphere; and he would want you for another, where you would feel more at home in spite of the heat."

"I was about to say that I despised a liar."

"You did say that; and the royal father of lies would have decided to take you as the person he wanted."

"I am not tempted to reply to that charge, for what I said was strictly true. I did not finish what I had to say before you picked me up. In the line of his duty a man must sometimes tell falsehoods; and what I intended to say was that a man or boy who tells an unnecessary lie was to be despised; and it must be left to a person's own conscience to determine whether his lies are necessary or not. The general of an army"—

"I beg to suggest that you are not the general of an army," interposed Louis, still looking about him to increase his knowledge of the situation, and feeling very little interest in the conversation.

"Excuse me, but I am a general, at least in a figurative sense," replied Frinks quickly. "My commander-in-chief sent me on shore to visit Von Blonk Park, and procure the attendance on board of this vessel of Mr. Louis Belgrave and his most respectable mother; and I beg to submit that I have done so. In carrying out my instructions I was under the necessity of uttering what would certainly have been regarded as falsehoods under other circumstances, to say nothing of having to overhear conversations at the fat man's house and elsewhere."

"I think I will not dispute this point any longer," added the young man, weary of the conversation.

"Knowing you to be a reasonable young man, I was sure I could convince you that I was right," answered Frinks, with the air of a victor.

"I will leave the matter to the decision of his satanic majesty when he comes for you; and I am sure he has no more faithful subject than yourself."

"You alluded to Miss Lambold: I am sorry to be obliged to admit, for my own sake, that the lady is an unmitigated myth; and so is her excellent papa, Sir William Lambold; I shall not have the pleasure of presenting you to either of them. I am sorry I cannot; but truth is mighty and must prevail."

"I have no doubt it will prevail; and I shall be sorry to see what becomes of you when that time comes."

"Don't distress yourself in the least on my account, my dear Louis. When you understand my character better you will appreciate it more highly."

"If I don't get ahead any faster than I have so far, I am afraid I shall have a very mean opinion of you," replied Louis, trying to keep up with the raillery of his companion.

"Don't forestall your judgment. In time you will love me as a model of integrity and truthfulness."

"Speed the time when the serpent shall become a new creature. But will you kindly answer a few questions?" continued Louis, who was still burning to know what had become of Captain Ringgold and Felix, without whom he felt that he could do nothing to redeem the situation.

CHAPTER 6
A DISAGREEABLE REVELATION

"CERTAINLY, MY DEAR FELLOW, I will answer your questions if I can do so with propriety," said Mr. Fobbington in reply to Louis.

"Was there any truth in those yarns you reeled off to me on the piazza of the hotel? Probably you could tell me the truths in your story quicker than you could the falsehoods."

"You are quite right so far as time is concerned, though I did tell you some truth; but the proportion to the lies was ridiculously small," answered the helmsman with a laugh. "I am a graduate of one of the colleges of Oxford; I spent a year in Paris; I had a fortune of about one-twentieth of the sum I mentioned, but I spent it all in 'riotous living,' as the Scripture has it; I never had the least difficulty in spending my income, and should not have had if it had been ten times as great."

"I am much obliged to you for this frank statement. Perhaps you will allow me to ask a few more questions on other subjects," continued Louis, who was becoming somewhat accustomed to the situation, and was considering how he should get out of the scrape into which he had so easily tumbled.

"I will permit you to ask any questions you please."

"Where are my friends who went below?" asked Louis very anxiously.

"I did not expect you would bring a crowd with you when you accepted my friendly invitation, and your two masculine friends are in the way. In fact, their presence on board was really embarrassing; and when they went below to examine the timbers of the vessel, I was under the painful necessity of confining them in the hold by putting on the lower hatch," returned the wheelman.

Louis realized that he was actually alone for the present. If Uncle Moses had been on board he would have seen that his *protégé* had an excellent opportunity to practise his calling as a knight-errant; for even in the days of chivalry these worthies had to use their skill, ingenuity, and prowess in getting out of scrapes, as well as in plunging into them. But "Sir Louis" could have conclusively proved that he had not sought this adventure. If he achieved any greatness in the conduct of the affair, it would be "greatness thrust upon him."

If his mother had not been on board at this moment sick in the cabin, without a suspicion that she was in the power of her villanous husband, he would have felt differently, and might have been in the mood for an adventure. The particular Fate that arranges adventures does not always adapt them to the pleasure and convenience of the hero; and it was a gross error in this instance to put Mrs. Belgrave on board of the vessel. It might have been fun to the knight without her; but it was positive misery to have her in the trap with him.

"Then Captain Ringgold and Felix have not been drowned, had their throats cut, or their brains knocked out?" said Louis, when the disappearance of his friends had been explained.

"That is cruel, my dear Louis, and you shock me. I shall not love you if you talk like that," replied Frinks, with an intensely deprecatory expression on his face. "We are men of brains, but not of blood. Do not do me the injustice to suppose I would engage in any affair that called for the shedding of blood, or the shedding of brains, for that matter. We simply make your friends comfortable in another part of the vessel; for their presence on deck might lead you to commit some act that would create unpleasantness on board."

"Precisely so; and I cannot help seeing how kind and considerate you are with me," added Louis, bestowing a sarcastic look upon his excellent friend. "May I venture to ask where this vessel is bound?"

"She is bound to England, though I cannot now inform you just what port she will make, for that will depend upon circumstances."

"What circumstances?"

"The principal one is the pleasure of the captain."

"In other words, your own pleasure."

"Bless you, no, my dear Louis! I am not the captain," protested the wheelman, shaking his head.

"May I ask who is the captain?"

"Captain Wade Farrongate," replied Frinks without hesitation. "Of course you are aware that he is the husband of the lady in the cabin. I assure you, Louis, I am telling you the strict truth; for it would be useless to lie about a matter you understand better than I do."

"Fobbington and Farrongate are horses of the same color, and both of them are myths," said Louis with a palpable sneer.

"Perhaps you can tell me who is the captain of this frisky schooner."

"I can; one John Scoble is the captain of her."

"I don't know him."

"If you don't know your commander, I can introduce you to him so far as his character is concerned, for I know him well. John Scoble was a deserter from the British army, and he is a robber, a swindler, an embezzler. There are warrants out for his arrest in New York and New Jersey at the present moment," said Louis with a good deal of vim.

"That's an excellent character you give him," replied Frinks, shrugging his shoulders.

"My mother and my two friends in the hold would tell you the same story, if you wish to examine them."

"It's none of my affair, and I shall not trouble myself to look into the matter. I only obey orders, and it makes no difference to me what the captain's name is."

"I am not to believe that this schooner is the Oxford, I suppose?" continued the victim.

"Not unless you insist upon it. I took care not to let you see the name on her stern," replied Frinks.

"She is the Maud, I have no doubt."

"You are a Yankee, and you guessed right the first time."

"I have been on board of her before. She has been painted white since I saw her."

"Three coats," laughed the wheelman.

"If John Scoble is the captain, what are you, devoted lover of the truth?"

"I am the mate."

"If you are bound to England, do you intend to take my two male friends with you, Mr. Frinks?" asked Louis, who had learned to "mister" the mate on board of the Blanche.

"I must refer you to the captain for an answer to that question, my dear Louis, for I don't know what will be done with them. We did not expect them, and did not provide for their accommodation beforehand."

"I am very much obliged to you for the information you have given me, Mr. Frinks. So far as I can see, what you have told me gives me no advantage if I should desire to make any change in the present situation," said Louis as he moved away from the wheel.

"If I had supposed it would, I should not have given it you; for I am employed by Captain Farrongate, and it is my duty to be loyal to him," returned the mate. "But, my little lark, must I remind you that you are on the broad Atlantic, where you can't swim ashore? You are caught in the captain's fly-trap, and you can't do a thing to help yourself. As your true and faithful friend, I advise you not to attempt to squeeze milk out of a paving-stone, for it can't be done."

"Certainly it cannot; but the exercise might strengthen the muscles of the hand and arm," replied the victim as he moved forward.

He looked in at the galley as he passed it, rather to measure the size of the cook than to observe his culinary operations. He was not of large stature, and did not look at all formidable, for his expression was mild and meeching. The victim continued his walk forward, where he found the two seamen seated on the forecastle. They were men of medium size, who might be serviceable in an affray, but Louis did not regard them as invincible.

Like a good general, the victim had carefully estimated the force on the other side, and he went to the open hatch to consider the approaches to the prison of his friends. The wind was north-north-east, and the Maud was beating out of the lower bay of New York. As the schooner tacked, all hands on deck were occupied, and Louis found his opportunity to look at the lower hatch, as the mate called it. The main hatch opened into the between-decks, not often found in small crafts. Directly under it was another, with the hatches on, secured by a broad iron bar, bent to fit the curve. Beneath this closed hatch, if the mate had told him the truth, Captain Ringgold and Felix were imprisoned.

Louis examined the iron bar with interest, and discovered that it was held in place by a large padlock. Of course it was locked, and the key was probably in the mate's pocket. If he attempted to release the prisoners, it would take a long time to break the lock, and Frinks would sound the alarm if he should jump down the hatch. He would have at least three men upon him in an instant, and it was not prudent to undertake any movement in this direction.

If the victim had examined the between-decks, he would have found that it was fitted up for second-class passengers, with rude berths on the sides. He wondered if there was any means of getting from the cabin to the steerage, as the place was called, or sometimes the fore cabin. He remembered the door he had seen opening from the pantry, and he had a hope that he might effect an entrance by it.

The motion of the schooner was very uneasy, and the wind seemed to be increasing to a gale. The Maud was carrying all her principal sails, and she was making rough weather of it. The sea broke over her at times, and it must soon be necessary to close the main hatch. But it was time for Louis to inquire into the condition of his mother, and he descended the companion-way to the cabin. He looked about him as he entered, but he saw nothing of Scoble, though he was confident he was close at hand. He entered the stateroom, and found his mother in just the position he had left her.

The son wondered if Scoble had been near her; but he could not answer the question. He bent over the sick lady and listened to her breathing. It was very seldom that she was ill, and at these times her son was her only nurse, so that he was not altogether unskilled in the duties of the sickroom.

"Are we going back to the shore, Louis?" she asked, when she was conscious of his presence.

"How do you feel, mother?" inquired he, without answering her question. "I hope you are better."

"I am a great deal better, my boy; and I should get up if I were not afraid it would make me worse," replied Mrs. Belgrave, raising her head. "Are we going back to Southfield now?"

This was a hard question to answer. He could not tell her a falsehood, and it would be useless to do so if he could, for she would soon find out for herself the painful truth. It was worse than folly to lie to her; he must tell her the actual situation, and he might just as well do it then as a few hours later. The Maud was bound for England; and Scoble had no doubt bought the vessel for the sole purpose of taking her and her son there.

"You don't answer me, Louis. Why are you silent?" she asked, fixing an anxious gaze upon him when he hesitated.

"We are not returning to Southfield, mother, I am sorry to say," replied he, seating himself by her berth, and taking her hand. "You must be very strong and brave, mother, for my news is very disagreeable."

"What is it, Louis?" she demanded with a gasp.

"This vessel is the Maud; John Scoble is in command of her, and we are bound to England."

The poor woman covered her face with her hands and said not a word.

CHAPTER 7
THE CONFERENCE IN THE STATEROOM

LOUIS FELT THAT HE had done no more than his duty in telling his mother that they were in the power and at the mercy of the enemy; and he regarded John Scoble as an enemy in the worst sense of the word. He was not disposed to give way to despondency, though the prospect before him and his mother was anything but assuring. His two male friends were prisoners in the hold, and until he could deliver them he could hardly hope to accomplish anything for the party, of which the circumstances appeared to have made him the leader.

Scoble did not yet show himself; for he seemed to be satisfied that he had won a complete victory in the capture of his wife and her son, and was willing to let them recover from their astonishment before he took a second step. What the next step would be was a trying question to Louis, and he wished to make himself ready, if he could, to meet it. He could hardly believe that the conspirator would take Captain Ringgold and Felix to England with him; and he was anxious to free them before any other disposition was made of them, for he needed their aid.

Louis was not afraid of Scoble; all he really feared was that his mother might grow weak in the battle with the enemy. He felt that he must strengthen her, and if possible increase her power of resistance to the insidious magnetism of her former husband. There could be no better time than while she lay in her berth recovering from the effect of her sea-sickness, and he might not have another opportunity to converse with her. He might be defeated in any enterprise in which he engaged, and then be a prisoner in the hold with his friends from the Park.

"I suppose I am to blame for this misfortune, mother," said Louis, as he bent over her, and spoke in a low tone, fearful that Scoble might be within hearing distance of them.

"I do not think you are to blame, my son, for you could not possibly have known that this Fobbington was an agent of Scoble," replied the poor woman, removing her hands from her face and trying to smile upon her boy to assure him she did not blame him.

"Of course I did not intend to get you into this trouble, and I had no possible reason for supposing that Frinks, for this is his real name, was in the service of Scoble. He heard me talking to the professor, and spoke to me. I had not heard from the jockey for so long that I had almost forgotten he ever existed. Besides, Frinks is a scholar, and I took him for a gentleman, as his manners indicated that he was."

"I do not blame you in the least degree, my dear boy," she added, taking his hand and tenderly pressing it. "We must all have our light afflictions in this world, and this is one of ours; and I trust the Lord will give us strength to bear up under whatever trials are before us."

"That's it precisely, dear mother," said Louis, encouraged by the view of the situation she appeared to be taking. "You must be as firm as the immovable rocks on which the mountain rests, with no change or shadow of turning. It is for your salvation in this world and the next, as well as mine, that you are to battle, and any shrinking may be the ruin of us both. For my sake, as well as for your own, do not yield a hair to this villain, however softly and smoothly he may address you."

"I will not, Louis!" she exclaimed in a louder voice than it was prudent to speak.

In the face of danger he had never seen her so strong and determined, and he felt more hopeful of the situation. It was not the annoyance, not the suffering, that might be in store for them, which troubled the young millionaire; it was the fear that his hitherto nervous and timid parent would yield to the fascinations of Scoble, and renew her matrimonial relations with him.

If his mother would only be firm and resolute in her purpose never again to join her existence to that of the man who had kidnapped them, Louis cared little for anything else. He could defend himself and her from violence if any were attempted; and he was better prepared for such an event than his mother suspected; and certainly his enemies were equally ignorant of his resources in this direction.

Mrs. Belgrave was recovering from her sickness, though it was still prudent for her to remain in her berth; and Louis found her in a vastly better condition, morally and mentally, than he had dared to hope for. He had more to say to her; but he was afraid Scoble might be listening to the conversation, and he went out into the cabin to survey his surroundings. When he felt sure of his mother's strength of mind in her trying situation, he would be ready to do something for the release of his companions.

He looked about the cabin, and examined every one of the dozen berths it contained, and went into the other stateroom; but Scoble was nowhere to be seen. As he was not near his mother he did not care to look for him any farther.

He returned to his mother's room. Though the motion of the vessel became more and more uneasy, the sick lady had ceased to be affected by it.

Louis had been out in the Blanche enough to learn something about the moods of the ocean, and had once been caught in a smart gale; and it seemed to him that the Maud was running into a storm. He had never been sea-sick himself, and he believed he should not be affected in that way, whatever the weather.

"I am afraid we are going to have bad weather, mother; for the vessel pitches and rolls more and more every minute," said Louis, as he seated himself at the side of her berth.

"I don't think I shall be sick any more; after I once get better, I don't have any more trouble," she replied; and Louis was astonished to see how self-possessed and even cheerful she was.

There are many women who are timid and nervous under ordinary circumstances, and given to borrowing trouble, who become firm, patient, and self-commanding in the presence of great trials, who are resolute in the face of danger and in the midst of affliction; and Mrs. Belgrave was demonstrating that she was one of them.

"I hope you will get over it now, for I am afraid you will have other and more serious trials to encounter," added her son. "I am going to be frank and candid with you, my dear mother, in this terrible trial."

"I hope you are always so, my son."

"No, mother, I have not always been so; for you are nervous and timid, and I have tried to save you from all mental suffering. I have not told you that I met Scoble face to face nearly a month ago, and that I struck him down with a club, so that he fell senseless at my feet."

"You meant kindly to me, Louis; but I am not sure that you did the best thing in concealing the truth from me," she replied.

"Mr. Woolridge and Uncle Moses thought I did; but we will not talk about that now. It was the first time we went out in the Blanche. I will tell you the whole story now," said Louis; and he proceeded to do so.

"But is this the same vessel?" asked Mrs. Belgrave. "It does not look like her; that one was black."

"Her captain and owner has evidently taken her to some small place to the southward, and painted her white; but it is the same vessel. Now, mother, the only thing of which I have any decided dread in this adventure is that you will permit Scoble to influence you to the extent of restoring former relations between you. That would be the worst calamity that could happen to both of us."

"You need not have the slightest fear of me, Louis," replied Mrs. Belgrave very earnestly. "I know I have been weak and faltering, and I have given you reason to distrust my firmness; but Heaven will give me strength this time to be true to you and to myself;" and she drew him towards her and kissed him on his brow.

"I am satisfied, mother; and as long as you continue resolute in your present purpose, I shall not care what happens to me."

"But I shall care what happens to you, my son," she interposed. "I hope you will not rashly undertake any wild scheme; I trust you will not try to be a knight-errant."

"We are in a bad scrape, and you surely do not expect me to fold my arms and do nothing, do you, mother?" demanded Louis, with something like indignation in his tones, as nearly like it as it could be in speaking to his mother.

"What can you do, Louis?"

"For one thing I can make an attempt to release Captain Ringgold and Felix from their dungeon in the hold of the schooner. They are my friends, and they are having the worst of it."

"Perhaps Scoble will release them if you ask him to do so."

"I shall not ask him. I know better than to do that," replied Louis decidedly, as he heard a tremendous racket in the cabin, with a voice speaking in a loud tone.

Louis hastened out into the cabin to ascertain the cause of the disturbance. The first person he saw was Frinks, who was standing near the pantry door, pounding with his fist upon the panels near him.

"It is blowing half a gale, and it looks as though we were going to have a tough north-easter," shouted he in a loud tone, as Louis stopped at the stateroom door.

"Did you speak to me, Mr. Frinks? If you did, I beg to suggest that I am not deaf," said the passenger when he saw the mate.

"No; I did not speak to you, for you are nothing but a landlubber," replied the mate, who did not seem to be in as good humor as when he was on deck. "Where is the captain? He is the man I want to see just now, before the blow takes the masts out of the vessel. Where is he?"

"I have no idea where he is, and I can't say that I care. I saw him when I first came into the cabin, but not since."

The mate cared more about the matter, and, crossing to the pantry, he pounded on the door of it loud enough to wake the dead, if any had been within hearing distance.

"Below there! Captain Scoble!" yelled the mate at the top of his lungs.

"In the cabin!" replied a voice, which Louis recognized as that of Captain Scoble; and it appeared to come from the bowels of the vessel, forward of the cabin. "What's the row now?"

"Row enough!" replied Frinks, entering the pantry, and trying the door leading to the steerage, which was fastened. "You had better show yourself on deck, Captain Scoble, if you don't want the masts taken out of the schooner."

The mate stepped back, and the captain emerged from the door inside the pantry. He followed Frinks out into the cabin, and looked as though he was in no better humor than the second in command.

"I ordered you not to come into the cabin till I told you to do so," said the captain, who had the expression on his face with which Louis was most familiar, for he was angry with the mate.

"But you did not order me to take in sail if it came on to blow a hurricane," answered Frinks, as smartly as his superior had spoken.

"I thought you had sense enough to do that without any orders," growled Scoble.

"It can't be done now without all hands, including the captain and cook," added Frinks.

"I have business below, and I can't go on deck at present," said Scoble.

"You will have business below in Davy Jones's locker if you don't attend to the working of the vessel."

"No more jaw! Go on deck and take in the foresail!" continued the captain beginning to be furious.

"That will not prevent the mainmast from being taken out of her, for you know both sticks are half rotten," returned the mate.

Mr. Frinks evidently believed he was quite as good a man as Scoble.

CHAPTER 8
BOUND TO ENGLAND

AT THIS STAGE OF the discussion, Louis happened to step out of the stateroom to which he had retired on the appearance of Scoble, for he did not wish to provoke a quarrel with him at present. But if the vessel was in danger, as the mate intimated, he wanted to know something more of the situation. It would have been better, so far as preserving the peace was concerned, if he had kept out of sight.

"Go on deck, Mr. Frinks, and put a reef in the mainsail!" stormed the captain; and his wrath seemed to be freshly rekindled at the sight of Louis.

"It can't be done without more hands. If you don't care what becomes of your schooner, I am sure I don't," replied Frinks, who did not seem to be a model sailor, for he had not learned the duty of passive obedience.

"Here is a stout boy; take him on deck with you!" said Scoble, concentrating a look of hatred upon Louis. "He shall work his passage. Take him on deck with you! He's of no use below."

"He is a lubber, and good for nothing," answered the mate, glancing at the victim. "I expect every minute to hear the mast snap off; but I shall wait till you get ready to go on deck, Captain Scoble."

"What do you mean by calling me Captain Scoble?" demanded the commander; and it was clear that Frinks had forgotten his instructions in the excitement, and that Scoble had not noticed it till he realized that Louis was present to hear the name.

"I stand corrected, though Farrongate is not your name, all the same," added the mate in sulky tones.

"We will not quarrel, Mr. Frinks," said the captain, doubtless seeing that he was tipping his own fat into the fire. "I will go on deck with you, and we will reef both the fore and the mainsails."

"All right, Captain Farrongate," added Frinks, who had carried his point, and went on deck.

"Come, Louis, you must do your share of the work in handling the vessel, and I shall soon make a sailor of you," said Captain Scoble, in a more pliable tone than he had used to him before.

"No, I thank you, Captain Scoble; I prefer not to be a sailor on board of this schooner," replied Louis firmly, but in a gentle tone.

"At your old tricks, are you?" demanded the captain, scowling maliciously at the passenger.

"I must decline to do anything to assist you and your crew in carrying off my mother," answered the brave young man.

"I don't intend to argue the point with you any more than with the mate," said Scoble, who had been beaten in the discussion with Frinks.

"I have no desire to argue the point, and shall not insist upon doing so," replied Louis, moving away from the stateroom door, for he was afraid his mother would be disturbed.

"I am the master of the vessel, and all on board of her obey my orders," retorted Scoble, following the boy farther aft, as though he intended to enforce his command.

"I have nothing to say," added the passenger, not desiring to irritate his tyrant if he could avoid doing so, though that was an almost hopeless task.

"I have something to say, you young rascal!"

"Say it if you wish; I do not object."

"I ordered you to go on deck."

"I am aware that you did; but I did not go."

"For cool impudence, you beat all the boys I ever knew!" exclaimed Scoble, who seemed to be a little bewildered for the moment.

"Do you think my impudence will compare with yours? You ask me to assist in carrying off my own mother," added Louis, as quietly as though he had been in the squire's parlor.

At that moment the Maud gave a lee lurch, and the passenger could hear the water pouring in over the bulwarks. Captain Scoble did not stay to bandy any more compliments with his opponent, but rushed on deck, though even Louis did not apprehend any serious danger. Mrs. Belgrave was not alarmed; and her son went part way up the steps to see what was the matter. The sea looked more angry than when he had last seen it; but he had been out in a rougher time on board the Blanche.

"Put on the hatches, Stowin!" shouted the captain as soon as he reached the deck and saw that the water was pouring down the hatchway into the steerage. "Why didn't you have the hatches put on before this time, Mr. Frinks?"

Louis did not hear the reply, if there was any, but retreated to the cabin. His mother was not disturbed by any fears, and he answered all her questions.

"It was a lucky sea that made them close the hatches, mother; and now I am going to see if I can find Captain Ringgold and Felix," said Louis, anxious to do something for their release.

"Be very careful, my son, won't you?" pleaded Mrs. Belgrave.

"Certainly, I will; I am always careful."

"Don't provoke Scoble if you can possibly avoid it."

"I have tried not to irritate him, though my blood is boiling every time I set eyes on him. But I have been firm and decided; for he is one of those men who would be ten times worse than they are if you did not keep a stiff upper lip and give them as good as they send. Now keep quiet, mother, and don't be alarmed at anything," said Louis, as he left the room and closed the door behind him.

The Maud had been fitted up as a passenger vessel, and her cabin was spacious enough to accommodate at least twenty persons. There was nothing new to be learned in this part of the schooner, and Louis went into the pantry from which Scoble had come out when the mate made the disturbance in the cabin.

In the pantry he discovered a couple of lanterns hanging on a beam overhead. He took down one of them and lighted it with a match from the tin safe. He expected to explore some dark places in his search for his friends, and he was prepared for the emergency. He thought it must be dark between-decks since the hatches had been put on.

He opened the door leading forwards, for the captain had not locked it when he came out, and stepped into a passageway, which was as dark as Egypt ahead of him. He closed the door through which he had passed, and finding the key in the lock, he turned it. By the light of his lantern he found a door on his left, which he opened. Then he found himself in what he took to be the second cabin. There was a skylight in the deck overhead, and he left his lantern in the passage. The apartment was full of tobacco smoke, and he readily concluded that this was where the captain had passed his time before he came into the cabin. He remained there but a few minutes.

Proceeding towards the forward part of the vessel, he found that his light was a necessity, and it soon enabled him to make out the lower hatchway, which he had seen before from the main deck. His first inquiry was into the strength of the padlock that held the hatch-bar in place. It was large and heavy, and the task of breaking it looked like a formidable job.

He had no tools of any kind; but there was a stove in the second cabin, and he had seen a heavy poker lying by the side of it. It was but the work of a moment to procure this implement. He thrust the small end of it under the hasp, and then applied all his strength to it. Salt water is not good for iron ware, and the fixtures were rusty. A few vigorous twists with the poker drew out the staple that held the hasp, and the lock was removed. The operator made short work with the iron bar; and in less time than it takes to tell about it, he had removed one of the hatches.

At the same moment Captain Ringgold appeared at the opening with Felix, for they had heard the noise made in getting to them. Louis could hear a heavy pounding and rattling on deck, with the voice of Scoble rising above it, and he concluded that the captain was attending to the reefing himself of the mainsail. He was therefore so far aft that he was not likely to hear anything at the main hatch.

"Arrah, Louis, me darlint, is it you?" asked Felix. "What are ye givin' us?"

"I'm giving you your liberty," replied Louis in a low tone. "Don't speak out too loud."

"It's a good thing ye're givin' us. I had nearly broke me bachk in thinkin' they moight have kilt ye, me darlint."

"Not yet, Flix; and I shall not be the first one to drop, if it comes to that," replied Louis cheerfully. "I hope you have not suffered much, Captain Ringgold."

"Suffered? Oh, no, I have not suffered at all; for I found a pile of old bagging, or something of that sort, and I have been asleep most of the time for the want of something better to do," replied the retired shipmaster in a pleasant voice, evidently taking his cue from his companions. "But I should very much like to know what all this means."

"I think you had better come out of the hold before we have any more talk," answered Louis, as he extended his hand to assist the captain.

"Thank you; I don't need any assistance," added the shipmaster, as he mounted to the lower deck by the aid of the notched stanchion which supported the forward deck-beam, Felix following him in the same manner.

"Now come with me, and we shall soon be in a place of safety," said Louis, as he led his friends aft, feeling that their captivity could not last much longer.

"Faix, the darkness is broighter than the loight down here," said Felix, as they groped their way through the gloomy passage; for their leader had put out the lantern, fearful that it might be seen through the skylight in the steerage.

"You shall have more light in a minute; and don't let the darkness dazzle your eyes, Felix," added Louis.

The conductor soon reached the door of the second cabin, which he had decided to make the headquarters of the party for the present. He threw it wide open, and the light from the apartment pervaded the dark gangway. Leading the way into the steerage, he closed the door as soon as his companions had both entered.

"I think we shall be comfortable here for a while," said Louis, as he seated himself on one of the benches under the berths that surrounded the apartment. "Sit down, Captain Ringgold, and make yourself at home if you can."

"Faix, a man that was raised in a bog couldn't ask for onything better nor this," added Felix, as he took a seat by the side of Louis, while the captain was on the other side of him.

"It seems to be getting a little rough out from the shore," said Captain Ringgold, as the Maud made a heavy roll. "If I had known that you intended to take a sail in this craft, I should have told you that it looked as though a north-easter was coming up."

"I had no intention of taking a sail, captain; and I have to confess that I have been made the victim of a trick," added Louis.

"But how much of a trip do your friends intend to make of it?"

"My enemies on deck would express it better; and the word is especially applicable to the captain."

"Who is the captain of the Oxford?"

"The schooner is not the Oxford, but the Maud; and her captain is John Scoble, whom you will better recognize by his assumed name of Wade Farrongate," Louis explained.

"Farrongate!" exclaimed Captain Ringgold. "Then I begin to get an idea why Felix and myself were shut up under the hatches."

"This was a trick to get my mother and myself on board of the Maud. Fobbington is a fraud; and we are bound to England."

This was startling information to Captain Ringgold and Felix.

CHAPTER 9
A DINNER IN THE SECOND CABIN

"BOUND TO ENGLAND, IS it?" exclaimed Felix, jumping up from the bench on which he was seated. "And will we shtop in swate Ireland on the way? That would give me a chance to foind where me grand-dad is buried in the province of Munshter, in the county of Watherford, and the parish of Ballinyfad."

"I don't believe we shall stop on the way, Flix; at least not so far over as Ireland," added Louis. "I am very sorry, Captain Ringgold, that I have got you into such a bad scrape."

"It is no worse for me than for you and your mother. It will stir up my blood a little; for I was getting so lazy and rusty that I needed something to wake me up," replied the captain as cheerfully as though he had a personal interest in the proceedings of the party. "My first idea was that, as you are a millionaire, the banditti had captured us in order to get a big ransom out of you. If I had seen you again I intended to advise you not to pay them a red copper; and I am one to help you hang the whole troop at the fore-yard arm."

"I don't know what is the fore-yard arrum, but that is what I'd loike to have you do, me darlint!" exclaimed Felix with enthusiasm.

"Don't talk so loud, Flix; I don't care to attract the attention of the villains before we are ready to receive them," interposed Louis.

"Whisht, is it?" whispered Felix.

"I am not in the hanging business, and I should rather send Scoble to Sing-Sing for a term of years than suspend him to the fore-yard arm," replied Louis. "There are warrants out for his arrest."

As Captain Ringgold was likely to become an actor in the drama in progress, the leader decided to inform him at once in regard to the history of his mother's marriage to Scoble, and to the subsequent events connected with that union.

It did not take him long to relate enough to enable the captain to understand the present situation fully; and the shipmaster promptly volunteered to do all in his power to enable the party to get out of the hole into which they had tumbled. In fact, he was enthusiastic enough to become a knight-errant himself in the service of the lady in the cabin; for she was still fair, and popular enough at the Park to enlist all his sympathies.

"The vessel is easier, and they have doubtless put a reef in the foresail and mainsail," said Captain Ringgold, after the history of the Belgrave family had been fully considered. "I suppose it is about time to expect a visit from the captain of this craft, and it is rather important to agree upon the ceremonies with which he is to be received."

"'Pon me wurrud I don't believe in any ceremonies at all, at all," said Felix, "unless we eshcort him to the fore-yard arrum to the music of a brickbat in a tin pan, and h'ist him up while we all whistle 'Pop goes the weasel!'"

"Be quiet and reasonable, Flix; this is not just the time to make fun," added Louis. "I think you will be comfortable here if I leave you for a time, Captain Ringgold; for my mother is in a stateroom in the cabin, and I must look out for her."

"Will I go wid ye's, Louis, darlint?" asked Felix, rising from the bench.

"No, you will not go with me, Flix."

"Perhaps Oi'd betther go wid ye's," replied the Milesian, as he put his hand in his right hip-pocket.

"No; you don't need that now."

But Felix drew from the pocket a revolver of medium size, and held it up before his companions.

"Put it away, Flix!" said Louis sharply. "You have no use for that now, and you are not to show it except in an emergency, such as I explained to you."

"I just wanted to look at the pretty toy," replied Felix, as he returned the weapon to his pocket. "It does me hairt good to luk at it, and it gives me a whole tub full of stringth and confidence in meself. I advoise ye's to luk at the one in your pocket, darlint, for it'll be loike puttin' an exthra man inside your coat wid ye's."

"I know that I have it, and that is enough for me. If my mother thought I was likely to shoot a human being, even her worst and only enemy in the world, I believe she would jump overboard; and I don't know but I should do so myself if I thought I should do such a thing," continued Louis.

"What call have ye's to a revolver if ye's wouldn't shoot such a blackguard as Shcoble?"

"Perhaps I would shoot him if my mother's safety required it."

"Faix, ye's have a bone in your bachk, and ye'll do it."

Louis left the second cabin and entered the first through the pantry. He had about him the means of defending himself in case of an emergency. His arsenal consisted of a revolver in one hip-pocket and a box of cartridges in the other. But he had no murderous thoughts in his head or in his heart. His idea of an emergency was that last extremity when he might have to use the weapon to save his mother's or his own life.

He believed that Scoble was a coward at heart, as all villains and bullies are apt to be; and he expected to use the "pretty toy," if at all, as a means of intimidation, rather than for the purpose of killing or maiming any person, even the great enemy of the Belgraves.

Governed by these reflections, he had purchased two revolvers of moderate size, but of the best quality the expert keeper of the shooting gallery could recommend to him. Scoble had already appeared on the stage, and Louis was likely to be obliged to confront him even when he was totally unprepared for an encounter with a man trained to arms, and of large experience in the ways of the world.

As Felix was his constant companion, he had given him one of the weapons. He informed Uncle Moses what he had done, and added that both of them were practising with the toys in a gallery in New York. The worthy lawyer looked serious, and even troubled; but he made no objection, though he read the boys a long lecture on the danger of carrying concealed weapons.

Louis was as conservative in his views on this subject as the squire, and he did his best to elevate the sentiments of Felix to the same high standard. After what had occurred, it could not be denied that the young millionaire was in peril at all times while Scoble was known to be on this side of the Atlantic; and he carried his weapon everywhere he went, and slept with it within reach of his hand. As a further precaution both of the boys had taken lessons in fencing and the art of self-defence, though neither of them took the least interest in prize-fights, or even amateur boxing.

When he entered the cabin where his mother was, Louis found no one to dispute his passage. The captain of the Maud was probably on deck listening to the report of the mate on his operations. The vessel was going along comparatively easily, though she still had a considerable pitch and roll, and it was evident that the storm Captain Ringgold had predicted was coming down upon the Maud. As nearly as Louis could make it out, the vessel was somewhere to the southward of Long Island, and not far from the shore.

Mrs. Belgrave declared that she needed nothing; and preferring to be alone, she begged Louis to leave her: she thought she could sleep; and he complied with her request. He went back to the second cabin, and told his companions that nothing could be done at present, as his mother was still sick. He was sorry to prolong their imprisonment; but Mrs. Belgrave was not yet in condition to bear the excitement of any movement.

"Don't disturb yourself in the least degree, Louis," replied Captain Ringgold. "Let this cruise continue for a week or a month. I have nothing in the world to do at the Park, and I was thinking of taking a trip to the South, for the sake of something to occupy my mind; but this excursion will answer my purpose just as well."

"Me, too!" exclaimed Felix. "The only thing that's bodthering me is whether or not we'll get ony dinner."

"I was thinking of that myself," added the captain. "An excursion without anything to eat is not wholly to my mind."

"I think I can settle that question very soon," replied Louis, as he returned to the pantry, where he had seen a whole boiled ham and other eatables on the shelf.

He placed the ham on a tray, with bread, butter, pickles, and an apple pie, and carried it to the second cabin. He put the eatables on the table, and then arranged them in proper order, bringing knives and forks from the pantry. Though he had not thought of dinner before, the sight of the food stimulated his appetite, and he ate a hearty meal with his companions. With the help of Felix, everything not consumed was restored to the pantry.

Louis returned to the first cabin, and listened at the door of his mother's room. He could hear nothing, and he did not disturb her. He seated himself and began to consider a plan he had thought of to redeem his party from their imprisonment. While he was thinking of this subject, a man came down from the deck and began to set the table for dinner. He put on the cloth, arranged the dishes, and then brought out the remains of the ham.

"I wonder who has been cutting into this 'am," said the man, who was the cook. "I boiled it this morning, and took it out of the pot since breakfast, which it was only three hours ago, and no one hadn't any occasion to touch it. These dishes are all dirty, which it was me that washed them all this morning. I don't understand it at all."

Louis understood it all, but he said nothing.

"All the pickles is gone that I took out, and more than half the butter has been gobbled up, as the Yankees say. Have you taken a lunch, sir?" asked the cook, turning to the involuntary passenger, "or was it the sick lady that ate up 'alf this 'am?"

"It was not the sick lady," replied Louis.

"Then maybe it was yourself, sir?" interrogated the puzzled cook, who appeared to be also the steward.

"I did not eat half the ham; but with my two friends, we helped ourselves to what we wanted of it," answered Louis, as coolly as though he had owned and commanded the vessel. "I am very much obliged to you for putting it where you did, and here is a five-dollar gold piece to help you out in white silk handkerchiefs, or any such things as you may need."

"Thank you, sir, which it is very 'andsome of you; and if you and your friends want anything more in my line, which it is cook and steward, I shall be very pleased to serve you."

"Thanks, cook and steward," added the passenger. "Do you happen to know which is the captain's stateroom?"

"Of course I know, which it is the room where the lady is," replied Bickling; "which it was his name."

"Is that ham all you have for dinner, cook?" inquired Louis, in order to change the subject.

"Which it is all I have; but I did not know that all your party were to lunch off it first. For a gentleman as treats me so 'andsomely, I will cook a beefsteak, or some 'am and heggs."

"I have already dined, and I don't wish for anything more."

Louis thought he heard his mother moving in her room, and he softly opened the door. She was sitting up in her berth, and wanted to know if it were possible to obtain a cup of tea. He assured her she should have it, and asked the cook for it. He had made his peace with Bickling, who hastened to the galley to make it. He returned to the room and seated himself in front of the berth.

CHAPTER 10
A SKIRMISH WITH LIGHT WORDS

"This is Captain Scoble's stateroom, mother," said Louis, as he seated himself.

"Then I must move," she added.

"No, you shall not move, mother; there is another room in the cabin, and he may sleep there, for I will not permit you to be turned out of this one," replied Louis, as he began to make a careful survey of his surroundings.

"You talk as though you were the captain, my son. Do not quarrel with Scoble if you can help it," she pleaded.

"I will not; but I shall not submit, or bow my head to him."

Louis had not asked for the captain's room without a purpose, which he was now carrying out. Under the berth he saw a trunk; he drew it out and opened it. He found nothing but a thin package of letters which he cared to possess, and he slid it into his pocket.

"What are you doing, Louis?" asked Mrs. Belgrave, whose attention had been attracted to his operations.

"Preparing for the future, mother; nothing more. But don't ask me any questions. Scoble must soon come down into the cabin, and I wish to be prepared for him."

She said nothing more, though she watched him closely till they were disturbed by a knock at the door. It was Bickling with the tea, which Louis handed to his mother, and closed the door. While she was drinking the contents of the cup, her son busied himself in ransacking a case of drawers in front of the berth. In one of them he found two revolvers of twice the size of the one he carried, and two boxes of cartridges. He took possession of these, and closed the drawer from which he had taken them.

"Do you think it is right for you to look into the drawers of other people, Louis?" asked Mrs. Belgrave, as she finished drinking her tea.

"Here is what I found in one of them, mother; do you think I had better put them back?" he replied, showing her the pistols and the ammunition. "Shall I leave them for Scoble to use when he wants to get nearer to the missing million? as probably he still regards it; for I am confident Frinks brought him no report of the finding of it."

"No; throw them overboard!" exclaimed she, as she sank back in the berth.

"I will not throw them overboard; but I must leave you."

The cook had left the cabin; and he carried the revolvers to Captain Ring-gold, giving him no explanation in regard to them. When he returned to the first cabin, Captain Scoble was just coming down the stairs. He looked better-natured than when the passenger had last seen him, possibly because he did not find himself in the presence of a rebellious subject.

"How is your mother, Louis?" asked Captain Scoble, halting at the foot of the steps, and looking the young man full in the face, as though he had nothing to blush for.

"She is better," replied the passenger, gently enough; for he had resolved to be as firm as a rock, even while he was conciliatory. "She would have left her berth, but the vessel began to roll worse than ever, and she had to remain where she was."

"The Maud rolled worse while we were reefing, for we had to throw her up into the wind," added the captain; and the listener thought he had never seen him in a pleasanter frame of mind; and he was sure he must have given himself a severe course of training before he came below.

"I noticed that she rolled very badly at one time."

"My stupid mate ought to have reefed her before," said Scoble. "He is not much of a sailor when called upon to act on his own responsibility, though he does very well under the direction of one who knows his business."

"I supposed Mr. Fobbington was a very skilful seaman," replied Louis.

"Who?" demanded the captain, looking as though he had never heard the name before.

"I beg your pardon: I mean Mr. Frinks, who, in a fit of pleasantry, assumed the name of 'Fobbington,' just as, on a former occasion, you took the name of Farrongate," answered the passenger with a chuckle.

Scoble frowned so that his brow was covered with wrinkles at the allusion to the name under which he had married Mrs. Belgrave, and conducted all his operations as a jockey and pool manager. But he evidently realized that he could not make anything by assuming a stormy attitude with his present customer, and the wrinkles were suddenly banished from his brow.

"Mr. Frinks is not much of a sailor," repeated the captain, choking down the passion that began to boil up.

"Not much of a sailor!" exclaimed Louis, who was playing a part as really as the commander of the Maud. "Why, he speaks French like a native."

"I know he does, for I have talked with him in that language myself; but we Englishmen don't go to France to look for our sailors," replied Scoble, with a fine show of self-sufficiency, for his knowledge of French consisted of half a dozen phrases he had picked up.

"I thought he had learned his French so thoroughly that he must have made himself equally proficient in his seamanship."

"Not at all. Frinks is the son of a merchant who spent a good deal of money on his education. He died about three years ago, leaving his son about ten thousand pounds. Frinks bought a yacht, and learned something about a vessel. He ran through his money in two years, and has been a sort of vagabond ever since. I took pity on him and made him mate of the Maud."

"He knows how to play the gentleman whether he is competent to play the *rôle* of mate or not," added Louis. "He managed the little comedy you laid out for him at the Park, as the presence of my mother and myself on board of the Maud abundantly proves."

"He did very well so far; but he failed totally to obtain the information I wanted. In fact, he could tell me nothing, though he hung round the office of that old lobster, Squire Scarburn, and heard some conversations that were of no consequence whatever to me. He knew nothing about you except that you wanted to buy a vessel."

"Possibly I may be able to give you the information you desire, Captain Scoble," suggested Louis.

"Why do you call me Captain Scoble?" demanded the commander of the Maud, with a gathering frown on his brow. "You have always been accustomed to call me Mr. Farrongate, and I desire still to be called by that name."

"I am sorry that I cannot accommodate you, Captain Scoble."

"What is the reason you cannot?" demanded the captain, subduing a rising flash of anger.

"I suppose you have heard of the German who explained why he called his son Hans, for it is a very antiquated chestnut."

"I can't say that I ever heard the German's reason."

"Der reason vot ve call our boy Hans is dot's his name. I can only plead the same excuse."

At this moment the cook appeared at the door with a dish of potatoes and a pot of coffee, announcing that dinner was ready.

"If you will excuse me, Captain Scoble, I will look into the stateroom and see how mother is getting along," said the passenger, moving to the door.

"Ask her to come out and have some dinner. I will order anything she likes," added the captain.

"I will deliver your message," answered Louis, as he went into the room without making any noise.

He crept gently to her berth, and found that she was asleep. As her slumber was doubtless doing her more good than a dinner would, even if she were disposed to eat it, he did not disturb her, withdrawing from the room as silently as he had entered. He reported the result of his visit to the captain.

"She will be better if she can sleep," replied Scoble. "The best thing in the world for her would be to get up and go on deck if she feels able to do so."

"She is not ready for that yet, Captain Scoble."

"Scoble again!" exclaimed the master; and the passenger understood why he was so anxious to resume his former name, for he desired above all things in the world to effect a reconciliation with Mrs. Belgrave. "May I ask you as a favor, Louis, to call me Captain Farrongate?"

"I am sorry it is not in my power in this matter to oblige you," replied the young man with courtly dignity. "Excuse me, but your mate called you by your right name, and you did not notice the fact till he had addressed you so half a dozen times; all of which goes to show that you have been called by your proper name on your voyage to this country."

"You were always a bit of a lawyer, Louis, my son," said Scoble, laughing, evidently because he could see no way out of the dilemma. "We won't jaw any more about it just now, though it will be necessary for me to pick up the point again at another time. Dinner is ready, my boy; sit down and make yourself entirely at home."

"I thank you, Captain Scoble; I am sorry that I cannot join you. I have already lunched, and that will pass for dinner to-day," replied Louis, still retaining his admirable self-possession.

"If you have lunched, you must have done so very early, and it is time for you to eat again. Sit down and take a slice of ham, which is better than most of the ham you get in America."

"I can most cheerfully testify that this particular one is an excellent ham, for I made a very hearty lunch off of it. By the way, Captain Scoble, where do you buy your hams?" asked Louis in an every-day, matter-of-fact tone and manner.

"This is a Scotch ham, and I bought a large supply of them in Southampton. The shop is just above the arch in the old court building; you can easily find it, and buy a stock for yourself. I can assure you there are no better hams in the world, though the French hams are very good," said Scoble, trying to keep even with his involuntary guest.

"Thank you, Captain Scoble. I judge that the Maud is bound to Southampton, and I may step into the shop you mention and buy a supply of hams. It will at least enable me to save my bacon out of this scrape."

"Oh, yes; you can get as good bacon as hams at that place," laughed Scoble. "I am very glad to learn that you made yourself at home on board of my vessel, and helped yourself when you were hungry, just as you did in the old house. But you had better sit down and take a cup of coffee, if nothing more; for I can say that Bickling makes almost as good coffee as your mother did when we all lived together."

"Thank you, Captain Scoble; I will accept your invitation to that extent," replied Louis, as he seated himself opposite the master. "We did not have any coffee at our lunch, and I have found that it goes very well at sea."

"I suppose when you use the plural number that you include your mother. Was she able to join you?"

"I did not mention the lunch to her, though I sent for a cup of tea for her."

"That was right, my boy; I am glad you made yourself at home."

It was really a combat between Scoble and Louis to see which should display the greater good humor, though the captain had to struggle at times to keep his temper in subjection. The time had come for the jockey to begin upon the great undertaking that had brought him to the United States in face of the danger of being arrested and sent to Sing-Sing as an embezzler. Doubtless he believed he could win back his wife if he could keep her away from her son.

CHAPTER 11
A BATTLE IN POLITENESS

LOUIS BELGRAVE WAS STILL seated at the table with Captain Scoble, and the skirmish of words was likely to become a pitched battle.

"You spoke just now as though you had been at sea some time in your life, my boy. It must have been since I left the Park," continued the master of the Maud.

"I have not been on any long cruises, but I have made several trips in the Blanche; and once I went around Long Island," replied Louis.

"The Blanche! I don't think I ever saw her."

"Oh, yes, you have! You remember the day the Maud went to the bottom in New York Bay. She came about just astern of you. You had discovered, with the aid of your spy-glass, that mother and I were on her deck, and you changed your course suddenly. That was the reason why the tug-boat ran into you and stove a hole under the counter of the schooner."

"Oh! That was the way it happened, was it? I did not know how it was before, and I am glad to be informed," replied Scoble, laughing as though it were a capital joke. "I was afraid of you, and I tried to run away?"

"Not exactly afraid of mother and me, but of the warrants in the pockets of Mr. Woolridge and Uncle Moses," added Louis very quietly, as though he did not understand that his remark had a terrible sting in it.

"What Woolridge was that?" asked Scoble, choking down his wrath, for he was bound to keep the peace for the present.

"He is the gentleman who had thirty-five thousand dollars in the little new valise you carried on board of the steamer two years since. It was long ago, and perhaps you have forgotten the circumstance. It was he also who sent a cablegram to London that a certain deserter would arrive at Liverpool in a certain steamer."

The commander of the Maud winced, bit his lips, and twisted about on his stool, but he still maintained his self-possession.

"I think you said you were bound to Southampton, Captain Scoble?" continued Louis.

"Undoubtedly; you shall have the chance to buy your hams."

"I suppose there is an office there from which I can send a cable message to Uncle Moses. I shall be out of funds when I get there, and I shall have to cable him to send me twenty thousand dollars, or so," said the passenger very glibly.

"You speak of twenty thousand dollars as though you had no great respect for such a large sum," chuckled the captain, who was not in possession of the news from the Park for the last two months, and perhaps not for the last two years.

"A mere bagatelle," said Louis, with supreme indifference.

"That is very juicy talk for a young fellow like you, Louis, with an income on which a country curate might starve," returned Scoble, who could make nothing of the magnificent talk of his passenger.

"Oh, Uncle Moses would send me fifty thousand, knowing that mother is with me. Yes; he would send me a hundred thousand if my mother joined me in the request, for she is my legal guardian, you know," continued Louis, who thought from the looks of his companion at the table that the shots he was pouring into him were rather warm, if not red-hot.

"Nonsense, Louis! You are blowing, swelling, and gassing. But you can't make me tipsy on tepid water. That old lobster couldn't raise twenty thousand dollars to save his mustard-seed soul from a single day's perdition. Have another cup of coffee, my boy: it will warm you up and help you to speak the truth."

"No, I thank you, captain. This coffee is not tepid water, and it might make me tipsy; and, judging from its effect upon you, who take it as a steady diet, I don't believe it would help me to tell the truth."

"Very good, Louis! You were always rather smart," replied Scoble, as he moved back from the table, having finished his dinner.

"Thank you for your generous compliment, and especially for the sincerity with which it is bestowed."

"Do you smoke, my boy?" asked Scoble, taking a cigar from his pocket.

"No, sir; I do not, and I never tried to do so."

"Then you are worse than a hot potato."

"And you are no better than a hot potato because you do smoke, for the smoke don't make the potato any hotter. But if you have a good cigar, I should like it for a friend, who has unfortunately acquired the vicious habit," said Louis, extending his hand to take the fragrant roll. "I did not find any cigars in the pantry where I discovered the Scotch ham, or I should have taken one for my friend."

"Who is your friend, Louis? Do you intend to keep that cigar till you get back to America?" asked the captain, as he held out his case to the passenger, who took a cigar from it. "I am afraid it will be all dried up by that time."

"Not at all; my friend will doubtless smoke it this afternoon."

"But who is your friend?" persisted Scoble.

"Captain Ringgold is the one for whom I desire the cigar, for my chummy, Felix McGavonty, does not smoke any more than I do," replied Louis in a matter-of-fact manner.

"Oh, yes! I see; Ringgold and Felix. But I beg leave to remind you that both of them are confined in the hold of the vessel; for I suppose you have found that out before this time."

"I learned the fact very soon after I came on board myself from Mr. Frinks; but they are no longer in the hold of the Maud. I think you owe me an apology, Captain Scoble, since we are getting to be so everlastingly polite."

"An apology! And for what can I possibly owe you an apology, my boy?" demanded the master, looking at his victim very earnestly.

"For doing me a serious injustice, captain. Do you take me for a young man with no bowels of compassion, no stomach for the duty of a Christian, no liver, heart, lungs, backbone, or gizzard to feel for the misfortunes of others?"

"Well, well! What has broke loose now?" queried the captain.

"My sense of justice, right, and duty broke loose pretty soon after I came on board of this craft. You have done me the injustice to believe that I had forgotten my friends, and left them to languish in the dark, damp, and gloomy hold of this vessel. You wronged me; for I have taken second-class passage for them, and dined them very nearly as well as you have dined yourself, though they had none of that excellent coffee."

"What do you mean by all this tirade of nonsense?" demanded Scoble, the wrinkles beginning to gather on his forehead again.

"Isn't my explanation plain enough? If it isn't, I will take the liberty to add that, as politeness is the order of the day,—and it was very impolite to keep a dignified gentleman like Captain Ringgold, or even my less dignified chummy Felix, in such a gloomy hole as the hold of this vessel,—I assumed the responsibility of letting them out. You were busy reefing the sails, and it was not convenient to consult you as the commander of the schooner."

"Do you mean to say that you have opened the hold and released Ringgold and that imp of Scarburn's?" cried the captain, shaking with rage.

"Pried off the hatch-bar and let them out, captain. But I thought we were to be polite. As you ask me a question, I feel obliged to answer it whether your courtesy is exhausted or not," replied Louis, unmoved by the increasing wrath of the commander. "As you were engaged at the time, I felt it to be incumbent upon me to do the honors of the vessel. I not only released my friends, but I invited them to occupy the second cabin, where they will doubtless be contented till I can procure accommodations for them in the main cabin."

"Then you intend to invite them into the first cabin, do you?" demanded the captain, with a curling sneer, and a sarcastic smile on his lips; but the passenger made such a long and deliberate speech that he had time to realize that he was ruining his case near his wife.

"It would be more proper, and therefore more courteous, for the highest authority on board of the Maud to extend the invitation, and conduct my friends to the first cabin. If you insist upon doing the honors of the vessel in this respect, I shall certainly step aside in your favor, for you are entitled to perform the ceremonies in person."

"As they are friends of yours, Louis, you shall do the honors; but you must not be impatient, for it may be a month before they come into this cabin," replied Scoble with an oath, which did not sound pretty to the young man, or to his mother, who could not help hearing it.

"Thank you, Captain Scoble, for taking such a pleasant and sensible view of the subject," added the passenger, bowing as politely as a French dancing-master.

At this moment the sick lady opened the door of the stateroom, and came out into the cabin, supporting herself against the partition till her son went to her assistance. She had heard the angry words of Scoble, and could no longer remain in her berth. She bestowed a single glance upon him who had been her husband. It was the first time in two years that they had met face to face.

In spite of the fact that they had been separated so long, Louis was glad to see that his mother manifested no decided emotion. It was evident to him she had so schooled her mind and heart that she had banished him from her affections. He appeared to be no more to her than any other person.

As to any affection on the part of Scoble, Louis did not believe any had ever existed. Though he pretended to be greatly moved by the sight of the lady, her son could understand that it was nothing but a pretence. He had no doubt the jockey had married his mother to get nearer to the lost million which she would leave behind if she became childless.

When Mrs. Belgrave came into the cabin, the captain sprang to his feet as though a whirlwind of emotion had swept through his being. He clasped his hands, and looked unutterably affectionate. He was better fitted for comedy than for tragedy; and his acting produced no impression upon the lady, who did not bestow a second glance upon him. She gave all her attention to her son. Louis supported her, for she was hardly able to stand on account of the uneasy motion of the vessel, and conducted her to a divan near the stern windows of the cabin.

Scoble, still standing by the table with clasped hands, gazed at her earnestly, though his expression was rather that of a sick monkey than of a man worthy of such a woman. He would have given all the cigars in his case if he could have got rid of Louis for a single hour, and something handsomer for a longer time.

Aside from his presence at this inconvenient time, the young millionaire was an enormous nuisance to him, an obstacle, a high wall in his path. The young man had defeated his first and grandest scheme by depriving him both of his wife and his stolen fortune, and had ruined his second when he struck him down in the boat. That he hated Louis is stating the case very mildly. He had looked upon his stepson at first with contempt; but he had learned that he was to be feared, and not despised.

Mr. Frinks came down to dinner, and his presence seemed to freeze all the parties for the time. Scoble left his place near the table, and moved farther aft, nearer to Mrs. Belgrave and her son. Either the mate was not very hungry, or he did not approve the viands set before him, and in a few minutes he had finished his meal. He did not speak a word, but, after looking at the persons in the cabin, he retired.

There was no one else to dine at the cabin table; and Bickling, in his capacity of steward, cleared the table, washing the dishes in the pantry, so that he was out of hearing of those at the after end of the cabin.

CHAPTER 12
THE POSSESSOR OF A MIGHTY SECRET

CAPTAIN SCOBLE ROSE FROM the divan in front of a berth where he had remained while the mate was at his dinner, his face covered with his hands, as though he were in a state of suffering, and walked toward Mrs. Belgrave.

"Maud" said he, pausing with folded arms in front of her after he had uttered her name.

They had been husband and wife for two years, and Louis was not disposed to embarrass them with his presence, especially as he felt that he could trust his mother to fight her own battle as far as their personal relations was concerned. He retired from his position on the divan at his mother's side, and seated himself near the pantry, where he could observe the operations of the steward. He did not intend to leave the cabin even for a moment, and he was ready to interfere whenever the comfort or the safety of his mother required.

Scoble had uttered the first name of Mrs. Belgrave as he had been accustomed to address her in the past. He had done so in the most impressive manner he could command, and the tone seemed to come up from his boots, its lowness perhaps indicating the depth of his feeling. The lady bestowed a single glance upon him, and then fixed her gaze on the carpet, which had been a new one at no remote period, devoting her mind to a study of the figures.

Probably the captain expected a reply from her. If he did he was disappointed. The lady was no actress, and if she had gone on the stage, which was an abomination to her, her face and form would have been her only stock in trade. She said not a word, either with her voice or her eyes.

"Maud, is it thus that we meet after a separation of two years?" continued Scoble, his voice still coming from the vicinity of his boots.

She did not answer him: she did not even look at him.

"You are silent, Maud," he proceeded, even more impressively than before; and in the absence of any evidence to the contrary, his vanity lead him to believe he had made a success of the first scene.

As she made no response, he seated himself at her side. Then he moved up a little nearer to her, as doubtless he had done in earlier days. The lady retreated to the farthest end of the divan. This movement did not please the practised diplomate, and he rose from his seat, taking a standing position in front of her. Louis was near enough to hear what the captain said, and to see what both of them did; and the last action on the part of his mother was particularly satisfactory to him.

"Won't you speak to me, Maud?" asked Scoble in a tone disconsolate enough to come from a graveyard.

"I have nothing to say," she replied, bestowing upon him a glance as blank as any coquette could have given in the practice of her art.

"You have nothing to say to me after a separation of two years, two long years that seemed endless to me?" said the melancholy master of the Maud.

"Nothing at all. I wish the separation had been fifty years longer," replied the lady in a tone that satisfied the son that all was going well at the other end of the cabin.

"O Maud! Can it be you who speak to me in this cruel manner?"

"You can have no doubt that it is I. If you have, I add that I have earnestly hoped I should never see your face again," returned the lady, with vim enough to satisfy the interested listener near the pantry.

"Am I so changed? Is my face odious to you now?" groaned the captain.

"Your face is the same; but you are all face: there is nothing of you but face. There is nothing at all behind it. You are utterly hollow and wicked."

"O Maud! How can you be so cruel! Am I not your husband?"

"No!" she almost shouted, as she sprang from the divan, and stood in front of him, looking him squarely in the eye this time.

"Did I not lead you to the holy altar in your own church? Were we not made one by your own minister?" demanded Scoble, becoming even more impressive as he proceeded.

"Never!" exclaimed Mrs. Belgrave in a loud and firm tone, such as Louis had never heard her use before.

"Have you forgotten the scene in the church?" he asked in a low, solemn tone.

"I have not forgotten it; for it was then that I was cheated, robbed of my name, and led into a trap by a villain!" replied the lady. "The marriage, as you call it, was a fraud, and long ago I ceased to regard it as a marriage. It was a sacrilege, a profanation of the holy temple in which the farce was acted."

"Still, *you* became my wife at that time," added Scoble with a tinge of triumph in his tone.

"I became your victim, not your wife!"

"We lived together as man and wife for over two years," suggested the captain, who was rapidly coming up from his boots, and abandoning his graveyard elocution.

"I did not know you then. I do know you now; and there would be no excuse for me before God or man if I recognized you as my husband. The marriage was a fraud, and the law dissolved it from the beginning."

"It would take something more than the law of that old porpoise you call Uncle Moses to undo what was done according to the law of God and man," said Scoble with a heavy sneer.

"You were never my husband in reality, for you cheated me. You pretended to be a person you were not."

"I supposed the marriage was legal; and I certainly intended that it should be so," replied the captain, resuming his argumentative manner.

"Then you were an idiot!" exclaimed Mrs. Belgrave.

"I am no lawyer, as your son is, and the church pronounced us man and wife," retorted the captain with one of his heaviest sneers.

"If you are ignorant, I will enlighten you out of pity. The name of the man I married was Wade Farrongate, as he gave it himself, as he was known in the community, and as you will find it on the church register. You are not that man."

"I beg your pardon, Maud, I am that man," persisted Scoble.

"It was a false name, and therefore the marriage was a fraud. I did not consent to marry John Scoble, deserter from the British army, and without consent there could be no marriage."

"I see that old lobster has posted you thoroughly in your lesson," said the captain furiously.

"If necessary, I shall bring suit in the courts to have the marriage, if there was any, annulled for fraud. You can defend yourself then," added Mrs. Belgrave more calmly.

"You know very well, Maud, that I am not at present in condition to defend a suit in a New Jersey court," said Scoble in a rather feeble tone.

"Why not? You have money enough, since your uncle left you ten thousand pounds. You could even sell your hotel if you came short."

"You seem to know all about my affairs," replied the captain, puzzled at the knowledge of him the lady betrayed. "I have money enough; more than you have now, Maud."

"Then you can defend your rights, if you have any, in court."

"Do not persist in misunderstanding me, Maud. You know very well I cannot show myself on shore without being arrested; but I have never been convicted of a crime."

"The arrest usually precedes the conviction," added Louis.

"I am not addressing my conversation to you, young man," said Scoble savagely.

"But I desire the assistance of my son in this matter, and if he cannot speak, I have nothing more to say, Captain Scoble," interposed Mrs. Belgrave with freezing dignity.

"Do not call me Scoble, Maud; my name is Farrongate."

"Do not stoop to a lie, even to defend a bad case, John Scoble, for that is your name. Under that name you deserted from your regiment, and under that name you were arrested for it. More than this, you told me that was your real name."

"No, Maud; you are mistaken."

"I heard you say it," protested Louis. "And your mate called you so a dozen times before you noticed it."

"We will not say anything more about the name at present, for it really makes no difference what it is," said Scoble, when the path in that direction was blocked against him. "My only grief now is that you are false to me, Maud."

"I hope you will make the most of your only grief," added the lady with pointed sarcasm.

"Let us be friends, Maud; let us heal our differences."

"We can only heal them when the leopard changes his skin, and the spots cease to exist, which can never be in this world. You have proved to me that you are a thief, a swindler, an embezzler, a highwayman; and these are the differences between us. They cannot be healed, and we journey in opposite directions."

"Do not use such harsh terms, Maud, for I am not a bad man. I am as good to-day as I ever was."

"Then you have been a villain all the days of your life!"

"I do not belong to any church, but I think I am better than the average of men," added Scoble complacently.

"Then may God have mercy on the average of men!" exclaimed the lady, lifting her hands towards heaven.

"You told me, my dear"——

"Silence, sir!" gasped the lady, as she started in the direction of the state-room.

"One moment, Maud," pleaded the captain, following her.

"Wait a moment, mother," interposed Louis, for he had a suspicion in regard to the villain's last point, and he was anxious to have him state it.

"If you ever address another term of endearment to me, not even my son shall call me back into your presence," said Mrs. Belgrave, with an intensified expression of scorn on her handsome face.

"You told me about a certain million of dollars left by your first husband's father"—

"By my husband's father! I have had but one husband," said she.

They talked for some time about the missing million; and it was plain that Scoble had not heard that it had been recovered. He admitted that he had heard of the lost treasure before he went to the Park to live, and had followed up his inquiries while residing there.

"Now, madam, as neither your son nor you are disposed to treat me with proper respect, I will say at once that I know just where that lost million is located at this moment, and I can put my hand upon it at any time," continued Scoble, with a tremendous flourish, as though he held the key to the situation, and all the obdurate woman and her son had to do was to bend the knee to him.

"I am speaking to you now, madam. I have the power to put a million of dollars into your family. Let us heal our differences, and the first thing I will do after we are married again will be to put you in possession of the money," Scoble proceeded, though he seemed to be somewhat disturbed by the coolness with which his important announcement had been received.

"Do you think I would foster and cherish a villain, a swindler, a highwayman, for all the millions in the world? No!"

Without another word she retreated to her stateroom. Louis told her to lock the door, which she did.

CHAPTER 13
CLOSING WITH THE ENEMY

LOUIS WAS QUITE AS tired of the battle of words as his mother, though it had given him a great deal of information that might be useful to him. He had been very anxious to ascertain whether or not Scoble was aware that the missing million had been discovered. He was now satisfied that he was entirely ignorant of the fact that the vast sum had been taken from its hiding-place, and safely invested by the trustee. It was evident that he had known for at least two years where the treasure was concealed, and he now offered his knowledge as a bribe to effect a reconciliation with Mrs. Belgrave.

Frinks had resided at the hotel at the Park only long enough to introduce himself to Louis. If he had talked with the people of the town, or with the clerk of the hotel, he would have been likely to learn the fact that the young man was a millionaire, though a few weeks had been enough to make it an old story. Even if the agent had obtained this knowledge, he had hardly had an opportunity to communicate it to the captain since his return.

Louis had certainly spoken to him about his inability to spend his large income; but most of their conversation had consisted of bantering and pleasantries, and doubtless Frinks regarded the alleged difficulty in spending his income as an idle boast; for he had claimed to be beset by the same trouble. His single mission was to get Louis and his mother on board of the schooner, and his mind had been fixed on this purpose. At any rate, he had not been able to inform Scoble that the missing million had been found; and the captain complained that his agent had not obtained for him the current news at the Park.

Louis thought there had been talk enough, and that it was time something was done. Of course he had not the least idea of allowing his mother and himself to be conveyed to England, and especially not in such a craft as the Maud, of whose sea-worthiness he had serious doubts. Captain Ringgold had not yet reported on the state of her timbers, but the mate had intimated that the masts were weak and rotten. The time for action had come. The excitement of the interview with the captain had certainly enabled Mrs. Belgrave to forget that she was sea-sick, for she seemed to be as well as when she was on shore.

It was now about three by the cabin clock, and when Louis had escorted his mother to the stateroom, he decided to visit his friends in the second cabin, and arrange his plan either to capture the vessel, or to effect the escape of the party. The captain was passionate and full of malignity, and Louis thought he ought to be afraid of him. He could not understand why he was not so, unless the presence of his mother on board explained it. He was prepared for anything that might happen, and he walked directly towards the pantry door, Bickling having gone to the galley long before.

"Where are you going now, Louis?" demanded the captain, moving towards his involuntary passenger, doubtless believing that he had some hostile intention in his mind.

"I am going into the other cabin to see my friends," replied Louis with all the self-possession a young fellow could need under such trying circumstances.

"No, you are not!" exclaimed the captain, his lips compressed, and his eyes glaring like the serpent he was. "Perhaps it is necessary for me to remind you that I command this vessel."

"Not at all necessary, Captain Scoble; I am fully aware of the fact, and I am perfectly willing that you should command her just as much as you please."

"Then you will remain in this cabin."

"Excuse me; you may command the vessel and the crew all you like, but I respectfully decline to be commanded," added Louis.

"Let me tell you that the passengers as well as the crew are under my orders."

"I am not in the humor for any more discussions; you may command as much as you please, and I shall not obey. I am a kidnapped prisoner, and hardly a passenger," retorted the young man, as he opened the pantry door.

"Stop, you young rascal!" stormed the captain.

"Louis!" called his mother in a tone which assured him that she was already alarmed at the situation, though it was likely to be a great deal worse before it was any better.

Whatever happened he could not turn a deaf ear to the call of his mother, and he started towards her. Scoble stood between him and her, and it was necessary to pass him. Beside the pantry door was a small stick of cord wood, not more than an inch in diameter, which the steward used to fasten the door back when he was at work on the dishes. Louis grasped it, for he did not care to take out his revolver in the presence of his mother if he could avoid it.

Armed with this stick, which he used as a cane, he moved towards Mrs. Belgrave. He was quite ready to use it as a weapon if necessary, though he was not belligerent enough to do so unless the occasion absolutely required it.

"What are you going to do with that stick, you young ruffian?" demanded Scoble, speaking in the imperative mood, as though he insisted upon an immediate answer.

"I do not wish to do anything with it; but I have seen the time when I found it convenient to have a stick in my hand. For instance, when you attempted to rob Mr. Woolridge of the ten thousand dollars in his pocket, between your stable and the station, I should have been very glad to have a club in my hand, though it might have cost you a broken head. As it was, Flix and I fought the battle with our naked fists. I came off with your collar and necktie, which mother identified as yours, and I have them still as mementoes of the occasion. You will admit that a stick is sometimes a handy thing to have in your hand, and I thought I would be provided with one on the present occasion, if you do not object," replied Louis, putting in a point not before touched upon.

"But I do object," growled the captain, though it was plain that he had been startled by the reply of the rebellious passenger.

"All right; I will hear your objections next summer," said Louis, as he came to his mother's side.

"I am afraid you will get hurt, my son," pleaded Mrs. Belgrave, as she took his hand.

"I am a hundred times more afraid that you will get hurt than that I shall," continued Louis, as he led her back into the stateroom. "Don't be at all alarmed about me; I can take care of myself. Go in, mother; lock the door, and do not come out."

"That is my stateroom, and I shall not give it up to any person, and especially not to one who treats me as that woman does," interposed the captain with a fierce scowl on his brow. "I say, I shall not give up my room!"

"Yes, you will, my dear captain, for you were always the most gallant man in the world, and you are not going to belie your record on this happy occasion," replied Louis, as he came out of the room, closing the door behind him, which his mother immediately locked.

"I would give it up to a lady," said Scoble with the most withering sneer he could paint on his handsome face, or it would have been handsome if he had not made it ugly at this moment.

"Thank you, captain; I knew you would give it up to a lady."

"Do you call that woman a lady?" demanded the captain, looking as ugly as sin itself, however personified.

"A word, Captain John Scoble," said Louis, stepping towards him, with the lower end of his stick raised from the floor. "You may call me anything you please, and I shall enjoy it as much as you do; but if you say an insolent or disrespectful word to or of my mother, I shall have immediate occasion to use this stick."

"This is mutiny!" roared the captain, dancing about the cabin floor in his wrath like a jumping-jack.

"I dare say it is; if it be mutiny to protect my mother from insult, I shall be a mutineer to your heart's content," returned Louis, as his mother opened the door again, and stepped out.

Her son hastened to her, and keeping one eye on the miscreant, gently crowded her back into the room.

"Now, my dear mother, do not be alarmed at anything you may hear. I am abundantly able to take care of this man without the help of our friends. I am going to bring them into this cabin, and I hope this circus will come to an end before night," said he to her.

"But don't be rash, my dear boy," she replied, drawing him hastily to her breast, and kissing him on his brow. "I am terribly frightened."

"There isn't anything to frighten you, dear mother. I shall be with you again in a minute or two," he added, as he disengaged himself from her arms.

He turned suddenly and discovered Scoble near the door, ready to make a plunge at him while his back was turned, or at least to go into the room. The moment he saw the face of the young defender of his mother, he retreated a few steps, still yielding a respectful homage to the stick.

"This is my stateroom, and though I might give it up to your mother, badly as she has behaved"—

"She has behaved like a heroic Christian woman, and whether you consent or not, she shall occupy this room," answered Louis firmly.

"Let her occupy the room!" exclaimed the captain, who seemed now to have some other object than to dispute the occupancy of the room in view.

"Thank you, Captain Scoble," said Louis, bowing, for he never forgot his politeness, which was something more substantial than mere bowing and scraping.

"But all my things are in that room, and I desire to go in and get some of them," continued the captain; and Louis concluded that he wanted to procure the pair of revolvers of which he had already obtained possession.

"I am sorry to disoblige you, but you cannot go into the room at present, for it is occupied by a lady," replied Louis.

"My night-shirt is in there."

"Then I am afraid you will have to sleep in your day-shirt if you sleep at all."

Louis moved away from the door, and the captain retreated before him, apparently expecting to receive a blow on the head from the club, as he had on another occasion; and he therefore knew that the young man had the pluck to strike.

"This is mutiny!" howled Scoble, evidently unable to control himself any longer.

"So you suggested once before, and I dare say it is mutiny," replied Louis indifferently.

"I will have you put in irons!" gasped the captain, almost foaming at the mouth.

"Bring on your irons," added the mutineer carelessly.

Captain Scoble took a pair of rusty handcuffs from the table drawer, and marched towards the rebel as magnificently as though he had already executed his terrible threat. He went as near his intended victim as he dared to go, and then cast them at his feet, the irons making a ringing noise as they struck the floor.

"There they are!" exclaimed Scoble.

"All right; but when you put them on it will be necessary for me to be present, and you will kindly let me know when you are ready to perform the ceremony."

"I will let you know, you young scoundrel!"

"Thank you, captain. The things won't do any harm on the floor, and I am willing to let them remain there till you are ready to put them on. By the way, don't you think you had better have them cleaned before you make use of them? for they look as though they were too rusty to be comfortable."

"You will find them very comfortable when you are shut up in the hold, you impudent rascal!" cried the captain, dancing about in his inability to contain himself.

"Probably I shall when I am shut up in the hold. Very likely you will look upon it as mutiny, but I can't help hinting that I have not the least idea of being shut up in the hold. I am at liberty just now, and I intend to remain free."

"You won't be free long!" yelled the captain, as he darted towards the companion-way, no doubt with the intention of calling some of the crew to his assistance.

Louis stepped between him and the stairs with the club in the air; and this movement caused the captain to retreat again. At the same time, he took his revolver from his pocket, for he thought he had better make things a little plainer to the enemy.

"Captain Scoble, you will do me the favor to retire to the after end of this cabin," said he, pointing the weapon at him.

The villain could not stand the pistol, and obeyed the command. Louis remained near the pantry till Scoble reached the divan, under the stern windows.

CHAPTER 14
THE VICTORY IN THE CABIN

Louis Belgrave knew Scoble perfectly, and believed with all his might that he was a coward; otherwise he would hardly have dared to drive him to the farther end of the cabin, though he had the means in his hands of enforcing his command. With a revolver in one, and a club in the other, he felt strong enough to do anything.

He was grievously tired of the long discussions, useful to some extent as they had been, which had taken place in the cabin, and the necessity of some more decided action had been pressing upon him for some time. The sickness of his mother had prevented him from doing anything more than release his companions in the second cabin from their prison in the hold; and the long talks had been forced upon him by the presence of the captain.

He had not had an opportunity to consider the situation of his mother and himself as calmly and judicially as he desired. Even if he could get out of the present difficulty, Scoble would be in the field to make another attempt upon the tranquillity of his mother at another time. He believed it would not be a difficult matter, after the preparations he had made, to escape from the vessel; but the schooner and the villain would still be in the vicinity of his home, and he could renew his assault at a future time.

As he stood by the pantry with his eyes fixed upon the captain, he could not help asking himself if he had done wisely in not telling the villain that the missing million had been recovered. That was the object of his visit to the United States, and he had bought the Maud for this special purpose. For the hidden treasure he had married Mrs. Belgrave; for that he had tyrannized over his wife's son; and for that he had intended to take them both to England, where the boy would be more under his control. In fact, all that he had done had been with the single object of obtaining eventually the possession of the million.

Even if Scoble knew that the money had been found, and was held in trust for Louis, he was aware that the boy's only heir was his mother, and every-thing would remain practically the same. Nothing would have been gained by announcing the discovery of the treasure to the villain. After he had looked the matter over thoroughly he was satisfied that the situation was quite as well as it was.

He had hardly come to this satisfactory conclusion before the Maud began to behave in a very violent and unruly manner. She pitched and rolled furiously, so that it began to be rather difficult for the young landsman to keep on his feet. Either the gale had increased in force, or the vessel had reached a more exposed position. The water was breaking over the schooner, and it could be heard pounding upon the deck. Some of it poured down the companion-way into the cabin; and then Louis heard the mate order one of the sailors to close the doors, and draw the slide.

Captain Scoble did not offer to leave the divan under the stern windows where he had been driven, and Louis went to the pantry. He opened the door leading into the steerage, and shouted the name of Captain Ringgold. He was absent from the cabin but a few seconds, for he knew he could not trust Scoble to keep quiet. Before the shipmaster appeared, Mr. Frinks came down into the cabin. He must have heard some of the loud talk in the cabin, for the skylight was not far from the wheel. He had shown no disposition to interfere with the captain's affairs, at least not till he was called upon to do so.

The mate seemed to be greatly astonished to find everything so tranquil in the cabin. He looked at Louis, and then cast his eyes about, evidently in search of the captain. He did not see him at first; for that worthy, in the absence of anything better to do, appeared to have lain down and gone to sleep.

"Where is the captain?" asked the mate.

"He is somewhere about here," replied Louis indirectly.

"It is about time for him to come on deck, for it is blowing great guns, and we have just got out from the lee of the north shore. It is wet on deck, and I want my rubber coat," replied Frinks, as he went to the stateroom opposite that occupied by Mrs. Belgrave.

He procured the coat and came out again; but he had enabled Louis to ascertain where he berthed in the cabin. He asked Louis to tell the captain that he had better go on deck if he saw him, which he did not promise to do, and then returned to his duty. He had hardly closed the slide before Captain Ringgold came out of the pantry.

"I saw that you had company, and I waited till the mate had gone," said the captain. "I saw that you were having no trouble, or I should have come at once. What is going on here?"

"I will tell you all about it in a few minutes, for"—

"How is your mother, Louis?" interposed the shipmaster, fearful that something had happened to her.

"She is all right; she has got over her sea-sickness. I want you to tell me where we are, if you can, and what makes this violent kick-up of the vessel," said Louis, who was ready to act, but did not understand the situation of the Maud.

"I can only guess where we are, for I have not had a sight of the sea or the shore," replied Captain Ringgold. "I don't believe this vessel has made more than two and a half knots an hour since she got under way. I should say that we were just outside of Sandy Hook; and the last kick-up began when she got out where she could feel the swell of the broad ocean."

"Is the vessel in any danger now?"

"Bless you, no! Not if she is well handled."

"Then we will proceed to business," said Louis.

"What is the business to which we are to proceed?" asked the captain.

"Call Flix, if you please, and I will tell you both all about the situation," continued the leader, who still held his revolver and stick in his hands.

"Shall I bring the cook also, for he has been with us in the fore cabin for some time?" inquired the shipmaster.

"No, I think not," replied Louis, though he believed he had made a friend of Bickling.

In a few minutes Captain Ringgold returned, followed by Felix, who looked about him with curiosity and interest. Louis proceeded at once to inform his friends briefly what had transpired in the cabin, and added that his mother was in the stateroom.

"I think you said you were ready to proceed to business, Louis," said the shipmaster. "What is the nature of the business?"

"To capture the vessel and go to New York in her," replied the leader bluntly and to the point.

"That is plain talk; and I don't think we should call the taking of the schooner by any such hard name as piracy. We were all kidnapped; and I do not believe this is a legal voyage, for I doubt if the craft has any papers. But you are the chief of the party, and I will follow your orders as long as they don't lead us into hot water, for you have got the run of this affair, and I have not," said the captain.

"And what am I to do, my darlint?" asked Felix.

"I will tell you what to do when the time comes. Now, Captain Ringgold, the first thing is to put the captain in irons," added Louis. "The irons are all ready, for Scoble got them out for me."

"I'm wid ye's, me darlint!" exclaimed Felix; and perhaps the business in hand was more to his mind than to that of the others.

Louis led the way aft, but he halted between the two staterooms, one on each side of the cabin. He pointed out the unoccupied one as belonging to the mate, and suggested that he might be provided with one or more revolvers, as Captain Scoble had been. He thought it would be well to take possession of them if there were any in the room, and he sent Felix to look for them, telling him to open the drawers corresponding to those from which he had taken the master's weapons.

While he was absent, Louis and his companion moved towards Scoble, still lying on the divan. He did not notice them, and he appeared to be asleep. It had been a mighty calm to him after the excitement of his interview with Mrs. Belgrave, and a sailor drops asleep very readily. Felix joined them presently, with a single revolver in his hand, saying he could find no more.

Louis had brought with him the handcuffs the captain of the Maud had cast upon the floor. He had examined them, and found they closed with a heavy spring, and worked well enough. Scoble did not move as the trio approached him; and certainly he had been very accommodating to take his nap at just that time.

"Leave the rest of this matter to me, Louis; I can handle that man better than I could a live lobster," said Captain Ringgold, who was a rather large and muscular man. "You may speak to him, Louis, and then I will take care of him."

"Captain Scoble!" said the chief in a loud and sharp tone.

"Well, what is it?" replied the sleeper, moving a little.

"We are ready to put on the irons," added Louis.

"Oh, you are!" exclaimed Scoble, springing up to a sitting posture.

"But, if you please, we will change the programme a little, and put them on your wrists; and I hope you will find them comfortable," continued the young chief.

"Never!" yelled the master of the Maud, when he discovered three persons in front of him.

"Now, I think we will, Captain Scoble," said the stalwart shipmaster, as he seized his intended victim by his two shoulders, and threw him over on his back upon the divan. "Now, slip the bracelets on his wrists, boys, and don't let him hurt you."

Scoble struggled, twisted, kicked, struck out with his fists, and did all that a man in his situation could do. Louis got hold of one of his hands, and then sat down upon his lower limbs, while Felix grasped the other hand. The ship-master changed his grip to the throat of the prostrate villain, who was soon worn out with his struggles. Without any further difficulty the handcuffs were sprung upon his wrists, and he was powerless to do any mischief.

At this moment Mrs. Belgrave came out of the stateroom.

CHAPTER 15
AN OBDURATE PRISONER

CAPTAIN SCOBLE HAD MADE noise enough during the struggle on the divan to be heard in the stateroom where Mrs. Belgrave was passing her time in fear and anxiety. It was not for herself that she worried and trembled; but she was in constant dread that Louis would be overpowered and seriously injured in the conflict she was now assured was in progress.

"O Louis! Louis!" she screamed as she came out of her room in time to see the conclusion of the conflict, and hastened as rapidly as the uneasy motion of the vessel would permit to the scene of action.

"Don't be alarmed, mother," returned the son, as he ran to her support. "It is all over now, and you have nothing to fear."

"What is all over? What have you been doing?" asked the lady, hardly able to speak in the violence of her emotion.

"You can see that Scoble is in irons, and it is not possible for him to harm you or me just now," replied Louis.

"In irons? What does that mean?"

"He has a pair of handcuffs, which he brought out for me, on his wrists."

"But what are you going to do with him, my son?" asked the lady, who seemed to be hardly less terrified now than before.

"I don't know yet, mother: we have not decided what to do, though of course we shall get back to the Park as soon as possible. We have disposed of Scoble for the present, and we shall soon ascertain what we shall do next. What makes you tremble so, mother? You have nothing to alarm you now."

"I am afraid you will get hurt, Louis."

"But you need not be afraid, for there are three of us, and Captain Ringgold is a match for any two of the men on board of the Maud. Flix and I are not ciphers, and we can manage the matter very well, I assure you. I have no idea of being conveyed to England, or of permitting you to be conveyed there. I hope and expect you will be at the Park some time this evening. Now be a good mother, and go into your stateroom again, and keep very quiet there."

"But what are you going to do, my son?" demanded Mrs. Belgrave, still filled with terror and anxiety.

"I don't know yet. We have fought the battle in the cabin, and won the victory, and that practically settles the whole matter. Scoble can do none of us any harm now."

"But he and his men may be armed with pistols; and I am confident he would shoot you if you resisted him."

"You forget, mother, that I took his revolvers from his room, and I have given them to Captain Ringgold, who has them in his pockets at this moment. Our party are all armed, though I hope we shall not be compelled to use our weapons. Now come to your room, and as soon as we have decided what to do, I will see you and tell you all about it," said Louis, as he took the arm of Mrs. Belgrave and conducted her to her room. "Now lock the door, and lie down in your berth. Make yourself as comfortable as you can, for this state of things cannot last much longer."

She went into the stateroom, though she was plainly very reluctant to do so. Nervous and timid as she was, she would have thrown herself physically into any affray in which the safety of her son was menaced. In the presence of Scoble she had manifested a courage and determination, which were a revelation to Louis. She was disposed to protect her son by the sacrifice of herself.

Louis called her his guardian-mother; and this was an expression that greatly pleased his fancy. He looked upon her as an influence greater and more powerful than all others on the earth combined. He was strong and energetic in the battle upon which he had just entered through the influence she exerted over him. He felt that life would be nothing to him without her. He heard her lock the door after he had kissed her and retired from the room.

Scoble still sat upon the divan at the stern of the cabin, where the stout shipmaster had cast him like an unclean bird after he had been ironed. He could not help realizing that he had been conquered, but he had not been subdued. Louis hastened to the after end of the cabin as soon as he had disposed of his mother. The captain of the Maud seemed to be dazed, confounded, and astonished at the result of the conflict in which he had been engaged. One so arbitrary and self-sufficient had some difficulty in believing that he had actually been overcome, and in his own cabin. But the violence of his wrath had apparently subsided, and he was silent, looking from one to another of his late assailants.

"What next?" he demanded, as he fixed his gaze upon Louis, evidently regarding him as the leader and chief engineer of the movement in progress.

"We are not disposed to make you any more uncomfortable than is necessary to prevent you from doing any harm to my mother and myself; and I think we shall be abundantly able to protect ourselves, Captain Scoble," replied Louis, taking upon himself the office of spokesman. "I wish to say for myself that, in spite of all you have done, I bear no malice towards you. I shall do nothing, and my friends here will not, to injure you, or even to annoy you, unless it shall be necessary to protect myself and mother."

"That is all very fine, you young scapegrace!" exclaimed Scoble, looking fiercely at the speaker. "We are on the high seas now, and you are engaged in a mutiny: you have captured the vessel, so far as I am concerned; and if I wished to get rid of you, as you say I do, I need only hand you over to the courts, and the penalty of your crime is death."

"Not much high seas just here, Captain Scoble," said Captain Ringgold, laughing at the threat of the other. "I have been to sea more than you have, and I know something about this matter. The principal idea is that four persons have been kidnapped on board of this vessel, and they are making an effort to save themselves, and to avoid being carried out of this country to a foreign shore. We will take our chances on the mutiny question."

"Captain Ringgold, you are a sensible man; but you plainly do not know this boy who is leading you about by the nose," continued Scoble, in quite a gentle tone for him. "That young thief robbed me of a good many thousand dollars."

"Which you obtained by robbing those who trusted you with their money. But this young gentleman restored all this money to the rightful owners," added the Park captain. "You are aware that warrants have been sworn out for your arrest as soon as you put yourself within the jurisdiction of the State of New York or New Jersey; and under these circumstances we don't shake a particle at the idea of being charged with mutiny. I am in the same boat with Louis, literally and figuratively."

"I suppose the next step will be to hand me over to a constable or sheriff," added Scoble; and this thought evidently had a very subduing effect upon him, for he fixed his gaze upon the cabin floor and was silent.

"Well, Louis, I don't think it will amount to anything to talk any longer over the matter. It is time something more was done," said Captain Ringgold.

"I quite agree with you, sir: I have done talking enough with this man since I came on board of the Maud. He understands the views and feelings of my mother; and that is the main thing with me. He knows just where she stands now; and I hope he will cease to pursue a woman who has no respect or regard whatever for him," added Louis.

"Maud Farrongate is my wife! You know it as well as I do, Louis; and I will follow her to the farthest ends of the earth, and compel her to return to her duty to me! I am not a spring chicken to be frightened away from my rights, and from my duty to my wife, by a boy who is trying to be a hawk. You understand me, Louis. Whatever happens to me, I shall struggle for my rights as long as there is any life, any soul, left in me!" said Scoble, crowding all the bitterness and malignity of his nature into his speech.

"That's enough!" exclaimed Captain Ringgold. "I am enlisted with you, Louis, for the war; and I will stand by you as long as there is any life, any soul, left in me. Let us proceed to business, and this fellow may fume and vapor to his heart's content while we are engaged in more telling employment. What next?"

"I propose to lock Captain Scoble into the stateroom on the starboard side of the cabin," replied Louis. "I will see that it is in condition for him."

The leader of the movement was afraid Felix had not been searching enough in his examination of the room; for he had brought out but one revolver, and he was afraid there might be another there. Calling his crony to accompany him, they went to the mate's room. Louis decided that it would be the most prudent way to remove everything in it to the cabin, and this they did, without finding a dangerous weapon of any kind.

"Now, Captain Scoble, if you are disposed to make things pleasant, you will take up your quarters in the room prepared for you without any useless opposition," said Captain Ringgold, when Louis reported to him.

"I have been outraged, my"—

"All right, captain; and four persons on board have been outraged besides yourself; but we have no time to talk about it. If you will be kind enough to move into the room made ready for you, that will save me the trouble of putting you there myself," interposed the shipmaster.

"I will not submit to this treatment! I will not do anything that looks like submission!" protested Scoble, squirming as much as he could with his wrists ironed behind him.

"Just as you please, captain," said Captain Ringgold, seizing him by the collar of his coat with both hands, and dragging him to the stateroom as though he had been nothing but a small boy, for he was powerless in the grasp of his stalwart conqueror.

With no difficulty whatever he thrust him into the room, and closed the door upon him. Louis was ready with the key of the lock, and promptly secured him so that he could not escape without breaking the door down. He seemed to be disposed to do this, and at once began to deliver violent blows, apparently with the heels of his boots, against the lower panel of the door.

"That won't do," said the stout captain briskly. "He is determined to be as uncomfortable as possible, and he shall have his own way. Unlock the door, Louis. Flix, go and find some cord, or rope; I saw some in the passage to the fore cabin."

Louis opened the door, and Felix hastened to procure the line required. Captain Ringgold went into the room, and took the prisoner by the collar, and shoved him over to a stool in the corner.

"You make more noise than the law allows, Captain Scoble," said his resolute captor, looking about the room to arrange his plan for dealing with the obdurate man.

"I told you I would not submit, and there is no such thing as submission in me!" howled Scoble.

"So much the worse for you, my man; but I shall keep you quiet in spite of all you can do."

"See if you do!" replied the prisoner, still manifesting persistent defiance of his stout adversary. "You may kill me, but you cannot subdue me! I am a free-born Briton, and I submit to no man!"

"You are a free-born thief that ought to be behind prison walls, and I hope to have you there soon," added the captain, who proceeded with the help of the boys to bind his ankles together, and then made him fast to the front of the berth.

CHAPTER 16
ALLEGIANCE TO THE POWERS THAT BE

Captain Scoble was an infant in the hands of a man as powerful as the ship-master, and he was soon made fast so that he could not move hand or foot. It was an uncomfortable position to which he had been reduced, but he had brought it all upon himself by obduracy. He howled and swore like a pirate; but nothing more was said to aggravate him, and as soon as he was securely bound to the front of the berth, the party left him to become a wiser and more docile man.

"Now, Captain Belgrave, what next?" asked the captain from the Park, as he looked at Louis with a smile.

"I will leave that to you, sir. I am not a captain, and I could not handle the schooner to save my life, or even to save my mother's life," replied Louis as he led the way to Mrs. Belgrave's stateroom.

"So far as the navigation of the vessel is concerned, I will attend to that; but I look upon you as the leader of the enterprise by which we are to be restored to our homes at Von Blonk Park. You know that man in the stateroom better than I do, and I think you ought to say what shall be done."

"We will arrange it all between us. But it seems to me that the Maud is tumbling about in a very wild way," replied Louis, as he grasped the handle of his mother's door to avoid being hurled over to leeward.

"We are going to have a violent north-easter, and one is due about this time of year. Whatever this schooner may be able to do with a free wind, she can't do much close-hauled. But that question will come up later," added the captain.

"What is all the noise I heard just now, Louis?" asked Mrs. Belgrave, opening the door of her room at this moment.

"Scoble is bound hand and foot and locked into the stateroom on the other side of the cabin," replied her son. "He can do nothing now, and you have no more to fear."

This explanation satisfied the terrified woman, and she retired again. Captain Ringgold and Felix had seated themselves on a divan, for it was exceedingly difficult to stand in the cabin. The time had come to decide what was to be done with the vessel; for she was still in the hands of the crew, consisting of the mate and two men, besides the cook. She had hands enough to manage her; but there were still four men against one stout man and two stout boys.

Whether or not the crew would stand by their captain and fight for him was an interesting question; and when they were preparing to face it Bickling, the cook, came into the cabin from the deck. He at once announced that he had been sent below to ascertain the occasion of the noise by Mr. Frinks, who said it sounded like blows with an axe upon one of the doors.

"Which it was a great noise, for I 'eard it myself in the galley," added the cook, steadying himself by holding on at the table.

"Perhaps the mate had better come below himself and have the noise explained to him," replied Captain Ringgold.

"Which 'e can't leave the deck, sir, for the vessel is making very bad weather of it; and Mr. Frinks is wondering where is the captain that 'e don't come on deck and attend to the vessel," said the cook.

"Do you know anything about the affairs of this vessel, cook?" asked the captain sharply.

"Which I don't know anything at all about anything, sir."

"You don't? How long have you been on board of her?"

"Only two weeks and three days, sir."

"Didn't you come over from England in her?"

"No sir, I did not; I was cooking at a 'otel in Baltimore when Captain Farrongate engaged me. I took the lay because I wanted to go home to Hengland."

"Who was the cook that came out in the Maud?"

"Which she 'ad no cook coming out, sir; but one of the seamen did the cooking."

"Why do you call him Captain Farrongate when his name is Scoble?"

"The ship's company all called 'im Captain Scoble till a few days ago, and then we were all told to call 'im Captain Farrongate, which it is true we all called 'im after that."

"Did you know that all the persons who came on board this forenoon were kidnapped, and that two of us were confined under the lower hatch?"

"Kidnapped! Bless my body, no sir! I never 'eard a word said about any such thing sir!" protested the cook, with energy enough to be telling the truth.

"Didn't any of the hands say anything to you about it? Didn't they tell you they had put the hatches on when two of us went into the lower hold to examine the vessel?"

"Not a word about it, sir; which I mind my business, sir, and I have nothing to do with the foremast hands except to give them a kid of beef and a dish of h'ard bread."

The party wondered if this man was telling the truth. Louis stated that he had seen but three men leave the Maud at the time she was sunk, which confirmed a part of the cook's story, that he had been on board but about two weeks, and had not come from England in her.

"We have made some changes about the schooner, cook, and we should like to know how you stand. Captain Scoble has been put in irons, and is locked up in the starboard stateroom," added Captain Ringgold, in an impressive manner. "We were all kidnapped, including the lady in this stateroom, and Scoble was intending to take her and her son, and perhaps the rest of us, to England. We have taken possession of the vessel, and I mean to take her to New York."

"The captain in irons! Bless my body!" exclaimed the cook, apparently overwhelmed by the news.

"It is just as I state it, and the noise you heard was made by Captain Scoble, trying to get out of the room where we have confined him. But we have bound him hand and foot, and made him fast to the front of the berth, so that he can do nothing more to help himself. Now, my man, do you want to fight on Scoble's side?"

"Bless my body! No, sir! Which I always run away when a fight is coming on," protested Bickling.

"If you wish to take part in this conspiracy with Scoble and the mate, I shall be under the necessity of binding you hand and foot, and making you fast to a stanchion. You will obey no order given by Scoble or the mate," continued the shipmaster, taking from his hip-pocket one of the revolvers with which Louis had provided him.

"Bless my body! Revolvers!" groaned the cook, as though one had already been fired at him; for both of the boys imitated the example of the captain and produced their weapons, though the exhibition was only for its moral effect. "I see you have the hupper 'ands, sir, and I will obey your orders in all things."

"All right, Bickling. Now you will go on deck and tell the mate all you have learned, and we will be with you in a few minutes," said the captain; and the cook made all haste to get out of the reach of the revolvers.

"I measured that man about right," said Louis, after Bickling had gone. "I did not look for any powerful opposition from him."

"As he says, he minds his own business, and don't care who is king. Probably we shall have to serve Mr. Fobbington as we have the captain."

"His name is Frinks; and I think he is a smarter man than Scoble; but I am sure we can handle him."

"I am used to this sort of thing, Louis, for I once had occasion to put down a mutiny on the north-west coast. Frinks may give us some trouble; but the seamen will be about such fellows as Bickling. They work for their wages, and don't care who is captain of the ship. Now, Louis, we will go on deck, and when I have seen what the wind and weather are, I shall know what we had better do in a nautical point of view."

Louis expected there would be some sort of a brush with Frinks, for he must be familiar with the whole length and breadth of the plot to capture Louis and his mother. He could not plead ignorance of the designs of Scoble, for he had really managed the whole affair. The stick with which the rebellious passenger had intimidated Scoble lay on the floor where he had left it, and he picked it up, ready to make use of it with regret if occasion should require.

It was not an easy thing for the landsmen to mount the companion-stairs, for the Maud was leaping like a running horse, and the sea was breaking over her bows at every plunge she made. The two seamen had been driven to the shelter of the caboose, for there was nothing for them to do. The scene on the quarter-deck, where the mate still kept the wheel, was likely to be a stormy one in a double sense.

Bickling had not yet finished his story relating to the condition of things in the cabin. Frinks was plainly very much interested, and the situation had evidently been anticipated by him. Louis had told Captain Ringgold all he knew about Frinks, who was a good deal of a humorist; but whether or not he was a fighting character was yet to be ascertained, though in the opinion of the shipmaster it did not make much difference.

"I salute you, Mr. Frinks," said the captain, politely addressing the mate. "You have heard the whole story from the cook, and I suppose there is nothing more to be said of a descriptive nature."

"Who the dickens are you, my fine fellow?" demanded Frinks, who knew nothing at all about the gentleman who addressed him.

"Well, sir, I am Captain Royal Ringgold; and I have been to sea enough to see that you are handling this craft in a very lubberly fashion; and I am about to relieve you of the helm, and have the vessel better managed."

"Thank you, Captain Royal Ringgold; I shall be under very great obligations to you for doing so. If you can make this old tub do any better, I should like to see it done; but I think we shall soon find that we have two lubbers on board instead of one," replied the mate as pleasantly as he had talked to Louis.

"I think we had better attend to one or two preliminaries before we do anything. You assisted Captain Scoble to kidnap four persons at this moment on board of the Maud. Is this a true bill?" demanded the captain, placing himself close beside the mate.

"Yes, sir; as true as the comic almanac," answered Frinks squarely, with a smile on his spray-covered face.

"That is honest and candid."

"Do you suppose if the Prince of Wales should succeed to the throne of the United Kingdom, it would make any difference to me?"

"Give it up!" laughed the captain.

"He would be the king and I should still be the subject, just as John Scoble is commander of the Maud and I am the mate. It is all the same to me who is captain. I am informed by the cook that you have taken possession of the vessel, and put the captain in irons, locking him up in my stateroom."

"The cook informed you correctly."

"All right. I am not such a fool as Scoble, who has been jawing all day with my particular friend, Louis Belgrave, whose acquaintance I had the honor to make at Von Blonk Park. As to kidnapping you, my dear Captain Ringgold, I had not the least intention of doing anything of the sort. I would have given ten shillings out of my own pocket to get rid of you and the other young gentleman, when I saw you at the station. In a word, Captain Scoble did not want you."

"At the same time I am glad to be here for Louis's sake."

"I dare say. If you are now the captain, I am ready to swear allegiance to the powers that be." The mate resigned the wheel to the captain.

CHAPTER 17
A CHANGE OF MASTERS

LOUIS WAS NOT A little astonished at the ready yielding of Mr. Frinks to the new order of things on board of the Maud, for he had expected serious opposition from him, and that he would carry it even to fighting for Scoble. If he was disposed to resist the new masters of the vessel, probably the physique of Captain Ringgold was not encouraging to him. The shipmaster took the wheel, and immediately gave his whole attention to the management of the vessel.

"I suppose you have no further use for me on deck," said Mr. Frinks, after he had given up the wheel. "I don't know what course you intend to take, but, with your permission, I will go down into the cabin."

"I should be very sorry to incommode so amiable a gentleman, but you will oblige me by remaining on deck," replied the captain. "You are acquainted with the Maud, and I am not; I may need your counsel and assistance."

"I did not suppose you would require anything of such a lubber as I am," replied the mate.

"On the contrary, I must ask you to continue to discharge the duties of mate. It is possible that the men forward may not be inclined to obey me; and I should prefer to escape the necessity of disciplining them into obedience, though I feel perfectly confident that I can do it."

"As I said, Captain Ringgold, it makes no difference to me who is captain of the Maud. I am a soldier of fortune; I have no home on the wide earth, no place to lay my head; and I had as lief go one way as another. I am entirely at your service, and ready to obey orders in all matters relating to the schooner."

"All right, Mr. Frinks, and we will be friends."

"I shall serve you faithfully as long as I remain on the deck of the Maud; and I think you will have no trouble whatever with the men forward, especially if you issue your orders through me."

"Did it occur to you, Mr. Frinks, while you were at the wheel, that this vessel is not making above two knots an hour?" asked the captain.

"I don't think she is doing as much as that, Captain," replied the mate, laughing. "When she has a leading wind she does very well; but on the wind she is not good for much, especially when she is reefed down as she is now."

"It seems to me that you chose a very bad time to carry out your little scheme, for you could not help seeing that a north-easter was coming up."

"The fact is, as I suggested before, that we got more than we bargained for when you and that youngster you call Flix came on board. We could easily have taken care of Mr. Belgrave and his amiable mother, and anchored under a lee; but with so many of you it was not prudent to remain too near the shore."

"Precisely so."

"I thought I had taken good care of you when I put the hatches on which confined your peregrinations to the lower hold. I don't exactly understand yet how you happened to be in the cabin."

"Louis Belgrave can explain that to you in full when you have time to listen to him, for he took the liberty to take off the hatches and let us both out like a Christian as he is. But, Mr. Frinks, I am not disposed to keep on this tack any longer, for we are getting it worse and worse every minute."

"You have the wheel, and all hands will obey your orders, so that you can go where you please, Captain," replied Frinks.

"Ready about!" shouted Captain Ringgold. "Stand by the jib-sheet!"

The mate went forward and placed the hands at the jib-sheet. The helmsman put the wheel over, and the dull sailer threw her head slowly up into the wind, leaping and rolling and bouncing about like a log. But she came about after a while, and her jib began to draw on the starboard tack. The mainsail went over on the traveller, and the men forward attended to the fore-sheet.

Captain Ringgold laid a course due west, which indicated that he intended to return to the bay, or some point near it, from which the vessel had departed in the forenoon.

"Ease off the jib-sheet!" shouted the new captain.

"Ease off the jib-sheet!" repeated the mate, to assure the master that his order was understood; and it was promptly obeyed.

"Now ease off the fore-sheets!" continued the captain.

Frinks could see from the course of the schooner what was required; and if he had sworn allegiance to the present commander of the craft, he could not have discharged his duty more promptly and faithfully.

"Send a couple of hands aft!" called the captain; and the mate came himself with one of the hands. "Ease off the main-sheet!"

After the change in the course, the Maud took the wind on the starboard quarter, and behaved much better than before, though she still pitched and rolled violently in the heavy sea. With two reefs in her principal sails, and with the stormy sea, her progress through the water was anything but rapid. The mate had gone forward, and he was now talking with the two sailors on the forecastle, which was no longer washed by the head sea.

"Flix, you are not much of a sailor, I dare say," said Captain Ringgold, calling the Milesian to him.

"Not a bit of it, sir; I don't know the fore to' gallant bobstay from main top-mast hatchway," replied Felix.

"Then your education has been neglected. I want you to go forward and ascertain what the mate and the hands are talking about; for they may be hatching up treason, and it is well to be on the lookout, though I don't think the mate means mischief," continued the captain.

"It don't take much of a sailor to do the like o' that," replied Felix, as he started to go forward, clinging to the rail to enable him to keep on his feet.

"Do it in a mild and gentlemanly way, and don't let the mate understand that you are listening to them," added the captain.

Felix sauntered as leisurely forward as the motion of the schooner would permit, keeping his gaze fixed on the shore, which was Rockaway Beach, distant about two miles. He took a seat on the windlass, where he could hear all that was said, if anything was said, and continued to gaze at whatever was to be seen. Of course his presence prevented the mate and the men from hatching up any treason; and this was the principal object of the new commander in sending him there.

"I don't know where you are going, Captain Ringgold; but it is all right, wherever you go," said Louis, who was clinging to the after part of the cabin skylight for support.

"We are bound to the Great Kills, which is the bay from which we sailed this forenoon," replied the captain. "That is just about twenty miles from where we are. The Maud is not making more than six knots an hour, and we can't make the Kills till after eight o'clock. It will be low tide then and very dark in this weather; and I am not a pilot in the inside waters. It is rather unfortunate; but there is no help for it. We may have to stay there all night; and Uncle Moses will have fits over your absence."

"I thought you would go directly up to New York, where we could hand Scoble over to the police at once," added Louis.

"That is just what I would do if it were possible; but the wind is now blowing a smart gale. It is likely to be a great deal worse before it is any better. You see, after we made The Narrows, it would be a dead beat to windward for about ten miles, and we never could do it in the world in this old tub."

"I understand now."

"It occurs to me, Louis, that it is about suppertime; and we had better attend to that matter before dark," suggested Captain Ringgold.

"I see that Bickling is in the galley; I have been keeping an eye on him, for I did not know but he might take it into his head to let Scoble out of his prison, and take off his bracelets," replied Louis. "I will tell him to get supper at once;" and he made his way to the galley.

The cook was ready to attend to his duties, and he promised to "'ave some 'am and heggs" ready in a very short time. Louis went below, and after listening at the door of Scoble's prison, hearing nothing to excite alarm, he knocked at the door of his mother's room.

"I am so glad to see you!" exclaimed Mrs. Belgrave when she saw her son. "Have you been hurt?"

"No, mother; no one has been hurt, and we are in full possession of the vessel, which is now headed back to the place from which we started this forenoon," replied Louis, after his mother had embraced him. "We are all right now, and you have nothing whatever to fear. We may have to stay all night on board of the vessel; but you can sleep very well in your berth, and some of us will keep watch all night."

"I do hope we shall get home without any more trouble. I shall not sleep a wink on board of this vessel, and I wish there was some way to get ashore," added Mrs. Belgrave.

"Perhaps there will be; we will see when we get into the bay, where we shall have smooth water. But how do you feel, mother?"

"Very well indeed. I should like a cup of tea and some toast, if I could get them."

"We are going to have supper pretty soon, and I want you to eat all you can, for it will do you good."

Bickling was already setting the table in the cabin, and putting on the "fiddles," which the motion of the vessel rendered necessary, for the dishes would hardly have stayed on the table. In less than half an hour the meal was ready, with tea and toast in addition to the heavier fare the cook had promised to provide. Louis seated his mother, and then went on deck to call Captain Ringgold, who summoned the mate to take the helm, though Felix was left to keep watch of him and the men. The Milesian stationed himself at the companion-way, where he could call the captain and Louis if anything went wrong; and he kept one hand on the revolver in his right hip-pocket, perhaps rather anxious for an opportunity to use it.

Mrs. Belgrave had so far recovered her appetite that she could eat ham and eggs as well as toast, and made a very satisfactory meal. The violent emotion to which she had been subjected seemed to have been a panacea for her sea-sickness. The captain praised the ham, and praised the cooking, very much to the satisfaction of Bickling, and testified more fully to his pleasure by making a very hearty meal. He returned to the deck a happy man in his present condition, and sent the mate down for his supper. Louis remained below while Frinks and Felix ate their rations, and they imitated the example of the captain in doing ample justice to the fare.

Louis gave the cook two ten-dollar pieces, and asked him to feed the men before the mast as well as he had those in the cabin; but the difficult business of the hour was to feed Captain Scoble, for the young millionaire would not permit him to be deprived of his supper as the captain suggested.

The shipmaster attended to this duty himself after the mate had returned to the deck. The sailors were invited to the cabin one at a time for their supper, and a fresh supply of ham and eggs had been provided by the cook. The captain took off the handcuffs of Scoble, who had become quite mild and tractable under the discipline of confinement, and he ate his supper as though he enjoyed it. In fact, everything on board seemed to be pleasant.

It was half-past eight in the evening when the Maud ran into the bay. It was very dark; and as soon as Captain Ringgold got the schooner under a lee, the anchor was let go, and the voyage was at an end.

CHAPTER 18
SOME SIGNS OF TREACHERY

THE SAILS OF THE Maud were furled, and the vessel rested as easily under the lee of a sort of promontory, which rose up from the marsh, as though a gale were not raging outside of it. Captain Ringgold would have proceeded to the town from which they had embarked in the forenoon if the tide had not been entirely down; but he was not familiar with the navigation of the bay, and he would not run the risk of getting aground in the middle of it.

Mrs. Belgrave declared that she was very comfortable in her stateroom; but she very much preferred to go on shore, even at the expense of some hardship from the weather, and the perils of the marshes. Louis desired to gratify her if it were possible. One of the men had been left on deck as an anchor watch, and the captain and mate had seated themselves in the cabin.

"I don't think you would have any trouble at all in getting up to the town," interposed Mr. Frinks, when he had heard the conversation of the passengers.

"Do you mean to go ashore here and walk up?" asked the captain.

"It can't be much over a mile," replied the mate.

"But we may come to creeks and mud-holes we cannot cross with a lady," suggested the shipmaster.

"I think not, for I got some idea of the locality when we came into the bay, and while we lay at anchor here for about two days," added Frinks. "There is something that looks like a creek or the mouth of a river over to the northward of us; but we can land the lady beyond that with the jolly-boat."

"I'll tell you what we will do," said Captain Ringgold suddenly and loudly, as though a satisfactory idea had come to his mind. "We will take the boat and go on a little exploring expedition, for I don't believe in taking Mrs. Belgrave out on a night like this without knowing where we are going to fetch up. This bay is big enough to be well shaken up in a gale like this; and I think we had better feel our way before we expose her to anything in the way of danger."

"I am not afraid, Captain Ringgold," protested Mrs. Belgrave. "It was not very rough when we went out of the bay this forenoon."

"Very true, madam; but it blows more than four times as hard now as it did then," added the shipmaster. "Perhaps we had better wait a couple of hours or so, for the tide is dead low now, and by that time we shall have water enough to get about in the jolly-boat, and perhaps in the schooner. There is a good channel up to the town if we only knew where it was; but it is very crooked, I remember, for I was in here in a schooner twenty years ago."

"I think that it is a capital idea to explore the bay to the northward of us; and I am confident we can land on that creek not more than half a mile from the anchorage," said Frinks with considerable enthusiasm, as though he desired to do all he could to comply with the wishes of the lady passenger. "I will go with you, and do what I can to assist, for I know something about the bay from my stay here."

This plan was agreed upon, and Louis was very glad to have the mate accompany the exploring expedition, for he regarded him as the only dangerous man at liberty on board the Maud, and he could easily be kept under control in the boat, or on the desolate shore of the bay at the north, though it had a town on the west side, whose cheerful lights could be seen from the deck of the schooner.

Louis advised his mother to lie down in her berth and sleep a part of the night, for they could not be ready to take her ashore for at least three hours. She complied with his request, rather to please him than because she expected to sleep under the present circumstances. Felix had already gone to sleep on one of the divans under the berths, and Louis was inclined to follow his example. He went on deck with the captain to take a more careful survey of the surroundings, so far as they could make them out in the gloom of the night.

"I suppose there is no danger in leaving mother on board while we go on this exploring expedition," said Louis, after they had peered into the darkness for a while without being able to make out anything.

"I don't think there is; if there were any danger I certainly would not leave her," replied Captain Ringgold. "Scoble can do no mischief in his present condition, and we are to take Frinks with us. The mate seems to be in a very friendly mood towards us, and I don't believe we have anything to apprehend from him."

"Certainly not, if we take him with us," added Louis. "Who is to go in the boat besides the mate?"

"You and I must go, for in spite of appearances Frinks may be tricky and make trouble when we get away from the vessel, and are buried in the darkness. The safest way is to trust no one; and that is just what we will do."

"That is the better way."

"We take Frinks with us, and both of us have revolvers within reach of our hands on the instant. Of course Scoble can do nothing with his wrists ironed behind him, and made fast to the front of the berth. We shall leave Felix on board, and we are absolutely sure that he will be faithful."

"There is no possibility of a doubt so far as he is concerned," replied Louis heartily.

"One thing more, my boy. We have to dispose of Scoble, and what are we to do with him? No officer in Southfield would arrest him on your statement or mine; and it would not be right for any one to do so. Uncle Moses, you say, has one warrant, and Mr. Woolridge has the other. One of us must go home with your mother, and that will weaken our force. I have not much doubt a tug can be had in the town, and if we find a practicable way to get there over the marshes, one of us had better go and obtain it, and at the same time telegraph to Squire Scarburn to send an officer with the warrant to make the arrest. As I am the stronger man of the two for duty on board, you had better attend to this duty."

"Of course I am willing to do anything I can to get the villain inside of a prison," added Louis.

Captain Ringgold had no intention to take a nap, and for an hour longer he discussed the situation and the plan, for Louis found himself wide awake again as soon as the safety of his mother was under consideration. There was nothing to be seen in any direction but the lights in the town, which were growing less and less as the evening advanced; and vessels going into New York, if there were any on such a stormy night, did not go so far to the southward as the entrance to the bay.

"We left Felix asleep in the cabin," said the captain, after they had been on deck at least an hour and a half. "Perhaps you had better go below and see that all is well."

"I will do so," replied Louis, as he went to the companion-way.

Felix was still fast asleep on one divan near the door of Mrs. Belgrave's room, and Bickling was apparently in the same condition on the one just forward of the stateroom in which Scoble was confined. If Louis had hurried his steps he might have seen Frinks leap hastily into the berth next aft the prison room. By the time the young man reached a point abreast of the late captain's wooden cell, the mate had buried himself in the bedclothes of the berth abaft the cell, and was snoring like a trooper, so that Louis could have no doubt from the sounds that reached his ears as he passed that the occupant of the bunk was sound asleep. In fact, it appeared to be a very sleepy time in the cabin, though appearances are sometimes very deceitful.

When Louis returned to the deck he found the captain heaving a hand lead in the waist of the vessel; and he had done it before at the bow and stern. The messenger to the cabin reported upon the state of things there, and it was entirely satisfactory to the shipmaster.

"It is about eleven o'clock, Louis, and the tide has made about two feet since we anchored here. It is about time for us to get off on the exploring expedition," said Captain Ringgold as Louis joined him.

"You have not said yet who is going in the boat, captain. Do we take any one of the Maud's crew except the mate?" asked the young man.

"The mate and I can pull the boat, and you can look out ahead, though I do not object to another, provided it is not Felix, who must keep guard over your mother," replied the captain, as he led the way to the cabin to call the mate.

On the stairs they encountered Bickling, who put his hand on Louis's shoulder in a rather mysterious manner, and led him to the deck again, while the captain continued on his way down the stairs.

"You are going away in the boat," said he, as he halted near the companion. "Will you take me with you? I can be of service to you."

The cook seemed to be in mortal terror of something, and the hand he laid upon Louis's shoulder trembled, and his manner was very strange.

"Why do you wish to go in the boat, Bickling?" asked Louis.

"Which it is very kind you 'ave been to me, and"——

At that moment Frinks rushed upon deck from the companion-way, closely followed by Captain Ringgold.

"I hope I have not delayed the expedition; but I was tired and dropped asleep in my berth, and lost all idea of what was going on," said the mate, as the captain joined him.

The cook could not say another word, so terrified was he at the appearance of Frinks, or rather when he heard his voice near him, for he could not see him in the darkness. The two men forward were ordered to bring the boat up to the gangway; and when the mate discovered the cook, he told him to assist them. In a few moments the boat was ready for use. Frinks seemed to be in a great hurry, and got into it at once.

"I should like to have Bickling go with us, captain," said Louis, as the shipmaster was about to follow the mate.

"We will take the cook with us, if you don't object, Mr. Frinks," added the captain.

"I don't object; and I think we can find enough for him to do. Bickling! In the boat!" replied the mate.

But Louis was not quite ready to go, and said so to those in the boat. Then he rushed down into the cabin, where he found Felix still fast asleep on the divan. He roused him at once, and then charged him in the most earnest manner not to fall asleep while the boat was absent. Felix promised faithfully to keep awake, and declared that he would keep on his feet all the time till the boat returned. Louis, satisfied that he would keep his promise, went on deck, and took his place in the boat.

Frinks shoved her off, and the craft went off into the darkness. Bickling had been put at one oar while the mate pulled the other. The captain was to occupy the stern sheets, and Louis took his place in the bow as the lookout, for he was supposed to have the sharpest eyes. Keeping the lights of the town, rather more than a mile distant, on the port hand, the boat went to the northward. At the mate's suggestion, the course was made more to the westward, to enable them to find the creek or river he had seen before.

There was plenty of water for the boat, and most of the way for the schooner, for the captain had brought the hand lead with him, and was taking the soundings at frequent intervals. In less than half an hour Louis reported that he could make out the opening in the land leading into the creek. The boat presently made a landing, and Louis and the captain leaped ashore, followed by Bickling, to whom no order to that effect was given.

"If you find a way to the town that suits you, come back as quick as possible, and we will bring off the lady," said Frinks.

The other three were no sooner ashore than Frinks pulled with all his might for the schooner.

CHAPTER XIX
EUCHRED ON THE SHORE

Captain Ringgold and Louis Belgrave did not at once understand what Frinks was doing, for the boat could hardly be seen in the gloom of the dark and stormy night. They heard the noise made in getting away from the shore, and then the dip of the oars in the water. The young millionaire was the first to suspect that something was wrong, but he did not feel well enough assured of it to say anything, for he was strongly opposed to becoming a prophet of evil under any circumstances; but he halted in the march which had already been begun in the direction of the town.

The young man stopped short a few rods from the shore, and listened with all his ears for any sounds which would afford him further information, while the shipmaster and the cook continued on their way. He could plainly hear the hurried dip of oars, and the rattle of the looms in the thole-pins. Beyond a doubt there was a movement of some kind on the part of the mate, and Louis rushed in hot haste to the bank of the creek, for there were signs of treachery on the part of the Maud's officer in the boat.

"Halloo! Hallo! Mr. Frinks!" he shouted at the top of his lungs, which were not weakened by consumptive tendencies.

"On shore!" replied the mate, as he ceased rowing.

"What are you about, Mr. Frinks?" demanded Louis.

The boat was already too far off for an easy going conversation; but if the mate condescended to explain his movement, it might do something to restore the young man's confidence.

"I am going to look along the shore towards the town to see if there is another creek you will have to cross, and to ferry you over if I should find one," answered Frinks, still laying on his oars.

"What is the matter, Louis?" asked Captain Ringgold, hastily returning to the shore, followed by Bickling.

"I don't know that anything is the matter," replied Louis. "The mate shoved off in the boat, and says he is going towards the town to see if there is another creek, in order to ferry us across it if there should be one."

"I don't quite like the looks of that movement, and I am decidedly in favor of keeping the mate on shore with us. If a boat-keeper is needed, let the cook attend to that duty," replied the captain; and his tones indicated that he also discovered some signs of treachery.

"All right; order him to bring the boat back to the shore, captain," answered Louis.

"In the boat!" shouted the shipmaster.

"On shore!" replied Frinks. "What do you want now?"

There was something in the tone of the mate, and in the little word "now" with which he ended his sentence, that indicated a sort of contempt for the one who hailed him.

"Bring the boat to the shore!" added Captain Ringgold, loud enough to be heard half-way across the bay.

"Very well, captain! I will come ashore as soon as I have taken a look across this point of land," answered Frinks; and Louis thought there was something of the raillery with which he had mixed up his speeches when he explained in what manner he had made the capture of the party in the forenoon; in other words there was something like triumph in his tones.

"Come ashore at once!" cried the captain, fortified in his suspicion that all was not right by the manner of the mate.

"All right! You wait till I come!" was the response of Frinks.

At the same moment the rattle of the oars and the dip of them in the water were heard, and it was evident that the treacherous mate was pulling with all his might away from the spot where he had landed his late companions in the boat.

"Come ashore at once! If you don't I will fire upon you!" yelled the captain, as he drew one of the large revolvers from his pocket.

"Fire away!" returned Frinks in tones of derision, mingled with a chuckling laugh that fully indicated the treason of the mate.

Captain Ringgold got the direction of the boat as well as he could from the sounds that came from it, and then discharged his revolver, which he had loaded in the steerage when the pair of weapons were given to him.

"Good!" shouted the mate contemptuously.

The shipmaster, using all the care the situation permitted, fired again; but it was very much like shooting at the moon, so far as the chances of hitting were concerned. The darkness was impenetrable, and the shipmaster had nothing to guide his aim but the sounds from the boat.

"Good again!" returned Frinks derisively, and the sound of his voice grew less distinct as he increased his distance from the shore.

"No use to fire at him any more, captain," replied Louis in a tone of utter despondency, as he realized that the battle, according to present appearances, was utterly lost.

But the captain continued to fire until he had discharged all the barrels in his two pistols. The mate could hear the reports, and he responded to every one of them in tones of the utmost contempt, as though he was enjoying the chagrin of the young millionaire and his stalwart companion. He had certainly won the victory again over the young Parkite, and he appeared from his tones to be enjoying it heartily.

"There is a light off there now, and it must be on board of the Maud," said the captain, as he peered through the gloom in the direction from which they had come in the boat. "All I have to say, Louis, is that we have been euchred!"

"So it appears," added the young man bitterly. "And my mother is on board of that craft still, with no one to protect her from the wiles of that villain. I am afraid I have been stupid in trusting to appearances. We had Scoble bound hand and foot, and we brought the mate off with us. I ought not to have believed a word that oily-tongued rascal uttered."

"It is no use to groan over it, my boy; we must act," added the shipmaster, evidently ashamed that he had permitted himself to be overreached, but not so utterly cast down as his young companion, as he had less reason to be.

"What can we do?" demanded Louis, suddenly rousing himself from his despondency.

"Oh, I don't give it up yet, my boy! All we can do is to make our way to the town, procure a tug-boat, and give chase to the schooner. I think we have taken away all the firearms there were on board of her, and with such officers as we can procure in Southfield, where I am somewhat acquainted, we may yet be able to arrest the villain, and save your mother from further persecution. I feel that I am somewhat to blame for the accident which has happened to us, and I pledge you all my time, and all my fortune, which is nothing near as large as yours, to follow this Scoble all over the world if necessary, till we have him behind the iron bars," continued Captain Ringgold with a heartiness that made Louis his friend for life.

"Whatever fortune I have is nothing compared with the safety and happiness of my mother, and I would spend every dollar of it, if my trustee will allow me to do so, to redeem her from the power and possession of John Scoble," said Louis earnestly.

His million and a half, as that was the amount of it in round numbers, seemed like a bagatelle to him at the present moment, for he could neither pay it out nor pledge it to procure the return of his mother to her new home at the Park. But the captain did not despair of being able to accomplish something in the pursuit of the villain who had again brought grief and shame to those it had once been his duty to protect.

"It is certainly the time for action, as you say, Captain Ringgold; but what shall we do? What can we do?" he demanded.

"That is the question to be immediately settled," replied the captain, looking about him as if to obtain further information that would assist him in taking some action. "This creek is too wide to be crossed without a boat; and there seems not to be even a punt about here."

"What good would it do to cross the creek, if we could do so?" asked Louis.

"Perhaps none. If we could get over to the hill that shelters the vessel from the gale, we should still be too far from the Maud even to shoot those on board of her; and we could not get on board of her without a boat. It is no use to look in that direction," was the captain's conclusion. "The only thing we can do is to make our way over to Southfield; and I hope we shall find a tug-boat there, though it is by no means certain. It is plain enough to me now that Frinks knew more about this bay than he pretended, for he made sure to land us this side of the creek so that we could not get near the Maud again. He has managed his case very well."

"That light was not exhibited on the Maud when we left her," suggested Louis.

"It was not; but the mate is expected to come back, and the light is hoisted to enable him to make the quickest time on his return. I have no doubt Captain Scoble will put to sea the moment he is on board. I dare say the reefed sails are set, and the anchor hove short by this time."

"We have seen that the Maud can't do much in the way of sailing in such a heavy sea, and with the wind nearly ahead of her," added Louis, taking comfort from the reflection.

"That is very true, my lad; but the ocean is almost boundless, and it is very hard to find a vessel, even a slow sailer, on its vast expanse," replied the captain. "I was an ensign in the navy during the last part of the Rebellion, and my ship was looking for months for the Alabama; but we did not find her. Scoble may not sail before morning, and we may get a steamer on his track by that time. But we can't waste any more time in talking about the matter; let us move towards the town."

Captain Ringgold led the way, and Louis kept at his side. Bickling came up behind them. He had been forgotten in the excitement of the stirring event of the evening; and then, for the first time, the young man recalled the application of the cook to be taken in the boat with him. He called him to his side, for they were walking over a salt marsh which was dry enough at that stage of the tide, and there was room enough for all of them to march abreast.

"Why did you desire to go in the boat with me, Bickling?" asked Louis, in opening his inquiry.

"You have been very kind to me, sir, which I appreciate a good friend, sir, and I wanted to be of some service to you, which I am afraid it is too late now," replied the cook.

"Then, why didn't you speak out before?" demanded the young man indignantly.

"Which I couldn't do it, sir, though I would gladly 'ave done it, sir," protested the man, who even now seemed to be frightened about something, though he had no reason to fear his present companions.

"Why couldn't you do it? You had a tongue in your head!" added Louis very warmly, for it was clear to him that the cook knew something about the plot which had just been sprung upon them.

"I 'ave to mind my own business, sir, and I can't hafford to meddle with hother people's haffairs, which it is just as plain to you, sir, as it is to me, sir, who am a poor man," replied Bickling. "I tried to do something for you, sir, but I failed."

Louis thought that he was perhaps unjust to the poor man, and softened his manner.

CHAPTER 20
IN PURSUIT OF THE MAUD

LOUIS BELGRAVE RECALLED THE circumstances under which Bickling had applied to him for permission to go in the boat with the exploring expedition. He had asked to be taken with the young man, saying that he could be of service to him. Before he could say anything more the mate came on deck, and the cook seemed to be in mortal terror of him, for he had noticed the fright of the fellow at the moment.

It did not occur to Louis at the time that anything could be wrong in the arrangements for visiting the shore; but he realized now that the cook had discovered some signs of treachery on the part of Frinks; but his fears prevented him from uttering a word.

"It looks now as though you knew something about the trick which has been played upon us, Bickling," continued Louis, more gentle in his manner than before.

"Which I didn't know anything at all about it, sir, but which I thought there was something wrong goin' on in the cabin, sir, and I did not know what," pleaded Bickling.

"I am sorry you did not speak to me."

"Which I should 'ave done if I 'ad known what was hup, sir."

Though Louis had given the cook twenty-five dollars, rather for the service he rendered him and his party as cook than for any other reason, he could not feel that he had any claim upon the fidelity of the man. He had made an advance towards telling what he knew; but he was sadly wanting in pluck, and he had failed, so that the intention must be taken for the deed.

"Did you know that it was the mate's purpose to abandon us on the shore, and return to the schooner?" asked Louis.

"Which I hope to die when my time comes, sir, if I 'ad the smallest idea of what he was goin' to do, sir!" protested the cook vehemently. "If I 'ad, sir, I wouldn't 'ave let you and the captain go in the boat. I thought I'd 'ave a chance to tell you what little I knew when you got to the shore. If I 'ad let Mr. Frinks know what I was tellin' you, that would have spoiled, the 'ole, and the mate would have killed me dead on the spot, sir."

"That is sensible, Louis," interposed the captain. "He could not afford to blow on the mate; it was not safe for him to do so, as he did not belong on our side of the question."

"Which the young gentleman has been very kind to me, and I was glad to do him a good turn if I could; and I am very sorry I could not, sir, which it is all I can say, sir," pleaded the cook.

"He meant right, Louis, and it is a pity he had not a small portion of your pluck," added the captain.

"Now tell me what you did know, Bickling," continued Louis.

"I was trying to get to sleep, sir, on one of the sofas, when I 'eard a noise near the mate's room. I looked that way, sir, but I did not move, and the mate thought I was asleep, no doubt. He unlocked the door of the stateroom, for he 'ad an extra key, and went in, sir. He shut the door after him; and then I heard him and the captain talking together."

"Could you make out what they said?" asked Louis, not a little excited at the revelation of the cook.

"Not much of it, sir, which they did not talk out very loud, sir. They were to get possession of the vessel, but 'ow it was to be done, I did not 'ear, sir. I put my hear to the partition, and tried 'ard to understand what they said, sir. By this time I reckon they 'ad fixed the plan to get the vessel; and I heard Captain Farrongate, or whatsoever his name might be, say that he should go to Bermuda, sir, while the friends of the lady would go to Southampton to look for her, sir. That is all, sir, and every syllable I could make out, sir."

The man had some education, and he did not mangle his h's very badly unless he became very much excited. It was easy enough to see that he was one of those men of no force of character that are often met in the world, but are at the same time filled with good intentions. The plot to leave Louis and the captain on the shore to the westward of the creek, the cook insisted, had not been mentioned in his hearing. He had made out the last part of the conversation, and that certainly was very important as a guide to future movements.

During this narration the trio had been walking at a tolerably rapid pace towards the town, finding a footbridge over the creek, and had accomplished a good part of the distance. It was midnight, and most of the lights in the houses had been extinguished. Another quarter of an hour brought them to the few wharves in the place, for the party had kept near the shore of the bay all the way from the creek.

With the most intense interest on the part of Louis, they passed from one pier to another, till they had gone beyond the water front of the town. Not a steamer of any kind was there; no tug-boat had taken shelter from the storm within the bay, so far as they could discover. There was not a light to be seen on the waters of the bay, and the few vessels in port were all made fast to the wharves, where they were partially sheltered from the violence of the gale.

With the midnight hour came a change in the aspect of the weather, which Captain Ringgold was the first to observe. The wind was hauling to the westward, and it had been what he called a "dry storm." He was confident that the sun would rise clear in the morning, for the wind had already measurably abated.

"That will be favorable to Scoble in getting away," suggested Louis.

"Yes, it will help him to get clear of the coast. Though the Maud is a very bad sailer on the wind, she seemed to be a weatherly vessel, and I have no doubt, by this time, she is pounding against the seas outside of this bay. It is an awful pity that there is not a tug within hail of us; but there is not, and I don't see that we can help ourselves."

"At this moment I wish I owned that steam-yacht you were telling me about yesterday," said Louis, who was musing sadly over the present hopeless situation.

"I wish you did! If you did, there would be music very soon at the heels of the Maud!" exclaimed Captain Ringgold. "But we must do something, and not stand here all night."

"I feel just as though all our hands were tied behind us, and I don't see that we can do anything," added Louis.

"We must do something! I used to know a certain Captain Boulong who lived in this town. He was the master of a coaster formerly, but I have not seen him for two or three years."

"Do you know his first name, captain?"

"I do; for he owed me a note, which he paid on time, and is an honest man. Captain Drench Boulong was his name, and is still if he is in the land of the living."

"Then he is the mate of the Blanche, which is Mr. Woolridge's yacht. I know him very well," replied Louis, who had heard the captain of the yacht call him by his first name when they were in conversation.

"If he is the mate of a yacht he is not likely to be at home, though he may be. I know where his house used to be, and I can find it. We will look him up, for we have nothing better to do."

Captain Ringgold led the way very directly to a small cottage on a side street, where he knocked loud enough to wake all the sleepers within a mile. The summons was effectual, for a man soon put his head out a window on the lower floor, and demanded who was there.

"Captain Royal Ringgold," replied the gentleman from the Park.

"And Louis Belgrave," added the young man.

"I know you both, and what can I do for you?" asked Mr. Boulong, whose voice was readily recognized.

"Is there a steamer of any sort to be had at this port?" inquired the captain.

"Not unless some tug has put into the Kills for the night."

"We could not find one. Is there any sort of a craft to be had?"

"Possibly," replied the mate of the Blanche. "Wait a moment, and I will let you in. Then we will see what can be done."

A few minutes later Mr. Boulong opened the front door, and showed them into his little parlor. In as few words as possible Louis explained the situation, declaring that his mother was a prisoner on board of the Maud, at that moment, without doubt, proceeding to sea. He told all it was necessary to know in order to understand the unfortunate dilemma of Mrs. Belgrave. The mate asked some questions, which were promptly answered.

"We brought the Blanche down here yesterday to clean her bottom, and she is at anchor just below the town, where there is a beach. I suppose you know that Captain Alcorn lives here as well as myself, Louis?" added Mr. Boulong. "As you and your mother are good friends of our owner, he may be able to do something for you, as I am sure Mr. Woolridge would if he were on the ground. If you will wait a few minutes I will call up Captain Alcorn; or we will go to his house if you like."

The party attended the mate to the residence of the captain of the yacht. He listened to the story of Louis, and then immediately volunteered to pursue the Maud in the Blanche. They proceeded to the beach off which the yacht was anchored, stopping at the railroad station to send a night message to the owner. All the ship's company of the Blanche were on board; the captain hailed the vessel, and the anchor watch sent a boat for the party. All hands were astir when the party reached the vessel, and in a very short time she was under way, standing towards the entrance to the inlet.

"You say the Maud is bound to Bermuda, Louis," said Captain Alcorn, after the yacht was fairly under way.

"That is what Bickling, the cook of the schooner, overheard Captain Scoble say," replied Louis.

"The wind has got round to the westward; it is fairing off, and we shall have a good day," continued the captain of the yacht. "As near as I can make it out, the Maud must have got under way about half-past eleven last night."

"That was about the time," added Captain Ringgold. "The wind has come round so that she can turn out her reefs and make a fair wind of it."

"Even if the Maud is bound to Bermuda, Captain, do you believe she will lay her course from Sandy Hook to the islands?" asked Captain Alcorn. "I believe you were in the navy in the war as well as myself, and you know what it is to chase an enemy even with no more than four hours the start of you."

"I was telling Louis this morning that my ship followed the Alabama for months without getting a sight at her," replied the shipmaster.

"The Maud has the advantage over any man-of-war enemy, for she can go into any port she pleases," suggested Captain Alcorn. "This Scoble, from what you have told me, is aware that his vessel is not a high-flyer. After the mischief he has done, or the crime he has committed, he may reasonably expect to be pursued by some fast craft."

"But he is not aware that we know he is bound to Bermuda, and if we chase him at all he will suppose we will follow him to Southampton," said Louis.

"Very true, and there is a good deal in that. Now, I believe the fellow will skulk into some inlet or bay where there is little or no population, and remain there concealed till he is satisfied any pursuers are half-way across the Atlantic," added the captain of the yacht.

"I have considered that idea very faithfully, and I think it is a reasonable supposition."

"There are plenty of openings all along the New Jersey coast, and probably Scoble went into one of them to have his vessel painted."

The course was agreed upon between the two sea-captains.

CHAPTER 21
FELIX McGAVONTY ON WATCH

MRS. BELGRAVE WAS SO exhausted by the violence of her emotion during the day, and by her sea-sickness, that she fell asleep almost in spite of herself; and she knew nothing of what transpired on board of the Maud during the evening. Louis had put his ear to the door of her room every time he went near it; but hearing no sound to indicate that she was awake, he had refrained from disturbing her.

Felix McGavonty was wide awake as soon as Louis called him. He had gone on deck with his crony, and watched the boat till it disappeared in the darkness. Then he walked the deck for a time, and all was as still as death. The single sailor who was doing duty as anchor watch was fast asleep on the windlass, as the other was in the forecastle. The Milesian had nothing to do and nothing to think about. Mrs. Belgrave was in her stateroom, and though he was in charge of her, he could do nothing in the line of the duty he had promised to perform. It was chilly on deck, and he went below.

He had assured Louis that he would keep on his feet while he was absent, and he was sure he should fall asleep if he even sat down on one of the divans. Faithful to his promise he marched from one end to the other of the cabin, occasionally listening at the door of Mrs. Belgrave's room, to satisfy himself that she did not require his services; but he could hear nothing, for she was sleeping soundly after the fatigue of the day, which had been a time of severe trial to her.

Sea-sickness is a curious malady, and no one can tell why it attacks some, and is not developed in others. Louis had never had the slightest symptom of it, while his mother was extremely susceptible to it. In a family of eight seven were always sea-sick even in smooth water, while one was always as well and hearty in the heaviest sea as on shore. The recovery is sometimes as curious as the malady itself, for an exciting event has been known to cure the patient immediately; and this appeared to be the experience of Mrs. Belgrave.

The gallant captain from the Park had attended to her at the table, and she had partaken heartily of ham and eggs as well as tea and toast for her supper. Doubtless the meal she had taken did something to incline her to sleep, and she had not heard a sound since early in the evening. She knew nothing whatever of the exploring expedition which had left the vessel at about eleven o'clock, when the tide had been coming in for a couple of hours.

Felix marched back and forth in the cabin. He had a duty to perform; but for the present it seemed to consist solely in keeping awake, for he could neither see nor hear the lady over whose safety he was watching. He was an active young man of sixteen, fond of excitement, and especially of fun, and something more stirring than the duty of an idle sentinel would have suited him better. When he had been engaged with Louis in any of his enterprises, he had been the shadow of his friend, willing and obedient, seeking no other glory than to serve him faithfully. But he was now alone, though Louis was not far off, and he felt a sense of responsibility with which he had rarely been burdened.

After his return from his promenade on deck, Felix had made but a few turns of his march in the cabin before something in the vicinity of the prison stateroom of Scoble attracted his attention. He halted near the after divan under the stern windows. He had a very great respect and regard for the revolver he had carried in his hip-pocket for some weeks, and he involuntarily grasped the handle of the dangerous weapon. In the opposite pocket he had another and larger pistol of the same kind, the one he had taken from the stateroom of the mate when sent by Louis to search for arms.

Both of these weapons were loaded, and he was well supplied with ammunition for each of them. But he remembered the solemn admonitions of Uncle Moses and Louis, in which he had been prohibited in the most positive manner from using the weapons he carried, unless it were to save his own life, or that of Louis or his mother. The worthy squire would not for some time assent to the carrying of these weapons, and the possibility of an attack on the part of Scoble had alone changed his refusal into a reluctant permission.

Felix was not a little startled when he saw the door of the captain's wooden cell slowly and cautiously opened. He had assisted in fastening the arms of the prisoner behind him with a pair of handcuffs, and had seen him made fast, with his ankles securely bound, to the front of the berth. He had looked at Captain Ringgold when he locked the door of the stateroom, and put the key in his pocket. He had observed the embarkation of the exploring party, and was fully aware that Frinks had been one of the four who went off into the darkness in the boat.

Under these circumstances if a ghost had accosted Felix as he made his round in the cabin, he could hardly have been more startled and mystified than he was when he saw the door of the starboard stateroom opened. If he inherited any superstitions he had long since got rid of them, under the instruction and raillery of the jovial lawyer with whom he had lived from his earliest years. It did not occur to him, therefore, that the door had been opened by any other than human agency.

He drew the smaller revolver from his pocket, and retreated to one side of the cabin, where the curtains of one of the berths afforded him an opportunity to conceal himself. He did not know who had opened the door. Of the ship's company the mate and the cook had gone with the expedition to the shore, and only the two seamen remained on board, with the prisoner in the stateroom. Felix felt his responsibility, and he wished to be wise in his action if possible.

Behind the curtain of the berth he watched for further proceedings on the part of the person who had opened the door. A lamp suspended from a deck-beam over the table gave him abundant light. He was not compelled to wait long for further developments, for presently he saw a head thrust out at the door. It did not require more than a glance to assure him that the head belonged to John Scoble, whom he had formerly known for a couple of years under the name of Wade Farrongate.

How he had been able to remove the cords and the handcuffs with which he had been secured was a mystery to Felix, for he had been fast asleep on the divan while Frinks had made his visit to the room. It was Scoble beyond the possibility of a doubt. He had often seen the man at the Park, had often been to the old house where he lived; but he had no acquaintance with him; in fact, he had hardly ever spoken to him in his life. His presence in the cabin, and free from the bonds which had confined him, made it painfully evident to him that the plans of Captain Ringgold and Louis Belgrave had utterly failed.

No one but the mate could have released the captain of the Maud; and it was plain enough to the Milesian that Mrs. Belgrave was again in the clutches of him who still regarded her as his wife. He was sure that something was about to happen, though it was possible that Louis and the shipmaster had been able to outwit the mate who was with them in the boat. He could only wait for further developments; and it was not likely that he would have to wait a long time for them.

Felix felt that he was on board of the Maud as the guardian and protector of Louis's mother, and he felt the responsibility imposed upon him to the deepest depths of his being. If Scoble attempted in any manner to injure or meddle with Mrs. Belgrave, he was ready to use one of the weapons in his pockets. In the face of both Scoble and the mate, he realized his own weakness, and that it would be useless for him to assume an offensive attitude. He could best watch over his charge by keeping out of sight for the present, and until something occurred to inform him more fully in regard to the actual situation on board.

He deemed it prudent to get into the berth behind the curtains of which he had concealed himself. Looking out from behind the hangings in front of him, he fixed his gaze upon the door of the prison stateroom. Scoble was looking about the cabin, still showing only his head. Probably he feared that Louis or Captain Ringgold was still on board. He continued to explore the cabin with his eyes for some minutes, and it was evident to the observer that he was also listening for sounds from the deck; but there was nothing to be seen or heard.

The absence of all sights and sounds appeared to assure Scoble that he had nothing to fear. He went back into the room for a short time, and then came out into the cabin. He walked from one end of it to the other, looking into all the berths, and then halted at the door of Mrs. Belgrave's room. Felix snored lustily while he was in the vicinity of his berth, though Scoble doubtless knew that he was to be left on board, and was not surprised when he discovered him apparently asleep in the bunk.

Scoble listened at the door of the lady's room; but she was still asleep. Then he went to the pantry, took down one of the lanterns, lighted it in the cabin, and then went on deck. Felix sprang from his bed as soon as he had ascended the companion-way, and followed him as far as the slide. He made the lantern fast in the main rigging, where the party on shore had seen it. Felix readily understood that this was a signal for the guidance of the mate on his return, and possibly to assure him that his superior was on deck.

Scoble then went forward, roused the anchor watch, still asleep on the windlass, and ordered him to call Bawkin, who was the man who had his watch below. The captain came aft as soon as the other man appeared. Felix retreated a few steps down the stairs; but returned to his position as soon as he heard the voice of the master.

"Take off the stops of the mainsail!" said Scoble, in an ugly tone, as though he was not in a happy frame of mind.

Felix was not sailor enough to know what this order meant, and did not understand what a "stop" was; and it is often called a "gasket." But in a few minutes more he saw the men, the captain working with them, hoist the mainsail, still reefed as when it had been furled. The foresail was then set, and both of these sails were banging and pounding in the gale, which could be felt to some extent behind the promontory.

Then the three men went forward, and the watcher followed them as far as it was prudent for him to go. They manned the old-fashioned windlass, and proceeded to heave up the anchor to a short stay, though Felix did not comprehend the manœuvre in which they were engaged.

The hoisting of the foresail and the mainsail indicated that the captain intended to go to sea again, and that he was ready to do so in a hurry. These preparations convinced the Milesian that Louis and the captain from the Park, as the latter expressed it, had been "euchred." As he understood it, the Maud was about to sail for Southampton again, and without Louis or Captain Ringgold. He had all he wanted to think of then, as though a hole had been made in the world, and he had dropped out of it.

Captain Scoble seated himself on the companion, and Felix caught an occasional glance at him. The watcher kept his eyes and his ears wide open, and in less than half an hour he heard the dip and rattle of a pair of oars. Something, that for which he had been waiting, was about to happen. The boat came up to the gangway, and Frinks sprang to the deck with the painter in his hand. The two men forward were called, and ordered to hoist up the boat to the stern-davits.

"You come back alone, Mr. Frinks," said the captain, in a dissatisfied tone. "Where is Bickling?"

"I had to leave him on shore, or blow the whole thing," replied the mate.

"But we can't get along without a cook," added the captain sourly.

"We can get along as well as we did coming over," returned Frinks.

"My wife is on board now."

Frinks refused to say anything more, and insisted upon getting under way at once.

CHAPTER 22
MRS. BELGRAVE'S PROTECTOR

THE MATE AND THE captain of the Maud did not appear to agree together any better than when Louis had listened to them in the interview in the cabin. Scoble took the non-appearance of the cook very hardly, while Frinks declined to say anything more about it. Without waiting for the command of his superior, he ordered the men to trip the anchor, and stand by the jib-halliards. The captain made no objection, and the schooner was very soon under way.

Frinks took the wheel, and ordered the men to hoist the jib. Casting on the port tack, he soon came about, and stood to the southward till the vessel reached the opening. Then he laid an easterly course, and stood out to sea. The gale had begun to moderate, though the sea was still heavy. The Maud began to pitch and roll as she had before; but, as soon as she was clear of the inlet, the sheets were started, and the vessel was headed for Sandy Hook Light, about nine miles distant. This change in the course gave her a free wind, and she behaved better than before.

The mate then called Stowin aft, and gave him the wheel. Instructing the helmsman to keep well to windward of the light-ship, he intimated to the captain that he was ready to talk with him in the cabin. Felix immediately retreated when he heard this remark, and sprang into the berth next aft of Mrs. Belgrave's room, where he had pretended to be asleep when the captain looked about the cabin. Whatever might be the subject of the conversation, he was anxious to hear all that was said.

"What has become of that other boy, Captain Scoble?" asked the mate as soon as they had descended the companion-way.

"He is fast asleep in one of the berths on the port side of the cabin," replied the captain. "He don't amount to anything at all, and is as stupid as an owl at noon-time."

"Thank you for the compliment," thought Felix. "Perhaps that is the kind of fellow I had better be under present circumstances."

The mate moved aft, apparently to satisfy himself that the intruder, as both of them now regarded him, was not in condition to listen to them. Felix opened his mouth partly, and snored musically enough to have suited the corporosity of Uncle Moses. Frinks looked at him, and listened to him, and left the berth evidently satisfied that the occupant was not in condition to hear what was said.

"What shall we do with that young cub?" asked the captain, as the mate seated himself opposite him at the table.

"I don't know, unless we throw him overboard," replied Frinks indifferently. "Never mind him now; we have better fish to fry."

"Everything seems to work right for those who have truth and honesty on their side," added Scoble.

"I don't think so, for the devils have got the weather-gage of the angels this time."

"What do you mean by that?" demanded Scoble, scowling fiercely.

"I consider the two persons we have just tricked and got rid of as honest and upright people, and I wish I were like them. I can't say as much as that of you or myself," replied Frinks bluntly.

"I claim to be an honest and upright man," added Scoble.

"Then the devil himself is one of that sort! But I don't want to discuss morality and piety with you, for you know nothing at all about subjects of that sort."

"Don't you think I have a right to my wife?"

"I don't know, and I don't care, whether you have or not. I haven't anything to say about that. You agreed to pay me five hundred pounds if I helped you out successfully with your business on this side of the ocean. You were to pay me a hundred pounds when I got the lady and her son on board of the Maud."

"But her son is not here now," pleaded the captain.

"He is not here because you wanted to get rid of him; and I got rid of him, and the man with him, who was big enough to turn your cake into dough. One hundred pounds now, Captain Scoble, or we quarrel on the spot."

"Don't be in such a hurry, Frinks. I will pay you every shilling I agreed to pay you," said the captain.

"I won't trust you a day or an hour. One hundred pounds now, or I will anchor the Maud where she was an hour ago! That is all that need be said about it. Pay, or lose every trick you have made!"

"But I can't pay just now," protested Scoble. "My wife occupies my state-room, and I cannot get at my money. I will give you the amount in the morning, as soon as I can get possession of my room."

"That won't do!"

"Would you have me turn a lady out of her room at this time of night?"

"Why not? I don't care anything about the woman," replied Frinks, rising from his seat at the table. "I will get her out of the room in something less than long metre."

"No, no, Frinks! Don't disturb her, for I am going to make my peace with her; and turning her out of her room would be a very bad beginning," argued Scoble, using his most persuasive tones. "It would be little better than an outrage."

"That is your affair, and not mine. One hundred pounds down, or we quarrel! Choose for yourself."

"If I can't help myself, I can't," muttered the captain.

"You can't, unless you want to go back to that bay. Of course you expect to be pursued; for Louis Belgrave is not going to let you carry off his mother without following you all over the world. The boy has grit and pluck."

"I have nothing to fear from him now."

"Shall I tumble the lady out of that stateroom so that you can get my money?" demanded the mate.

"I don't see that I can help myself," answered Scoble.

"But I can help myself!" shouted Felix McGavonty, leaping from his berth, and placing himself in front of the lady's door.

"Oh, you are alive, are you?" said Frinks, contemptuously.

"Faix, I'm aloive and I'm kicking!" replied Felix, with his hand on the handle of his smaller revolver, with which he had practised a good deal in a shooting gallery.

"Get out of my way, Paddy, or I shall pulverize that empty head of yours," added the mate, moving towards him with the evident intention of laying hands on him.

"Hould your hoult where ye air!" said Felix, elevating the revolver, and pointing it at the head of his assailant.

"That's it, is it Paddy? Two of us can play at that game, and perhaps one of us will get beaten at it," replied Frinks, as he retreated across the cabin and went into the stateroom he had formerly occupied.

Felix had intended to behave like a Milesian simpleton, assuming to be witless and stupid; but the proposed plan to disturb Mrs. Belgrave seemed to leave him no alternative but to stand up in her defence, though he was sorry the occasion required him to take this step.

The mate was absent some time, and had lighted the gimbal-lamp in his room. Felix kept his place in front of the door; but he fully understood the object of Frinks in going to his stateroom, and he was satisfied no shooting would be done in the cabin that night, however it might be at some future time.

The mate spent at least a quarter of an hour in his room, and appeared to be rummaging everything there; but he came out at last, and went to the table where the captain was still seated.

"Have you a revolver, Captain Scoble?" he asked in a more subdued tone.

"I have two of them; but they are in a drawer in my stateroom," replied Scoble.

"I don't know where mine is. I left it in one of the drawers, and that and the box of cartridges are gone," added Frinks, very much discontented at the situation.

"I don't see that you can do anything about it just now, Mr. Frinks," said the captain; and Felix thought he was pleased rather than disconcerted at the inability of the mate to meet him on equal terms. "It is time for us to go on deck and look out for the vessel."

Both of them left the cabin, and mounted the companion-way. Restoring his weapon to his pocket, Felix followed as far as the slide. He could see the light-house and the light-ship from the position he had taken. The sheets were started again, and the vessel was headed to the southward.

"Whether we are bound to England or Bermuda, we may be overhauled before daylight," the listener heard the captain say. "I have studied up this coast enough to know all about it; by daylight we shall be out of sight of any craft that floats in these waters. When we come to anchor we will put that young cub ashore."

At this moment the listener heard a voice in the cabin, and looking down discovered Mrs. Belgrave at her door. He did not like the task of telling her that Louis and Captain Ringgold were no longer on board of the schooner, and explaining the nature of the plot of which her friends were the victims. But he could not shirk his duty, and he hastened to the lady, who was calling her son by name.

"I am very sorry to say, Mrs. Belgrave, that Louis is not here," said he in tones of condolence.

"Not here? Where is he, Felix?" she asked with an expression of alarm on her face.

"He and Captain Ringgold went on shore."

"And left me here?" she gasped.

In gentle and sympathetic tones he told her what had occurred. The mate, who had been friendly and had offered to assist them in finding a suitable place to land the lady, had deceived them, and left them on shore. Mrs. Belgrave, trembling with emotion and terror, asked him to go into her room.

"What will become of me?" cried the poor woman, giving way to a flood of tears.

"Don't be afraid, Mrs. Belgrave; I will take as good care of you as Louis could if he were here," said Felix earnestly.

"What can you do against Scoble and the mate? I know you will do all you can; but you will be powerless against these men," sobbed Mrs. Belgrave.

"Not quite; I got the better of them a little while ago when they were going to turn you out of your room," replied Felix, giving her the details of the defence he had made.

"But you will not shoot them?" inquired she, fixing her gaze upon him.

"I should have fired if necessary; but I should have taken care to disable them only."

"But they would fire upon you, Felix."

"They have nothing to fire with, for we took possession of all the weapons on board this forenoon."

Mrs. Belgrave suddenly braced herself up, and her companion was surprised to see a smile on her face.

"Why am I weeping? I have been childish, and I am glad, as I ought to be, instead of sorry that things have taken this turn," said she a moment later. "Louis is not here, and he is out of the reach of Scoble! The villain will not harm me, and he has the wickedest intentions in regard to my son. I am happy now."

She looked as though she was really happy, and she begged Felix not to expose himself to any danger as he left the room. Neither the captain nor the mate came below again during the night; and at sunrise the Maud was at anchor in a little inlet sixteen miles south of Sandy Hook.

CHAPTER 23
THE SEARCH FOR THE MAUD

THE SUN ROSE IN a nearly clear sky, with a fresh breeze from the north-west, as Captain Ringgold had predicted, and the change in the direction of the wind had knocked down the sea. At sunrise the Blanche was over thirty miles south-east of Sandy Hook, for this was the course agreed upon by the two captains. They had no information whatever in regard to the course or the movements of the Maud. On the one hand she might have gone into some cove, bay, or inlet which she had visited before; and on the other hand it was possible that she had laid her course directly for Bermuda.

"The rascal knows that I am as much interested in this affair as though Mrs. Belgrave were my own sister," said the captain from the Park. "He knows, or he ought to know, that neither Louis nor I will give up the pursuit till we recover the lady."

"I don't know this Scoble, except as an exceedingly stupid skipper; but of course he cannot be aware that any vessel is in pursuit of him," suggested Captain Alcorn.

"He cannot absolutely know that we are chasing him; but I feel reasonably sure the fellow will expect to be pursued."

"He knows something about the Kills where he anchored, and he may not be willing to believe that we could find any craft in which to follow him at once. It was only by a very lucky chance that the Blanche happened to be where you found her. We can conjecture a dozen courses Scoble may take, and any one of them is as likely to be correct as any other," continued the commander of the yacht.

"It must be admitted that we are entirely in the dark in regard to his movements. He has laid his course for Bermuda, or he has gone into some hiding-place on Long Island or the Jersey coast," said Captain Ringgold. "I think there is no doubt on this point."

"I agree with you that he has done one of these two things, for he could not have done anything else. I am sorry to say I cannot leave the Blanche at your disposition any longer than to-day, for my owner ordered me to be off Twenty-third Street by one o'clock to-morrow afternoon," added Captain Alcorn.

"I have no doubt we shall be able to come to some conclusion before night," added the other captain. "The Maud had about four hours the lead of us."

"She got the change of wind not long after midnight, and then she could have turned out her reefs," argued the commander of the Blanche.

"With a leading wind very likely she made eight knots; I don't believe she could do any better than that."

"Thirty-two miles the start of us. We have been making twelve knots, for I have crowded her to the utmost," said Captain Alcorn, as he took a paper and pencil from his pocket, and began to figure up the time and distances. "If the Maud is headed directly for Bermuda, she is forty-six sea miles to the southward and eastward of Sandy Hook, at the most. My dead reckoning would give us thirty-six miles, or only ten astern of the Maud. In three hours more we shall either see her, or be ready to give her up on this course."

"Precisely so, captain," returned the other nautical authority. "Then we shall be satisfied that the Maud has not sailed directly for Bermuda."

"Then a course to the west south-west will take us to Barnegat Inlet, where we may obtain information at the light-house on the south side of the entrance, as to whether or not such a schooner as the Maud has gone in this morning."

This plan was adopted by the two captains. Louis was fast asleep in one of the berths in the cabin. He had been up till half-past three in the morning when the yacht got under way, and he was well-nigh exhausted. He was terribly anxious about his guardian-mother; but he had some consolation in the knowledge that Felix McGavonty was with her, and that he would protect and defend her from all harm.

Captain Ringgold had done his best to comfort him with the assurance that it would not be the policy of Scoble to annoy or persecute his mother. His sole object was to effect a reconciliation with her, and he certainly could not accomplish it by ill-treating her. It was sound reasoning, and Louis accepted it. The only thing he had to fear was that she would be overborne by the wily persuasions of the villain, though even in this respect he was tolerably confident that she would be unyielding after the strong position she had taken.

Solaced by the reasonable view of his excellent friend, he had consented to take to a berth in the cabin, and endeavor to obtain some rest. Captain Ringgold did not seem to require any sleep, so carried away was he by the interest he felt in the enterprise in which he was engaged. After all that he had said to Louis, he found Bickling, the cook, asleep on a divan in the cabin.

This man had given all the information that had been obtained in regard to the intentions of Scoble, especially that the Maud was going to Bermuda. It had been conveyed in a very hurried manner while the party were walking from the creek to the town, in the midst of the excitement of the occasion, and the shipmaster was not quite satisfied with it. He did not scruple to rouse the cook from his deep slumber for the purpose of examining him more at his leisure.

"You heard Captain Scoble say that he was bound for Bermuda, did you?" demanded the captain, as he seated himself at the cabin table, some distance from Louis's berth.

"Which I did, sir, and very plainly too, sir," replied Bickling after a long and heavy gape.

"Did he give any reason for going to Bermuda?"

"Which he did not then, sir; but Stowin, which it is one of the seamen of the vessel, told me 'e 'ad a brother there, which was the keeper of an 'otel in St. George's. Perhaps you don't know about the Bermuda Islands, sir?"

"I have been there half a dozen times, and know all about the islands. Stowin told you Captain Scoble had a brother there?"

"Which he did, sir, and that the captain had ten thousand pounds left him by his uncle in India, and 'e 'ad a bill for the same money for his brother, which his name is 'Enery Scoble, and I 'ave been to his 'otel in St. George, sir."

In answer to the questions of the captain, Bickling said he had first met Scoble at a restaurant in Baltimore, where he was order-cook. His furnace was in the dining-room, and the captain of the Maud had spoken to him about obtaining a cook for his vessel. As he wanted to return to England, he had engaged with him for the voyage, as Scoble said he was to have a lady passenger, and wanted to have a good table for her.

"But where was Scoble's vessel at this time?" asked Captain Ringgold.

"Which it was somewhere on the coast of New Jersey, sir, and I don't just know where; but he called it Dolphin Bay," replied the cook.

"I never heard of such a bay," added the shipmaster; "and I don't believe there is one of that same name."

"Which it is what Scoble called it; and I know nothing at all about it, sir. We went to Philadelphia, and then a long way farther by railway, and walked about seven miles over bogs and ma'shes, till we found the schooner made fast to an island."

The captain thought it more than possible that the Maud would seek the same concealment as on that occasion, when he was hiding his vessel and himself, and he was very desirous to obtain a better knowledge of the place. The cook was profoundly ignorant in regard to the situation of the bay, and he could obtain no satisfactory information. At three bells in the forenoon watch he went on deck; but no vessel could be seen that bore the least resemblance to the Maud.

Captain Alcorn was confident that he should have overhauled the schooner before this time, and it was agreed that it was useless to continue the pursuit in this direction. The yacht was then headed for Barnegat Inlet, and at half-past two in the afternoon a boat was sent ashore to make inquiries, in charge of Captain Ringgold. No such vessel as the Maud had passed the Light that day, and the course was laid to the northward.

Several inlets were entered, and diligent inquiry made for the Maud. No one on the coast had ever heard of Dolphin Bay, and it was evident that Scoble had given the name to the inlet himself in order to blind the cook, for he had strong motives for concealing the vessel and himself. It was impossible in the time at the disposal of the pursuers to make a thorough survey. In one of the inlets they approached they could find no inhabitants, and possibly this one was "Dolphin Bay." At nine o'clock in the evening Captain Ringgold and Louis were landed at the destination of the Blanche, just in time to take a train for home.

Louis was thoroughly cast down and disheartened at the ill-success of the search for the Maud. Devoted as he had always been to his mother, he had never known before how much he loved her, as one appreciates a parent more than ever before after he has lost her. He was so exhausted by his efforts and the excitement of the day, that he had slept a considerable portion of the time the yacht had been at sea.

The captain was not cast down; but he was very indignant and disappointed at the trick which had been played upon them, and at the failure to bring the guilty perpetrators of it to justice and retribution. He blamed himself that he had not been more cautious in leaving the mate alone in the boat for even a single minute.

The train moved on, and the shipmaster was silent and in deep thought for half the distance to the Park. He had not the slightest idea of giving up the battle, and he was willing to spend half his fortune in recovering the lady who had been kidnapped. Captain Alcorn had suggested to Mr. Boulong that the gentleman from the Park had a very deep and unusual interest in the fate of the lady, and they indulged in some sly remarks on the subject. Louis did not hear them, and he had no suspicion that his friend was actuated by any other than the most unselfish and disinterested motives.

The captain had been acquainted for years with Mrs. Belgrave, and at one time had been a rather earnest admirer of the lady. When Louis had asked him to visit the Oxford with him as an expert, he was very much pleased to learn that the mother of the young millionaire was to be one of the party. The widow of Paul Belgrave was hardly in a situation to marry till Scoble had in some manner been shaken off. But whatever the retired shipmaster was thinking about in relation to the lady, it was absolutely certain that she had not the remotest idea of marrying either him or any other gentleman.

"Louis, I hope you have given up the idea of buying such an old tub as the Maud for a yacht," said the captain as they approached the Park.

"I have thought no more about the matter, sir," replied Louis moodily.

"I have been thinking about the matter all day. I have an idea now. If you had been the owner of a steamer like that built for Colonel Singfield, we should get your mother back in the course of a day or two. She steamed sixteen knots an hour on her trial trip, and she is all ready to go to sea."

"If I had been the owner of such a steamer, my mother would not have been trapped on board of the Maud," added Louis with a faint smile.

"I wish we had her under our control at this moment," said the captain with a great deal of earnestness. "Louis, if Uncle Moses will consent to it, I will buy this steam-yacht with you!"

There was something like desperation in the manner of Captain Ringgold. He was popularly supposed to be worth half a million of dollars. He was a widower and had no children, and doubtless he felt at liberty to use his wealth for his own amusement. Louis was startled at the idea.

CHAPTER 24
THE GUARDIAN-MOTHER

CAPTAIN RINGGOLD AND LOUIS Belgrave reached Von Blonk Park just as the former expressed his readiness to join in the purchase of the new steam-yacht. The young millionaire was so startled at the idea, that he could say nothing, and they left the train after only a mention of the subject. As usual there was a crowd around the station, and they had no opportunity to discuss the question. It was late in the evening; but the shipmaster went with his young friend to the residence of Uncle Moses, the temporary home of Louis.

A steam-yacht that would cost in the vicinity of a hundred thousand dollars, and whose running-expenses would amount to a large sum, was a tremendously big question to the young man of sixteen who had always lived in plenty, but never in luxury. But he did not feel that he was to be responsible for the financial settlement of the question, for Uncle Moses could veto the plan without even a word of explanation if he was so disposed.

"How big is this yacht of which you speak, Captain Ringgold?" asked Louis, still appalled at the thought of such a heavy investment.

"I am not very sure on that point, though she is big enough for a voyage around the world," replied the captain. "My impression is that she is a vessel of about six hundred tons, though she may be considerably smaller than that."

"Do you believe we could get my mother back if we had her?"

"I feel reasonably sure of it, Louis. In fact, it looks like a very plain case to me," replied the captain with enthusiasm. "We could sail around that old tub a dozen times a day, for I don't believe the Maud can make more than eight knots an hour under the most favorable circumstances."

"How long do you suppose the Maud will remain in her present hiding-place, wherever it may be?" asked Louis.

"Less than a day, I should suppose. Scoble is as much bothered to know what our movements will be, as we are to understand what he will do. As you told me the villain has no suspicion that the missing million has been reclaimed, and that you are now worth a million and a half, he will not expect a pursuit on a grand scale, such as we are now considering. He supposes you have an income of less than a thousand dollars a year, and he will not believe it possible that we can pursue him with anything more than a small sailing-vessel."

"He may have come out of his hole before this time, and gone on his way to Bermuda."

"He may, but I don't believe he has. He will hardly believe that we can organize a pursuit before to-morrow morning, and he will hardly dare to come out before twenty-four hours from the present time."

"How long before the steam-yacht will be in readiness to sail?"

"I cannot answer that question definitely; but not in less than a whole day, I should say. I believe she has her crew on board at the present time, for Colonel Singfield intended to sail in her the very day he died."

"But Scoble will get away from us before that time," suggested Louis.

"I am confident he will not come out of his hole before to-morrow night, and perhaps not till the next morning; but all this is guess-work, and he may be on his way to Bermuda at this moment. It is no use to follow him in a sailing-vessel. But here we are at the squire's house, and there is a light in the office. I have no doubt he is very much worried about you and your mother."

Louis led the way into the office of Uncle Moses without the ceremony of knocking. The worthy lawyer was smoking his cigar very vigorously, and had probably exceeded his usual indulgence on this extraordinary occasion. The moment he saw Louis he sprang out of his big chair as briskly as though he had been a trained athlete, and rushed upon the young man, hugging him as his mother would have done on a similar provocation.

"My dear boy!" cried the two hundred pounder, shaking all over with emotion. "Where have you been? I expected you and your mother back by the middle of the afternoon. I am afraid something has happened."

"Something has happened, Uncle Moses," replied Louis, bursting into tears.

"But where is your mother, my poor boy?" demanded the squire, suddenly losing the cheerful expression on his fat face.

"She is John Scoble's prisoner on board of his vessel," replied Louis, dropping into a chair and covering his face with both hands, while he wept as though his heart was broken.

"Good-evening, Captain Ringgold," continued the squire, hardly able to restrain his own feelings, as he turned to the shipmaster. "What does all this mean?"

"It means that we have been tricked, trapped, outwitted by this Scoble!" exclaimed the captain, with a mixture of shame and indignation. "The vessel we went to look at was the Maud, and the whole plot was to get Louis and his mother on board of her."

"Take a cigar, Captain; sit down and tell me all about it," said the squire. "Don't cry, Louis; we shall find a way out of this trouble, as we have out of all others, though this appears to be the severest trial that has beset you, my dear boy," added Uncle Moses, as tenderly as a woman could have spoken.

Captain Ringgold lighted his cigar, and related very minutely all the incidents of the day; and his indignation waxed almost furious when he came to the part in which the mate had so cleverly tricked him. Squire Scarburn listened with his mouth half open at the exciting details. Then he asked a number of questions which the captain answered.

"It is not so bad as I feared it might be," said the squire when he was in possession of all the details. "We have had a heavy gale here since you went away this morning, and I was afraid you had gone out to sea to try the vessel. I concluded that you were out on the ocean, and that some of you had been drowned."

"Not so bad as that," replied the captain.

"Terrible as Louis considers the situation, I am greatly relieved to learn that it is no worse," added Uncle Moses. "That this Scoble is a rascal, there can be no doubt, but"—

"He has not the remotest suspicion that the missing million has been recovered, as Louis tells me, for the villain tried to effect his reconciliation with Mrs. Belgrave by informing her and her son where the treasure was concealed," interposed the captain.

"So much the better," answered Uncle Moses, nodding his head half a dozen times to express his satisfaction more forcibly. "As long as the money has been found, and even if it had not been found, Mrs. Belgrave has nothing to fear from her late husband. With Louis I believe it would have been different; and I wonder these conspirators have not contrived some way to have him fall overboard. But what is to be done? We won't waste even one of the dark minutes of the night."

"You are aware that just before we parted this morning I protested to you against the purchase of any old tub of a vessel for Louis," replied Captain Ringgold.

"I remember; and you said something about a steam-yacht, though I did not quite understand what you were driving at."

"I believe you ought not to permit Louis to risk his life in anything but the strongest and most seaworthy craft that can be built, and especially not in any such old death-trap as the Maud. Now will you excuse me if I ask what may seem to you to be impertinent questions?" continued the captain, very earnestly.

"Certainly, my dear sir; I know now, if I did not know it before, that you are one of Louis's best friends, and whatever you say will be for his good."

"I have something to propose, and I wish to know the extent of the young man's fortune," added the captain.

"He has one million four hundred thousand dollars, well invested, besides a surplus of about one hundred thousand dollars, which I have kept on deposit for any emergency," replied Squire Scarburn promptly.

"I think the emergency has come, even independently of the kidnapping of the boy's mother. Now, what is his probable income?"

"Seventy thousand dollars; for his money will pay an average of five per cent, and I am confident it is safely placed."

"Good!" exclaimed the shipmaster. "Better than I supposed."

Captain Ringgold then introduced the subject of purchasing the steam-yacht as yet without a name. The good squire was startled when he named the price it was expected to pay for the vessel, and shook his head rather ominously.

"I will give all I have in the world to get my mother back, and a hundred thousand dollars is nothing but a bagatelle compared with the safety and happiness of my mother!" exclaimed Louis, who had been listening eagerly to all that was said.

"But I propose to pay one-half of the price, and own one-half of the vessel," interposed Captain Ringgold. "And of course I shall pay one-half of the expense of running the steamer."

This proposition seemed to knock the squire entirely out of his self-possession; and he paused in silence, gazing intently at the shipmaster as if he desired to fathom his motive in making an offer so startlingly liberal. He had no especial interest in Louis, though he and the boy had always been warm friends. It occurred just then to the squire, and perhaps it had occurred to him before, that the captain had an especial interest in Louis's mother, as he certainly had had a few years before.

Uncle Moses was silent for some time, during which he did some heavy thinking, though no one could know precisely what it was all about. Perhaps he was considering whether or not he ought to make such a heavy investment in what he regarded as a mere plaything for the boy. But he soon came to a conclusion, and his fat face brightened up all at once, his habitual smile recovering possession of it.

"No, no, Captain Ringgold; I could not for a moment think of accepting your proposition. If Louis is to own a steam-yacht, he must own it himself alone," said the squire very decidedly.

"Of course I made the offer solely to help along the plan we have in view for the recovery of Mrs. Belgrave; more than this, I believe the purchase at the price it can be bought will be a good investment, for she cost a good deal more money than they ask for her," replied the captain, taken all aback by the firm and decisive conclusion of the trustee, though it possibly upset some hope he had been indulging.

The shipmaster's manner assured the squire that he had come to a correct conclusion, for he felt that he had no right to complicate the affairs of the mother in looking out for the welfare of the son. He did not consider that it would be proper for him to put the worthy nautical gentleman in condition to "make his way" with Mrs. Belgrave by permitting him to become half-owner in the steam-yacht.

"Now, my dear captain, can you give me an idea of the probable expense of running this steamer?" asked Uncle Moses.

"Fifty thousand dollars a year might easily be spent on such a yacht, but I believe it will not cost your ward more than half that sum. I believe that a trip around the world in such a craft would be worth more to him than a college course, especially if he took a competent instructor with him," replied the expert.

"That would just suit me!" exclaimed Louis.

"Buy the yacht for him then, Captain Ringgold," added the trustee. "He will not spend more than half his income at that rate."

"What shall her name be?" asked the shipmaster.

"The Guardian-Mother," replied Louis without an instant's hesitation.

CHAPTER 25
ON BOARD OF THE PHANTOM

CAPTAIN RINGGOLD EXPRESSED HIS astonishment in his looks at the name the young millionaire had chosen for his yacht, and Uncle Moses shook his fat frame with laughter. Probably they supposed he would select the "Thunderer," the "Skyrocket," the "Boomerang," or at least the "Sea-Nymph," the "Ocean-Bird," or some similar appellation, as most boys would have been likely to do.

"That is rather a strange name for a steam-yacht of six hundred tons," suggested the shipmaster.

"I would have called her the 'Maud,' after my mother, if Scoble had not given the name to that schooner,

'Built in the eclipse and rigged with curses dark.'

If I should set up an idol on earth, in a metaphorical sense, I should call it the 'Guardian-Mother,' and it would mean her who has watched over me all my life," replied Louis, the tears beginning to fill his eyes again. "If this steam-yacht means anything to me, it means the safety and happiness of my mother, with whom in my inmost thoughts I have for some time associated this name."

"There is not another word to be said!" exclaimed Captain Ringgold. "I know what it means now."

"It is not a bad name at all," added the squire. "I think it is rather poetical."

"I know what it means to me, and I don't care whether anybody else knows or not," added Louis, wiping away his tears.

"The question is fully understood now," said the captain, springing from his chair and consulting his watch. "The last train leaves in half an hour, and we must go to New York by it. Squire Scarburn, you had better have Mrs. Blossom pack up all Mrs. Belgrave's clothing, linen, and trinkets, with plenty of warm wraps."

While Louis was packing his valise, for he was not sure that he could return the next day, Uncle Moses drew several checks, payable to the captain's order, taking his receipt for the amount. The shipmaster went to his own house for his clothing, and they left for New York by the train. The squire hugged Louis again, and gave him a large check for the expenses of the expedition in which he was to be engaged. It was understood that Captain Ringgold was to go with him to Bermuda, or wherever else he might go.

"Now, Louis, you will soon be the owner of as fine a steamer as ever went out of New York harbor, and I hope that inside of ten days you will have your mother settled in the best stateroom on board of her," said the shipmaster when they were seated in the car.

"I hope so with all my heart; and when that comes to pass I shall feel as though I owed more to you for it than to all others," replied the embryo yacht owner warmly.

"Not at all, Louis; I am almost as much interested in this business as you are; and I pledge you my life, my property, and my sacred honor to stand by you to the end," said the captain very pleasantly.

"Thank you, sir; and when I see my mother I shall inform her that she owes more to you than to me for whatever has been done for her."

This remark pleased the nautical expert very much; but if Uncle Moses had been on the train, and could have prevented it, he would not have permitted his ward to make such a promise. The captain said no more about that matter, but his head was very full of business.

"I suppose you are tired out, Louis; but there is a good deal to be done even before morning. I am not quite satisfied to leave Scoble to himself till we are ready to 'go for him' in the Guardian-Mother," said he, beginning to state his proposed arrangements. "I cannot go down to Dolphin Bay, if there is any such bay, or to the coast of Jersey, for I have to attend to the purchase of the steamer, and the fitting of her out to-morrow. I know where I can find a small steamer commanded by a man I have assisted to purchase her, and I am going to send you down with him to be on the watch for the Maud. You can sleep all you want to as soon as you get on board of her."

Captain Ringgold proceeded to detail his plans. While he was doing so he happened to look across the aisle of the car, and discovered there, somewhat to his astonishment, Bickling, the cook of the Maud. He had gone with them by the train to Von Blonk Park; but in the excitement of the hour both Louis and the captain had forgotten all about him. He was busily engaged in conversation with a man in the seat with him, to whom the cook seemed to be telling some sort of a story.

The man with whom Bickling was talking was apparently about forty years old, with nothing particularly noticeable about him. As the cook had never been in this part of the country, it was hardly probable that he had ever met him before. The couple seemed to be very intimate for so short an acquaintance. On the ferry-boat Bickling approached Louis, and very politely and deferentially saluted him.

"I have been so busy that I forgot all about you, Bickling," said Louis.

"Which I got out of the railway carriage when you did, sir; and I waited a long time for this train, sir," added the cook.

"Who is the man with you?" asked Louis in a low tone.

"Which his name it is Flounder, sir; and I never saw him before to-night in all my life, sir; but he is a Hinglishman, sir, and we made friends at once, sir; for a Hinglishman is a Hinglishman all over the world, sir," replied Bickling.

"You were telling him a long story on the train."

"Which I told him about my little cruise in the Maud; 'ow the lady and 'er son 'ad been kidnapped, sir, and he was very sorry indeed, sir, for you, for he knew Captain Scoble when he lived 'ere; and he wished 'e could 'elp you get back the lady."

"I am very much obliged to him," replied Louis, who had already decided to take the cook with him, believing he might be serviceable to him on account of his knowledge of the vessel. "I am going down to the Jersey coast in a steamer; if you are willing, I should like to have you go with me, and I will pay you wages."

"Thank you, sir; which I shall be very 'appy to go, sir, and to serve you like a good master as you are, sir. This is my friend Mr. Flounder, sir," said the cook, presenting his companion.

The man bowed very obsequiously, and proceeded to explain himself. He knew John Scoble very well, for he had loaned him two hundred dollars from his savings, and the jockey had run away without paying him a cent. If he could see him again he would take it out of his hide, if he couldn't get it out of his pocket. He was out of work just then, and he would be glad to follow Scoble if he could and get his money, for Mr. Bickling said that his debtor had inherited a fortune.

"What were you doing out at Von Blonk Park so late in the night?" asked Louis.

"I went out to find Mr. Steinberger; I am used to horses, and I thought he might give me a job. I waited all the evening for him, sir, and he did not come home," replied Flounder.

Louis spoke to Captain Ringgold about him, and decided to take the man with him. He had a grudge against Scoble, and this fact seemed to assure his fidelity, though it was hardly a reliable recommendation. A carriage was procured, and the party drove direct to a pier where several small steamers lay. The captain soon found the one he wanted, and they went on board, of her. She appeared to have just come to her landing-place, and the steam was hissing still in her pipes. She was a screw steamer, somewhat larger than the ordinary tug-boats, and was called the Phantom.

Captain Brisbane, the owner and commander, had not yet turned in: he gave the shipmaster from the Park a warm welcome, and the latter explained the object of his visit at that late hour. Captain Ringgold had been very confident from the first that the Maud had gone to the southward, for that course gave her a fair wind. It required about half an hour to agree on the details of the intended trip, and by that time the Phantom was in condition to depart.

"Now, Louis, I don't much care whether or not you find the Maud; for as soon as I can get the Guardian-Mother to sea, we shall make easy work of this business," said the captain, as he grasped the hand of the young millionaire. "I have directed Captain Brisbane to look into all the openings on the Jersey coast as far as Barnegat Inlet, for I feel sure that the Maud has not gone any farther south. But the main thing is to observe the schooner if she comes out of any inlet on the shore, and keep watch of her. Keep her in sight, but don't attempt to board her. Captain Brisbane will follow your directions in all things. Now turn in, and the captain will call you at about four o'clock in the morning, when the Phantom will be off Squam Beach, or sooner if any schooner is discovered coming out of an inlet. Bickling slept enough last night, and he can identify the Maud; and it may not be necessary to call you unless the Phantom overhauls her."

The shipmaster took his leave of the young man, and proceeded in the carriage that was waiting for him to the residence of Captain Singfield, a brother of the late owner of the new steam-yacht, who had the disposal of the handsome craft in his hands. Captain Brisbane showed Louis to a stateroom, and he was between the sheets before the steamer got away from the pier. Flounder went to the forecastle to find a place to sleep, while the cook spread himself out on the divan in the pilot-house to finish his night's sleep.

It was about sunrise when Louis was called. He had slept five hours, and he felt like a new millionaire. He found that the Phantom had been off Squam an hour or more, waiting for the tide to make a little more. Every vessel that could possibly be the Maud had been followed and examined, but Bickling pronounced against all of them. The steamer was to make thorough work of the search this time. The plan had been laid out by Captain Ringgold, and if the schooner came out of any inlet on the high tide she would be intercepted by the steamer.

The Phantom ran into an inlet with an Indian name, and a boat was sent ashore to make inquiries at a life-saving station. The Maud had not been seen, and the men were sure that no such craft had gone in at the opening. The steamer then proceeded to the north about six miles to another opening in the coast. Louis had gone to the pilot-house, and was looking with all his might in every direction for any appearance of the fugitive craft. The captain rang his bell to stop her as soon as she had passed into a broad inlet which extended some distance to the north. The shore here was covered with pines, so that a portion of the sheet of water could not be seen.

"I wrote down all the facts, time, and distances, as Captain Ringgold gave them to me," said Captain Brisbane, as he took a paper from his little desk in one corner of the pilot-house. "The Maud left her anchorage last night at eleven o'clock, Mr. Belgrave. In my judgment, the schooner could not have got any farther to the south than we are now."

"Well, captain, what shall we do?" asked Louis.

"From the point where we are now, we can look out to sea and observe every vessel that goes along the coast, and we can intercept anything coming out of this bay," replied Captain Brisbane, with a long gape. "I have but a small crew, and the fact of it is that we are all about used up, I have not slept a wink for thirty hours; neither have my engineer and the hands. You have two men with you who ought to be fresh, for they have been asleep for the last six hours. I can't go in any farther, for the tide would leave me high and dry before noon. Now, if you are so disposed, you can take the boat, and explore the bay to your satisfaction, while the rest of us get a little sleep."

Louis decided at once to examine the bay, and his two men were called.

CHAPTER 26
AMONG THE PINES

BICKLING HAD CERTAINLY SLEPT enough, for he had been on the divan about ten hours during the evening and the morning, when Louis roused him from his slumbers. He sprang from his bed very promptly, and looking about him mildly inquired where he was. Then he went to the windows in front of the pilot-house and looked out for some time in silence.

"Do you know where you are now, Bickling?" asked Louis.

"Which I think I do, sir. It looks as though we were in Dolphin Bay again," replied the cook, as he continued his examination of the surroundings.

"Like Dolphin Bay!" exclaimed Louis, recognizing the fictitious name which Scoble had given the cook when he first went on board of the vessel; and he was satisfied that this was the locality where Scoble had concealed her appearance by painting her white.

"Which I am not quite sure, sir; but it looks like Dolphin Bay," answered Bickling, as he settled his gaze upon the expanse of water to the north of the steamer.

"I should think you would know the place if you had ever been here before," added Louis rather impatiently.

"Which it looks just like it, sir; but I was busy getting breakfast when we came out of the bay, and I did not watch the shore," pleaded the cook. "I was on board of the Maud two nights and a day before she sailed, which it was not in this part of the bay at all where she lay."

"Where did she lay, then?"

"Which I see it all now, sir!" exclaimed Bickling as he pointed across the bay. "Do you mind the point, sir, over on the other side, sir? It reaches over within a quarter of a mile of the shore on your left, and is covered with pines."

"I can see it plain enough."

"Which the water extends up beyond the point, sir, where you can't see it; and it was in there where the Maud was tied to a tree, sir."

This was definite enough. There was a considerable expanse of water at the south-west of the point, and the bay formed a W, upside down from the pilot-house, the space between the two acute angles forming the point covered with trees. The two deck hands of the steamer were getting the boat ready for the expedition, and Flounder had come up from the forecastle.

"Flounder, do you know how to row?" asked Louis, who had gone down to the main deck with the captain, followed by the cook.

"I do, sir; I made two voyages up the Mediterranean when I was twenty years younger than I am now," replied the recruit.

"I will pay you for your services, and I want you to row the boat with Bickling," added Louis.

"Now you must be very prudent, Mr. Belgrave," said Captain Brisbane, as the two men took their places in the boat. "If you get into any trouble over there, I can't do a thing to help you. The Phantom would be hard and fast on the bottom before I could get her over to that point, and I have only one boat."

"I mean to be always prudent, Captain," replied Louis, as he took his place in the stern sheets of the boat.

The young millionaire shoved off with the boat-hook, and the two men gave way very well together. There was no rudder to the boat, but Louis found an oar, which he used in the rowlock in the stern board.

The distance across to the point was about a mile, and Louis steered directly for it. He had decided to land there; if the Maud was concealed around the neck of land, he preferred not to come upon her in the boat.

The schooner still had four men on board of her, and he had no doubt Scoble would recognize him the moment he set eyes on him. He would then understand that his hiding-place was discovered, and in his desperation he was capable of being very wicked. It would be more prudent, as Captain Ringgold had cautioned him to be, and Captain Brisbane had repeated the warning, to land at the point, and move up among the pines on the shore till the Maud was discovered, if she was there.

"I beg your pardon, sir, but don't you think it would be better to run farther up the bay than the point, sir?" asked Flounder, who was pulling the stroke oar.

"I do not think so," replied Louis very decidedly. "I am going to land on the point."

"I don't believe the vessel you are looking for is up here at all, and I don't care about doing any more walking than is necessary," added Flounder, in a tone which bordered upon impudence to his employer. "By going a little way up the bay to the north, you can see all there is here that floats."

"Nothing more need be said about it; we are going to the point," replied Louis, quietly but firmly.

Flounder said no more. Whatever the recruit might be, there was evidently an element of insubordination in him. But he hated Scoble, and intended to get either money or revenge out of him. The boat reached the point, and Louis ran it up on the beach.

"Bickling, you may go on shore, and walk up far enough to enable you to see whether or not there is a vessel around the point," said Louis. "If you find the Maud there, and you will know her at once, come back immediately, and you need not go near her."

"Which I don't want to go near her, sir," replied the cook, as he stepped ashore, and started to obey the order.

"I think I will go with him," added Flounder, as he leaped out of the boat.

"Very well; but if the Maud is there, don't go near her," replied the leader.

"If I get my eye on Scoble, I shall want to know if he has any money in his pockets," answered the recruit.

Louis was not particularly well pleased with Flounder, for he had begun to develop a sort of lawlessness in his manner. But if Scoble got hold of him, and made a prisoner of him, it made but little difference to him, for he could readily dispense with the services of such a man. The two men disappeared around the point, where the ground seemed to be dry, though it was nothing but a bog on the south side.

Reasoning from the opinions expressed by the nautical experts, Louis expected to find the Maud in this bay, which the cook had recognized as the one where Scoble had concealed her before. She had come to the southward because that course gave her a fair wind; and she had not sailed directly for Bermuda, for the Blanche would certainly have overhauled her if she had done so. The chase must have put in at some inlet; and as Scoble had been into "Dolphin Bay" before, it was quite probable that he had sheltered himself here again.

Louis sat in the boat for half an hour or more, thinking over the situation, and wondering when the Guardian-Mother would arrive. She could hardly be expected before the next day, and all the Phantom had to do was to blockade the inlet, in accordance with the instructions of Captain Ringgold. While he was reflecting very busily, he heard a yell from the shore.

"Help! help!" was the appeal that came to him; and the voice was like that of Bickling.

He was startled at the cry, and he wondered if Scoble was in the act of recovering possession of his cook. Leaping from the boat on the impulse of the moment, he was about to rush to the assistance of the person who needed aid, when he discovered that the boat was afloat because he had moved his weight out of it. He drew it far up on the beach, but it reminded him that he was to use prudence. If the boat had gone adrift the tide would have carried it out to sea, unless the watch on the Phantom intercepted it.

"Help! help! murder!" yelled the voice again, and not very far from him.

Louis ran with all his might in the direction taken by the two men, and soon came upon them. The cook was on the ground, and the recruit was bending over him, apparently engaged in binding his arms behind him.

"What are you about?" demanded Louis, in good, vigorous English. "What are you doing with that man?"

"Softly, you little chickenpop! You needn't come any nearer, for this affair is mine and not yours," returned the ruffian.

"I shall make it my affair! Let the man up at once!"

"If you will excuse me, I will not do it," replied Flounder.

"I think you will!" added Louis, breaking into a run, and rushing with all his might to the scene of the outrage.

"Stop where you are!" shouted Flounder, as he rose to an upright position with one of his feet on the chest of his victim so that he could not move.

At the same moment the cook's assailant levelled a revolver at the head of the young man, who had not been intimidated by his threats. But Louis already had his hand upon his own weapon, and perhaps forgetting the lessons in prudence which had been given to him that day and often before, he drew it out, and fired instantly. The revolver which was pointed at his head suddenly dropped upon the ground, and the arm that held it fell to the side of the assailant.

Louis was prudent, though he had acted as quick as a flash. His bullet sped on its way before Flounder could realize what he was doing. One of the lessons he had taken at the shooting gallery had prepared him for just the practice he needed, to save himself. He had not intended to kill or mortally wound his opponent. All he desired was to save himself, and he had done so by disabling the ruffian.

As the revolver dropped upon the ground, Bickling sprang to his feet. He saw Louis; he also saw the weapon where it had fallen, and he picked it up. Evidently Flounder was suffering a good deal of pain, judging from the expression on his face. He seemed to be sort of dazed by the suddenness of his opponent's action, as well as by his injury. Bickling ran towards Louis. He was as white as a sheet, frightened half out of his senses, though he did not seem to be otherwise injured. He tendered the revolver he had picked up to his deliverer, who put it in his left hip-pocket.

At the same moment, the ruffian, conscious that he was utterly defeated by that single shot, started to move away from the others. The battle among the pines seemed to satisfy him. But the victor was not disposed to allow him to escape in that direction. He did not yet understand the situation, and had no idea what had caused him to fall upon such an innocent and pluckless person as the cook.

"Stop, Flounder!" called Louis, sharply enough to produce an impression on the ruffian, while he still kept his smoking revolver in his hand.

The man stopped; but he seemed to be very much disheartened and disgusted at the turn the affair had taken. Why he should move in the direction he had taken unless the Maud was there, Louis could not imagine.

"You threatened my life with a revolver, and you have been disabled. I have no ill-feeling towards you, and I propose to take you on board of the steamer, where you can be properly attended to," said Louis, in a mild tone.

"I shall not go on board of the steamer again," replied Flounder, gathering up somewhat from his depression.

"But you will go to the steamer!" added Louis sternly. "Bickling, did you see any vessel up the bay?"

"Which I did, and the Maud is there, sir," answered the cook.

"That is all I want to know now," continued the plucky leader, as he walked up to Flounder, and told him to march for the boat.

The ruffian refused to do so. Louis took him by the collar, and then a scuffle ensued; but the recruit could do nothing with his right shoulder disabled, and fell to the ground. With the assistance of the cook, Louis dragged him to the boat, put him into it, and then shoved off.

CHAPTER 27
AN AGENT OF THE ENEMY

BY THIS TIME LOUIS had come to believe that "Flounder" was not the real name of the recruit he had picked up. The fellow had been out to Von Blonk Park, but he doubted if he had been near Mr. Steinberger's residence. But he had not time to consider the matter then, for his prisoner was very restive, and protested against being conveyed to the Phantom in his present wounded condition.

"What do you wish me to do with you?" demanded Louis as he ceased rowing, for the boat was now at a considerable distance from the point.

"Put me back on the shore from which you had no right to take me," replied Flounder.

"Do you wish me to leave you, wounded as you are, in the woods there?"

"I can take care of myself better than you can take care of me."

"As I understand the situation, I engaged you to work for me, engaged your passage on the steamer, and agreed to pay you wages. I shall not desert you now that you are wounded," added Louis.

"Who wounded me?" asked the recruit.

"I did, when you threatened my life with your revolver. In self-defence I fired at you, and hit you just where I intended, for I did not mean to kill or seriously injure you; and I don't believe I have done so."

"Our contract ended when you fired at me, and I insist upon being put ashore," said Flounder, rising from his seat in the stern sheets, where Louis had placed him. "Either return me to the point, or I will jump over and swim for it, for I can do so with one arm left."

Louis felt that he had a stronger motive than the comfort of the recruit in retaining him; for the cook had informed him that the Maud was in the bay, and this man would be only another person added to the force of Scoble. Flounder had risen from his seat in the stern sheets, and turned to look at the distance between him and the shore, evidently measuring it with his eye, and estimating his power to accomplish it by swimming with one hand.

The wounded man was about the size of Scoble, and the young millionaire had already convinced himself that he was more than a match for him, at least in his present half-disabled condition. He judged that the fellow really intended to make the attempt to swim to the point, which was not more than a hundred feet distant. Rising in his place at the stroke oar, he seized Flounder by the back of his coat collar, and then sat down again, dragging his opponent after him.

The victim struggled, but taken at a disadvantage he could not make an effectual resistance.

Louis held him fast, and rolled him over to one side, so that he rested on the after thwart upon his left shoulder, his wound being in the right one. He kept him in this position, looking about the boat till he discovered a roll of spun-yarn, which he directed the cook to pass to him.

Still holding his prisoner upon the thwart, he ordered Bickling to make fast the left wrist of the man to his suspender behind, so that he could not use that arm any more than the other. In doing this the principal operator had been obliged to throw open Flounder's coat and vest. As he did so, he discovered a package of papers and letters in the pocket inside of the vest. He did not scruple to take possession of these, an act which excited the wrath of the victim to an ungovernable extent.

"Do you mean to rob me of my private papers?" demanded Flounder as Louis permitted him to roll off the thwart into the bottom of the boat.

"After a man has threatened my life with a revolver, I intend to ascertain as much about him as possible," replied Louis quietly. "Perhaps I know what I am about better than you think I do."

"This is an outrage!" roared the victim.

"I suppose it is; but I also think it was an outrage to fall upon a defenceless man, throw him down, and attempt to bind his hands behind him, as I found you in the act of doing, Mr. Flounder. I am willing to take the responsibility of everything I do."

"You will have to suffer for this! I will have satisfaction for this, if I have to follow you all over the world!" yelled the recruit, so beside himself with anger that he could hardly utter his words, and looked like a naughty boy crying in his fury.

"Give way, Bickling," said Louis, poising his oar.

"Are you going to leave me in this situation?" demanded Flounder, whom the pain suddenly reduced to something like subjection.

"Hold on a minute, Bickling," added Louis, as he left his place at the oar and stepped into the stern sheets.

Taking his victim by the collar of his coat, he raised him to the seat and placed him upon it. Flounder groaned heavily, and no doubt the movement gave him additional pain, which could hardly be avoided.

"Do you mean to kill me?" gasped the recruit.

"I do not; I am not disposed to give you any unnecessary suffering. Whatever pain you have you have brought upon yourself. Now if you will keep quiet, I will not molest you again; and when we get to the steamer, I will see that your wound is dressed and that you are properly cared for. Now, give way, Bickling."

The two oarsmen pulled till the boat reached the Phantom, which had drifted some little distance into the entrance to the inlet. Flounder had learned wisdom from his suffering, and he made no further attempt at resistance. One of the two deck hands of the steamer had slept on the passage down from the city, and he was now on watch on the forecastle. He hailed Louis to learn what had happened, for he could not help seeing the struggle in the boat.

"Call Captain Brisbane!" shouted Louis.

"What is the matter?" asked the man.

"Call the captain as quick as you can!" replied Louis sharply; and the man hastened to ascend the ladder to the pilot-house, where the commander was putting in his sleeping.

Before the boat could get alongside the steamer, Captain Brisbane came in sight, and rushed down the ladder to the forecastle. Probably the man who had been on watch had told him that something had happened to the expedition in the boat, for he manifested considerable excitement when he appeared on deck.

"What is the trouble, Mr. Belgrave?" demanded the captain.

"This man in the stern is shot in the shoulder, and I want him attended to before I say anything," replied Louis, who was a Christian at heart as well as in form, and was willing to heal the wound even of an enemy.

"Shot in the shoulder!" exclaimed the captain. "Have you been in a fight?"

The chief of the expedition did not answer the question, for the boat had come up to the gangway by this time, and he gave himself up to the duty of putting the sufferer on board. With the help of the captain and the deck hand, Flounder was easily transferred to the steamer, and conveyed to a stateroom, where he was put into the berth.

Like all masters of vessels, Captain Brisbane had some skill in prescribing for the sick, and in dressing wounds; for none but the largest vessels carry a surgeon. Somewhat to the astonishment of Louis, Flounder submitted to an examination, and behaved himself in a reasonable manner. His coat was removed, and his shirt turned down so that the wound could be seen.

"Not bad at all," said the captain, after he had looked the man over very carefully. "I have often cured worse wounds than this one on board ship. It is not in the shoulder, as you said, Mr. Belgrave: it is in the arm near the shoulder, but has not touched the bone. The ball went through the fleshy part and came out on the other side."

"I am glad it is no worse, though it seems to be painful," added Louis.

The captain proceeded to stanch the flow of blood, and then dressed the wound very skilfully for an amateur. He insisted that the patient should keep very quiet; and the party left the room. Louis insisted that he should be locked in, to which the captain assented, and declared that the man was as secure where he was as he would be in a cell in The Tombs.

"Now what is all this about, Mr. Belgrave?" demanded the captain impatiently.

"If you will direct your man on deck to watch that room, I will tell you all I know, which is hardly more than you have already learned," replied Louis, as he led the way to the forward part of the boat.

The captain directed the man on duty to watch the door of the stateroom; and the trio seated themselves on the forecastle. Louis said that Bickling must be the first one to tell his story, for he alone knew what had transpired on the shore before the leader landed.

"Which it was Flounder that fell upon me like a thief and a robber, sir, when I'ad done nothing in the world to vex 'im," replied the cook, not a little excited when he recalled the scene. "He knocked me down, sir, when I was thinking of nothing. Then 'e wanted me to go on board of the Maud, which"—

"Then the Maud, is really in this bay?" interposed, the captain. "I was sure she was here after all I had heard, if she was anywhere on the coast."

"Which she is there, and just where she was before when I first went on board, of 'er," continued Bickling. "Flounder knocked me down just as soon as we 'ad made sure the Maud was there."

"How far off were you when you saw her?" asked Louis.

"Which I couldn't say hexactly, but about as far off as that point is from us now. Then Flounder which 'e says to me that we would go on board the Maud, sir, and which I says no, I would not go any nearer to 'er, sir."

Bickling then went on to say that Flounder had threatened to kill him if he did not go with him, and had tried to tie his hands with his handkerchief. He had cried out with all his might, when the ruffian had stuffed his handkerchief into his mouth. He had struggled to get away from him, for he was afraid of him. Then Mr. Belgrave "'ad come up, which 'e was very glad to see 'im."

Louis related the rest of the narrative, including all that occurred in the boat. The final reduction of the prisoner to subjection reminded him of the package of papers he had transferred to his own pocket from that of the recruit, and he produced them. The first that attracted his attention was a letter, postmarked at Shark River the morning of the day before. The captain thought this was the nearest post-office to the inlet.

Louis did not hesitate to open the letter, for he felt that he was fighting an enemy in ambush. It was his first care to look at the signature, which was "Wade Farrongate;" and the letter was in the familiar handwriting of John Scoble. Turning to the address of the letter, he read the name of "Ovid Kimpton." Doubtless this was Flounder's real name. The letter instructed him to go at once to Von Blonk Park, find Louis Belgrave, and follow him night and day wherever he went.

The missive also contained some explanation of what he was about and where he was, including the statement of his intention to sail for Bermuda as soon as he could do so without the danger of being pursued. The movements of Flounder were thus explained. Probably he had gone to the Park, and, learning that Louis had gone away by train the day before, and that his return was expected, he had waited for him at the station, where he had met Bickling, who had told him all he wanted to know.

"What shall we do, Captain Brisbane?" he asked when he had finished.

"Nothing; Captain Ringgold told me to do nothing if we found the Maud." Louis was within a mile of his mother, and could do nothing.

CHAPTER 28
THE LAST OF THE PHANTOM

THE LETTER PROMISED TO pay Kimpton twenty dollars a day for his services; and perhaps this was the strongest reason why he wished to see his employer. Captain Brisbane went up to the pilot-house again to finish his nap, leaving Louis and the cook on the forward deck.

Bickling had certainly been faithful to his present employer, if his other recruit had not; and Louis wondered that he had mustered up pluck enough to resist the wishes of his late companion after he had resorted to violence. The cook's heart was in the right place; but he had not force of character enough to be a whole man.

The forenoon passed away, and Louis continued to be very nervous and uneasy. In spite of the injunction of Captain Ringgold, he was disposed to take the boat and make a visit to the Maud. But there were still four men left on board of her, and they were at liberty. If he put himself within reach of Scoble, he would be made a prisoner, and his power to do anything for his guardian-mother would have passed away.

Louis had been several times to a point on the steamer where he could see the man on watch at the door of the wounded prisoner. He had stretched himself on the deck, in the narrow gangway that was between the rail and the house on deck. Undoubtedly Kimpton was the most disappointed and disheartened man on board of the Phantom, for he had utterly failed in his mission near the young millionaire. Louis knew nothing more of him than the letter had revealed; but he looked upon him as a desperately bad character, in short, just such a man as Scoble himself. He had pluck enough for any person; but pluck may be manifested in a bad cause as well as a good one.

Louis not only watched the man at the door of the desperado, but he kept an eye up the bay in the direction where the Maud lay at her moorings. Whether Scoble heard the noise made by the cook when he was attacked or not, he must be aware of the presence of the Phantom at the inlet. He must realize that his project of getting off unseen to Bermuda had failed. He could not know, but he might well suspect, that this steamer was there to intercept him.

Scoble was not likely to remain where he was for many days without attempting to do something to effect his escape from the bay. Judging from what Captain Brisbane said, it would be high tide at noon and at midnight, or nearly at these times; and it was hardly probable that the Maud could get to sea at any other hours of the day.

While Louis was uneasily walking about the deck, fretting at his own inactivity while his mother was a prisoner in the hands of the enemy, he was startled by the violent yelling on the part of the watch at the door of Kimpton. This man had appeared to be asleep most of the time; but as he lay across the doorway so that the prisoner could not escape, Louis did not care to disturb the captain with a report of his neglect of duty.

"Fire! Fire! Fire!" shouted the man at the top of his lungs.

"Where is the fire?" demanded Louis, startled at the cry.

"Down below," replied the deck hand. "The deck is so hot you can't bear your hand on it!"

Louis found it very warm under his feet, and he remained in that part of the vessel only long enough to satisfy himself that the door of the wounded man's stateroom was still locked. While the man on watch ran forward to alarm the ship's company, Louis followed the narrow gangway to the stern, and then to the other side of the craft. He had hardly reached the after part when he made a discovery which appeared to explain the meaning of the fire in the hold of the Phantom.

The steamer was headed to the west, just as she had come in; and though Louis was not aware of the fact, the anchor had been dropped, and the fresh breeze kept the vessel headed in the direction of the point. The boat, after the prisoner had been put on board, had been made fast at the stern.

The boat was not where it had been secured, but Louis discovered it half-way to the shore on the north side, with Kimpton in it, sculling with all his might for the shore. He was using his left hand only; but he was so well skilled in the use of the oar in this manner that he was making rapid progress through the water.

By this time the watch had roused the ship's company, and the voice of Captain Brisbane was heard as he gave his orders for extinguishing the fire. The deck was so hot under Louis's feet that it made him step very lively, and he jumped upon the rail to escape the heat. Just then he observed that the door of the captain's stateroom, occupying the after part of the deck-house, was wide open. Rushing into this room, he saw a door leading into the room where Kimpton had been confined. The lock was secured to the outside of the door, and the prisoner had removed it by taking out the screws with his knife or some other implement in his possession.

The fire was just breaking through the deck in the wounded man's room, and Louis could remain there but a moment; but he had seen enough to satisfy himself in what manner the prisoner had made his escape. From the captain's room the incendiary had probably passed through the engine-room, where the engineer was sound asleep on the sofa, and descended to the fire room, making his way aft to some place where he found combustibles suited to his purpose.

As soon as he had finished his survey, Louis hastened forward to assist, if he could, in putting out the fire. The steam pump had been put in condition to be operated, and already was pouring water into the hold, but in a place, Louis thought, where it would accomplish but little in subduing the flames. He informed the captain that the fire was coming up through the deck farther aft. At this moment the fireman who had been sent below to start up the fires which had been banked in the morning, came up, and declared that the heat and smoke had driven him on deck. The hose was then carried farther aft; but the flames had taken full possession of both staterooms.

It began to look like a hopeless case, for the water poured in upon the fire seemed to have no appreciable effect. Those who were not at work with the steam pump worked with buckets, and Louis labored as earnestly as any of the hands. The flames were confined to the after part of the steamer, and it was now too hot for any one to remain there.

"Stand by your engine, Mr. Waters!" shouted the captain, as he rushed to the bow of the steamer, where he cast off the cable, and let it run overboard.

"All right, Captain Brisbane," replied the engineer, who was on duty at the machine, attending to the steam pump. "I am not sure that the screw will work, for something may have been burned away along the shaft."

"Start her forward!" shouted the captain, as he ran up the ladder to the pilot-house.

As soon as he had the wheel in his hands he rang one bell on the gong. The engineer started the machine, and ascertained at once that the screw was still in condition to work. The Phantom, with the flames pouring out abaft the engine-room, went ahead, and the captain headed her for the shore on the north side of the inlet, for that was the nearest land. It was not more than a quarter of a mile distant. The speed bell followed the stroke on the gong a moment later, and the vessel went ahead as rapidly as her low pressure of steam would permit.

The steam pump was still at work, and the fires had been replenished by the firemen before they had been driven from their post. Louis judged that Captain Brisbane had given up the battle with the fire, and had no hope of saving her. When the young millionaire found he could be of no further service on the main deck, he joined the captain in the pilot-house.

"This is a bad job for me," said Captain Brisbane, when Louis had taken his place opposite him at the wheel, where he could look through the window at the shore. "The Phantom is insured, but my loss will be large for me."

"I am exceedingly sorry for it, captain," replied Louis, whose first impulse was to make it good to him; but he was not confident that Uncle Moses would indorse his liberality, and he said nothing about it.

"I don't see how the fire got such a start upon us," added the captain. "We had a large supply of light wood for kindling the fires abaft the bunkers; but it was a good distance from the furnaces, and the fires were banked."

"Didn't you see that man in a boat about a quarter of an hour ago?" asked Louis, surprised that the captain had not yet ascertained the origin of the fire.

Kimpton had reached the shore and disappeared. Louis had not been able to observe his movements while he was at work on the main deck, and did not know what had become of him. He had had time enough to reach the shore, which was covered with stunted pines and firs, which were sufficient to conceal him from observation.

"I haven't noticed any boat; I was too busy with the fire to look to the right or the left after I was roused from my sleep," replied Captain Brisbane to his passenger's question. "What boat do you mean?"

"The first thing I saw after I got to the stern of the steamer was a boat with a man in it, sculling with all his might with his left hand; and that man was the prisoner whose wound you dressed this forenoon," added Louis, telling the whole story at once.

"Then the fire was set by that man," said the captain, grinding his teeth and shaking his head. "I should like to get hold of him again, and I would not wait for judge or jury!"

Louis explained in what manner Kimpton had escaped from his room, and how he supposed he had started the fire. Then he took the spy-glass from the brackets, and directed it to the shore. He could see the boat, but the man was not in sight.

"What time is it now, Captain Brisbane?" he asked.

"Just noon," replied the captain, glancing at the clock on the after bulkhead.

"At what time will the tide be up?"

"About half-past twelve."

The Phantom was approaching the shore at full speed, and the captain gave no further attention to his passenger. In a few minutes more the forefoot ploughed into the sand, and the steamer stopped short in a position where those on board could jump upon the dry land. The violent hissing of the steam indicated that the engineer was still at his post, hot as it was there. He had stopped the machine, and provided against a possible explosion of the boiler.

For the next hour all hands were kept busy in saving their own effects and such of the steamer's as were movable. Louis had landed, taking his valise, overcoat, the compass, and spy-glass from the pilot-house with him. With the glass in his hand, he climbed the highest pine-tree he could find, hoping that he might be able to discover the Maud at her moorings; but he failed to make her out.

Then he directed his glass to the other side of the bay. An inward trend of the shore-line enabled him to see across the water the extremity of a project-ing point of land on the peninsula where he had landed. On this point was a man seated on the sand, apparently very busy about something. This person must be Kimpton, for there was not a house or a hut within some miles of the spot, and the nearest life-saving station was south of the inlet. He had made good use of his legs after he landed, and Louis wondered what he was doing.

He was not obliged to wait long for a solution of the problem, for Kimpton hoisted a white cloth on a pole, and began to wave it violently. A few moments later Louis discovered a schooner under full sail, standing towards the inlet. The vessel was the Maud.

CHAPTER 29
LEFT ON A SANDBANK

THE HULL OF THE Phantom was now completely wrapped in flames, and it was impossible to save anything more from her. The ship's company had worked hard from the time the fire was discovered, and they were tired out after their exertions. They had seated themselves on the sand above the beach, while Louis maintained his position in the pine-tree.

Whether or not Scoble had discovered that a steamer was blockading the only egress from what he called "Dolphin Bay," Louis had no knowledge. He had not seen the Maud himself; but he had no doubt that Bickling's report that she was in the bay was correct. He had read Kimpton's letter from Scoble several times. In one sentence the writer said that he expected his confederate to assist him in getting out of the bay if he was pursued.

Kimpton appeared to have discharged this duty faithfully, for Louis did not question that he had set fire to the Phantom for this purpose. But there had been no communication between Scoble and his satellite so far as he knew. He wondered very much if the captain of the Maud was aware that the obstruction to his passage out to sea had been removed, for he had got under way as soon as the destruction of the steamer had been assured.

The Maud had a fresh breeze, and she was carrying a fore and a main gaff-topsail in addition to her ordinary canvas. She had the wind fair for her passage out. Those on board of her had plainly discovered Kimpton's signals, for the schooner had changed her course directly for the point occupied by him. Louis watched the Maud with his glass, and saw that she was getting out her boat.

Within an eighth of a mile of Kimpton, the schooner came to, and the boat pulled for the shore. The confederate was conveyed on board, and the Maud filled away. She was making at least eight knots an hour, for Captain Ringgold had said this was her maximum speed, and she had everything favorable.

His elevated position was no longer necessary to observe the vessel, and Louis descended to the ground. He was the first to notify the captain of the approach of the Maud. It made the heart of the young millionaire beat violently when he considered the fact that his mother was on board of the schooner, and he could do nothing to assist her, or even to comfort her, prisoner as she was in the hands of her only enemy on the face of the earth.

"She will get out in spite of anything we can do now," said Captain Brisbane when Louis had called his attention to the approach of the Maud.

"But can't you do anything? We have your boat still," added Louis in a pleading tone.

"Not a thing, Mr. Belgrave. I have lost my steamer in my efforts to assist you. What more would you have of me?" asked the disconsolate commander, as he glanced at the smouldering wreck of the Phantom; and there was a good deal of bitterness and reproach in his tones, as though he considered himself a much-abused man.

"Why cannot three or four of us go off in the boat and intercept the Maud as she goes through the inlet?" asked Louis earnestly.

"We cannot!" replied the captain sharply. "If I had known that I was to come down here on a fighting expedition, to overhaul a lot of cut-throats, I would not have come; at least not without a squad of policemen on board. What can you do if you go off in the boat, young man?" demanded Captain Brisbane sternly, and with a sneer on his lips.

"If we could get on board we could gain possession of the vessel," replied Louis with spirit.

"Do you take me for a pirate, Mr. Belgrave? I would not attempt a thing like that under any circumstances. Besides, Captain Ringgold directed me to watch the Maud if I found her, and follow her if she got out of any of these inlets. He told me not to meddle with her," returned the captain; and Louis had to admit to himself that he had the best of the argument.

"My mother is on board of that schooner, and am I to stand here like a mummy and do nothing to save her?" demanded Louis, somewhat excited.

"That is just what you are to do, young man. You cannot help yourself, and I cannot help you. I could not do anything more than I have done if it were my own mother they were carrying off," replied Captain Brisbane in a more pliable tone. "It would be madness to attempt to board a vessel making eight or ten knots an hour with a jolly-boat. We should all be shot down."

"I am almost sure there is not a firearm of any kind on board of the Maud, for I took care to obtain possession of all I could find."

"I did not ship my men for this kind of duty, and they would mutiny if I required them to engage in such a venture."

It was useless to argue the matter with the captain, or attempt to persuade him to embark in the foolhardy enterprise of capturing the vessel, and Louis could only watch the Maud as she continued on her course to the open sea. She kept well away from the point till she was about west of the inlet where the wreck of the Phantom lay, and then hauled her sheets till she had the wind over her port quarter. She dashed on her course with all the speed she could make, keeping as far to the southward as the depth of the water would permit.

By this time Kimpton had related his story, and Scoble was as wise as his pursuers. Louis looked at the vessel as she passed through the inlet, as both the bay and the passage into it are properly called, with the spy-glass. Frinks was at the helm, and no other person could be seen on her deck. Possibly the captain of the Maud feared that a pistol shot might disable him or some other person on board, and he had ordered all but the helmsman below; but the schooner was out of the reach of any weapon in Louis's possession, even if he had been disposed to use one.

Sick at heart, Louis watched the Maud as she dashed through the inlet, and laid her course to the south-east as soon as she had made an offing. While Mrs. Belgrave was thankful in her heart that her son was not on board of the schooner with her, he was groaning in spirit that he was not with her. The only consolation he had was that Felix McGavonty was at her side, or within call. Captain Ringgold had been very sure that the poor lady would be subjected to no hardship or indignity of any kind; and he was disposed to accept his assurance.

"Which the Maud is bound for Bermuda, sir, as you can see from the course she is taking, sir," said Bickling approaching him. "Which it is what I 'ad the pleasure of informing you, sir."

"I have no doubt she is bound to Bermuda," replied Louis, very sadly.

"Which it is a great pity that we have no vessel to follow her in, sir. With a fast yacht like the Blanche, sir, you could soon over'aul her, sir."

As the cook knew nothing about the Guardian-Mother, he could not have informed Kimpton in regard to her. Louis was sure that nothing had been said about the steam-yacht in the presence of either of the men he had employed. Scoble could have obtained no information from his confederate; and it was evident from the course he had shaped in sight of the shore that he did not expect to be pursued any farther, now that the Phantom had been destroyed.

"We shall soon have a vessel which is faster than the Blanche, Bickling," replied Louis after he had considered the subject for a few minutes.

"Which I am very 'appy to 'ear, sir," added the cook; and he seemed to be really pleased. "Which I am very sorry, sir, that Flounder turned out to be a bad man, sir."

"What did he wish you to do when he knocked you down?" asked Louis.

"Which he wanted me to go on board of the Maud, sir, and not tell you or the captain of the steamer that the Maud she was in there, sir," answered

Bickling. "Which I wouldn't do, sir; no, sir, not for the crown of Hingland, sir, to a gentleman as 'as used me kindly, as you 'ave, sir."

Louis had no doubt in regard to the honesty and fidelity of the cook; but his courage and intelligence were other things. The captain interrupted the conversation, which was of no importance at this stage of the adventure.

"The question just now is as to what we are to do next, Mr. Belgrave," said Captain Brisbane, as he seated himself by the side of Louis.

"I am compelled to answer in your own words, 'Not a thing,'" replied the young man. "We might as well be on a desolate island as here."

"Not quite so bad as that, for we have saved from the wreck provisions enough to last us two or three days. We have the boat, and we could cross to the other side of the inlet, and find our way to the life-saving station, or we could row up the river to the town where Scoble mailed his letter to Kimpton."

"I don't expect to suffer from hunger or cold, or anything else but impatience at being in such a desolate place while that villain is conveying my mother away from me."

"You ought to be old enough to do without your mother," added the captain rather coarsely, "I was ordered to remain on this coast by Captain Ringgold until he came himself in a steamer. Do you know when he will be here, Mr. Belgrave?"

"He did not know himself, and therefore he could not tell me."

"I doubt if any vessel will come into this bay in the next month. All we can do is to make the best of our situation. I suppose we might make a signal that would attract the attention of some vessel outside that would take us off."

"You can do that if you wish, Captain Brisbane, but I shall remain here till Captain Ringgold takes me off," replied Louis decidedly.

"He may not come for a week," suggested the captain.

"Perhaps not; in that case I shall remain here a week."

"You are not sure that Captain Ringgold will find you here."

"I shall wait and see if he don't, at any rate."

The captain took the spy-glass, and directed it out at sea.

"There are two schooners coming up from the southward," said he, still pointing the glass.

"Let them come," added Louis.

"As I said, Captain Ringgold may not come here for a week: I don't feel as though I ought to keep my men here on this sandbank any longer than is absolutely necessary," added the captain, calling his mate to him.

"Of course you will do what you think best, Captain Brisbane," replied Louis coldly.

The captain instructed the mate to rig a signal, and set it on the highest point of land in the vicinity. The order was executed at once; and the signal floated in the air till nearly sundown, when it attracted the attention of a tug-boat headed to the northward, which came within half a mile of the shore.

The little steamer, which had been towing a vessel down to Barnegat Inlet, ran her nose into the sandbank and hailed the party. He proved to be a friend of Captain Brisbane, and was all ready to take him and his ship's company to New York, with all they had saved from the wreck.

"I don't like to leave you here, Mr. Belgrave, but if you insist upon remaining, I can't help myself," said the captain, when all but him had gone on board of the tug.

"Don't disturb yourself about me, Captain Brisbane," replied Louis very stiffly.

"Very well, young man. Come along, Bickling!" added the captain.

"Which I don't leave the young gentleman, sir," replied the cook.

The remainder of the party hastened on board of the Rocket; and she steamed away, leaving Louis and the cook on the sandbank.

CHAPTER 30
A HUNGRY MILLIONAIRE

IT WAS A DESOLATE place where Captain Brisbane had abandoned Louis Belgrave; but the latter did not find himself in a desperate strait, or compare himself with Robinson Crusoe. He had been supplied with about half a cold ham, a quantity of hard bread, and a breaker of water, so that he and his companion were not likely to perish with hunger or thirst. The piece of sailcloth, rigged on a pole which the mate had prepared as a signal, had been left. A vessel in the distance could be hailed, and at worst a walk of six or eight miles would take them to an inhabited locality.

"Which we may 'ave to stay 'ere a week, sir," suggested Bickling, after he had walked about the sand hills for a time.

"It is possible, but I don't believe we shall," replied Louis cheerfully, for he had made up his mind to be contented, however long he was compelled to remain; and the only thing that troubled him was the absence of his mother.

"Which it is no worse for me, sir, than it is for you as is a gentleman, sir," added Bickling, gently opening his mouth in a grin which extended nearly from ear to ear, which was a surprise to his employer, for the cook generally wore a very solemn expression.

"It is about the same thing for both of us."

"'Ow shall we hever get hoff, sir?" asked Bickling, looking earnestly into the face of his companion, as though he was deeply interested in the expected reply.

"I expect a steam-yacht to take me off; but I do not know when she will come," answered Louis, who cast frequent glances at the ocean, though he hardly expected to see the Guardian-Mother so soon.

"A steam-yacht, sir!" exclaimed the cook. "And 'ow big might she be?"

"About six hundred tons."

"Which she is owned by Captain Ringgold, the fine gentleman as was on board of the Maud with you, sir?" asked Bickling, opening his eyes very wide.

"No; I shall be the owner of her myself, I think."

"Which it is you, sir, as owns a steam-yacht of six 'undred tons!" exclaimed the cook, rising from the ground on which both were seated, and involuntarily removing his hat.

"Nothing very strange about that, is there?" asked the yacht owner with an expansive smile.

"Which you are a very young gentleman to own a steam-yacht as big as that!" added Bickling, looking his companion all over as he would a live lobster. "Can it be possible? Which it must be as you says so. You must be as rich as Grease-us, sir."

"I shall not have to go to the almshouse this year. What is your name, Bickling?"

"Which it is Bickling, sir; and I never denies my name, sir," replied the cook, evidently very much surprised at the question.

"I mean your front name."

"Which Bickling is my back name, is it, sir? Which my front name must be Baldwin, sir; and people as I meets most calls me Baldy," responded the cook, taking off his soft hat, and passing his hand over the top of his head, which had no more hair on it than a pumpkin.

"Very well, my friend," said Louis, laughing at the close fit of the name to the head. "Which you will not think I am impolite if I call you Baldy?"

"'Ow could a gentleman like you be impolite, sir? Which you can call me as it suits your fancy, Mr. Belgrave."

As he had nothing else to do, Louis questioned his companion in regard to his previous history. He had been a servant till he was thirty-five, which explained his obsequious manners, and his slavish submission to those in authority, and to well-dressed people in general. He had worked about the kitchens of gentlemen and clubs till he had learned to cook. He had made two voyages as cook, and had gone to Baltimore in that capacity on board of a steamer.

He had worked in a restaurant there a year; but he could not get the "'ang of Hamerican ways," and wished to get back to England. For this reason he had shipped as cook with Scoble. He had no money, for he had been too simple to make a good bargain with his late employer, and had worked for next to nothing.

"I intend to go to Bermuda in the Guardian-Mother, Baldy," said Louis.

"The Guardian-Mother, sir!" exclaimed the cook. "And who is she, if you please, sir? Which I never 'eard of 'er before, sir."

"That is the name of my steam-yacht."

"Which it is a very hodd name, sir."

"It is the name by which I think of my mother, the lady who is a prisoner on board of the Maud."

"Then I takes hoff my 'at to the Guardian-Mother," added Bickling, suiting the action to the words.

"But she is going to Bermuda in pursuit of the Maud; and perhaps you do not wish to go there, Baldy."

"Which I should be very 'appy to go there, sir, if I can go with you, sir."

"I shall go to England sooner or later in the Guardian-Mother, though I shall probably spend the coming winter in the West Indies, and it may be a year or more before the steamer goes to Europe."

"Which it is all the same to me, sir. You 'ave been very good to me, sir, better as any other man now on the earth, sir. I should be 'appy to follow you all over the world, sir, wherever you go, never axing no questions, sir. I am not good for much, and I am the biggest coward as lives on the face of the footstool, sir," replied the cook in a rather more fawning tone and manner than usual.

"Not quite so bad as that, Baldy. You had pluck enough to refuse to go on board of the Maud when Flounder tried to make you do so," suggested Louis.

"Which he wanted me to be faithless to you, sir, and I was too big a coward to do that," answered the cook, with an extended grin. "But he would 'ave murdered me if you had not been near."

"All right, Baldy; you behaved very well, and I shall try to find a place for you on board of the Guardian-Mother," replied Louis, who felt that he was under obligations to his companion for his fidelity.

It was growing dark on the sandbank; and it became a question to the young millionaire how he was to pass the night. He was confident that Captain Ringgold would not come for him in the darkness, for he would have but little chance of finding him. After the conversation Baldy walked down to the water where the wreck of the Phantom lay, while Louis was seeking a place to sleep among the pines. The fire in the steamer appeared to have smouldered out. The west wind had driven the flames to the after part of the hull; and the crew had thrown a great quantity of water on the forecastle while they were saving their own and the vessel's effects.

Baldy went on board of the wreck by a gang-plank which had been left in its place. He soon discovered that the fire had not extended to the forecastle, prevented in its passage by the water above, and by an iron bulkhead below. He descended to the quarters of the crew, which had been stripped of everything movable, though some dirty coverlets remained in the bunks. Probably Captain Brisbane knew that the forecastle had not been burned out, for he and his men had been on board of the wreck an hour or two before they were taken from the sandbank by the Rocket.

The cook called Louis, and informed him of the condition of the forecastle. It was not a bad place to sleep, and it was too dark for the young man to see the dirt and grease that prevailed there. The cook had given him his supper before dark; and he found that his appetite was not impaired, for he partook heartily of the stinted fare. It was a dry meal for a millionaire; and Louis was no better off with his million and a half than his simple companion with nothing at all.

He turned in; and, while he was thinking of his Guardian-Mother now far out to sea, and his Guardian-Mother he expected to see the next day, he dropped asleep. He had not slept as much as a boy of his age required during the past three days, and he was very tired after the exciting labors of the day. He had covered himself with a greasy comforter, and he did not wake once during the night.

"Which it is about sunrise, if you please, sir," said Baldy at the side of the bunk.

"Thank you for calling me, Baldy," replied Louis, leaping hastily from the berth when he saw the daylight at the open scuttle; for it was time for him to be on the watch for the steam-yacht.

He had no toilet to make, but he took a plunge in the clear waters that washed the sandy beach. His first care was to look out upon the ocean; and he missed the glass he had used the day before, for Captain Brisbane had left him nothing but a scanty stock of provisions. He saw a steamer headed to the south far out to sea, and he watched her till she disappeared in the distance. Baldy gave him his breakfast, which was just what his supper had been; and when he ate the hard, dry ham, and the harder shipbread, he did not feel at all like a millionaire at sixteen.

It would require too much space to relate the tame incidents of Louis's stay on the sandbank. All day long he watched and waited to see a steamer approach the desolate locality, but none came. Several small craft came within a mile or two of the shore, but nothing that looked like the Guardian-Mother. He and Baldy slept another night in the forecastle of the wreck.

Again his slumbers were deep and profound, and the cook called him at daylight. He hastened to the sand-hill which afforded him the best view of the ocean. No steamer was in sight; breakfast and dinner were served, but the scanty stock of eatables was very nearly exhausted. Baldy was blessed with a tremendous appetite, and he had done double his share in reducing the supply. For his sake rather than his own Louis put himself on short allowance, in spite of his companion's protest. By dinner-time he was quite hungry; but he ate next to nothing, for the shipbread was all gone, and the ham was hardly eatable. He was a hungry millionaire by four in the afternoon, his stomach being badly pinched by the want of food. Baldy reasoned with him, and wished him to eat all that was left at noon; but he could beat the cook in an argument every time, and compelled him to finish the provisions.

At four o'clock in the afternoon Louis was sound asleep on the sand-hill, where he had laid down, actually suffering from the pain of an empty stomach. The change of position relieved, him, and, worn out with watching and anxiety, as well as by the loss of his usual meals, kind Nature had come to his aid in the form of sleep.

"Wake up, if you please, Mr. Belgrave; which there is a steamer headed this way, and it may be the Guardian-Mother, sir," said Baldy, taking him by the hand.

Louis sprang to his feet as quickly as his feeble condition would permit. The words of the cook made him forget that he was hungry. He did not believe that he was starving, though he had not eaten a "square meal" since the last one he had taken on board of the Blanche. The news which Baldy had given him was quite sufficient to make a new being of him.

From the sand-hill he saw a steamer feeling her way with the lead towards the shore. She was not half a mile distant, and she was a magnificent craft. Within a quarter of a mile of the shore she stopped her screw. A boat was lowered into the water, and pulled for the inlet with eight men at the oars, and an officer in the stern sheets. Louis had fixed the signal on the sand-hill, and it had been seen.

CHAPTER 31
THE MAGNIFICENT STEAMER

LOUIS BELGRAVE WATCHED THE boat, which was an elegant affair, as it approached the shore. When it had accomplished half the distance, the officer in the stern sheets took off his cap, and waved it vigorously in the air. Then the abandoned millionaire recognized the stalwart form of Captain Ringgold, and he returned the salute as earnestly as the other made it.

When he saw where the boat intended to land, Louis rushed to the shore and awaited its arrival. The men pulled with the precision of men-of-wars-men. At a short distance from the land up went the eight oars like a piece of clock-work. The bowman took his place in the fore-sheets with a boat-hook in his hand, and fended off as the keel ploughed into the soft sand. The boat looked like a fairy barge. The stern sheets were upholstered with crimson velvet; and the owner of the Guardian-Mother had never seen anything so luxurious, even in the cutters of the Blanche.

Captain Ringgold rose from his seat as soon as the keel touched the sand, and made his way to the bow, from which he leaped to the shore like a boy. Louis was there to receive him; and if there were tears in his eyes, they were tears of gladness, though perhaps his empty stomach was to some extent responsible for them. The captain rushed upon him with both hands extended, which Louis grasped with an energy which his feelings did not belie.

"I am exceedingly glad to see you, Mr. Belgrave!" exclaimed the captain, wringing the hands of the hungry millionaire.

"And I am heartily rejoiced to see you, Captain Ringgold," replied Louis, wiping the tears from his eyes, though he could not for the life of him have told for what he was weeping.

"But what is the matter with you, my dear boy? you are actually crying. Have you any bad news from your mother?" asked the captain, who was now the commander of the Guardian-Mother, though he had never been formally invested with that office.

"I have heard nothing at all from her, sir," answered Louis in a choking voice.

"What is the matter, then?"

"Which the poor young gentleman is 'alf starved, sir, if you please," interposed Baldy.

"Not quite so bad as that, captain," added Louis, trying to laugh. "I confess that I am hungry, and that I feel quite faint."

"Poor fellow! I don't understand it! But no talk till you feel better, my dear boy," said Captain Ringgold, full of sympathy. "Only one question, and then not another word. Where is the Maud?"

"She sailed from this place day before yesterday at noon, and headed to the south-east as soon as she got out into deep water," replied Louis. "She is forty-eight hours on her way to Bermuda."

"That's all now!" exclaimed the commander decidedly.

"I am able to talk, captain; I don't need any nursing. I have not lived very well since we left the Blanche; and I have eaten next to nothing to-day, for the ham was not good, and the hardbread was dirty and smoky."

"Have you anything to go on board of the steamer, Louis?"

"Nothing but my valise and overcoat."

Captain Ringgold ordered a couple of men in the boat to assist Louis to his place in the stern sheets, and a couple more to put his baggage on board. While they were doing so, he walked over to the inlet, followed by Baldy.

"If you please, captain, will you 'ave the kindness to take me on board of the Guardian-Mother? for the young gentleman as owns her—Mr. Belgrave—told me as 'ow I should go with him," said Baldy, who perhaps thought the commander had a veto on the promises of the juvenile owner.

"If Mr. Belgrave said you were to go on board, that is enough, in spite of any other person," replied the captain, laughing at the simplicity of the cook. "I should not be likely in any case to leave you, or any other human being, in such a desolate place as this sandbank. I don't understand this business at all. What is that wreck on the shore of the passage through?"

"That is the wreck of the Phantom, which she was burned the day we got 'ere by a hagent of Captain Scoble," replied Baldy.

The commander of the steamer realized that there was a history to the expedition he had sent down the coast to look for the Maud, but he did not care to hear it mangled by the cook; and he hastened back to the boat, anxious now only to relieve the discomfort, if not the distress, of the owner of the Guardian-Mother. He put Baldy in the fore-sheets, and took his place in the stern.

"Up oars!" said the captain, who seemed to be in the practice of naval discipline; and at the command six of the eight oars went up to a perpendicular position. "Shove off!" he added; and the two bowmen pushed the boat from the sand into deep water. "Let fall!" and the oars dropped into the water as one. "Stern all! Give way!"

The barge, for that was the name of the owner's boat, backed away from the shore, then came about, and pulled for the steamer. Captain Ringgold said nothing; and Louis did not feel like talking, for his stomach was still bothering him. He did not feel quite at home in the luxurious furnishings of the barge; but he looked the men at the oars over, and thought he had never seen a finer-looking set of seamen. They were all dressed in uniform, and on their naval caps were ribbons bearing the name of the steamer, Guardian-Mother, in gilt letters. The shipmaster had certainly attended to the smaller details of the fitting out of the vessel.

As the boat passed the bows of the steam-yacht, Louis discovered the name again; and he wondered at the expedition the captain had used in preparing the craft, though he had been thus occupied for three days. The boat went to the after-gangway, where the steps had been rigged out; and the commander assisted his youthful owner to mount to the deck. Louis was inclined to pause and admire the appearance of everything that met his gaze, but the considerate captain hurried him to the cabin.

"I am afraid you will get sick out of this affair, Louis," said the commander very tenderly, as he seated him on a sofa. "I am sorry to find you in this feeble condition."

"You need not be at all concerned about me, Captain Ringgold. I shall be all right as soon as I have had something to eat," replied Louis. "I always have trouble when I go without my regular food; but I am not starving, and I am not in the least injured."

"Sparks!" called the captain, and a colored steward came out of his pantry at the summons. "This young gentleman is the owner of the steamer. Get him some of the soup we had for lunch as quick as possible."

Sparks bowed low to the owner, and then rushed out of the cabin to execute his mission.

"Something not too heavy is best for you to begin upon. You need a little nursing before you can come out all right, my boy. I have to get underway now, and lay the course for Bermuda; but I will send Mrs. Blossom to look out for you, for you need a woman's care," added the captain.

"Mrs. Blossom!" exclaimed Louis, astonished to hear the name of Uncle Moses's housekeeper.

"She is the stewardess of the steamer. I went to see Squire Scarburn yesterday to ask him to recommend a woman to attend to the wants of your mother, after we have recovered her. Mrs. Blossom, who is the widow of a sea-captain, and has been to sea, heard me, and volunteered her services, saying that she needed a sea-voyage to restore her health. The squire consented, and that is why she happens to be on board."

The captain called the woman, and then left the cabin. Mrs. Blossom was delighted to see another Parkite on board, and sorry to find him in such a feeble condition. While Sparks was setting the table for his lunch, Louis explained what ailed him, and what had caused it. The good lady was quite sure she could relieve him, and she went to the pantry, from which she presently returned with a potion in a glass. She insisted that he should take it, and he did so. It was very hot, and it warmed up his stomach at once.

The owner seated himself at the table at the summons of the steward. The dishes and the table-ware were of the finest quality, and Louis was bewildered by the magnificence which surrounded him on all sides. In fact, he began to feel something like a millionaire after his late experience on the sandbank. The soup was very nice; but Mrs. Blossom would not permit him to take anything else, except some toast and some fancy biscuits.

He ate heartily of the soup, and then he claimed he was entirely well. His pain was all gone, for his malady was that unpoetical one which old ladies call "wind in the stomach" when babies have it. He was burning with curiosity to see the magnificent craft of which he had become the owner, and of which he had not seen even the outside till he left the sandbank.

"No, Mr. Belgrave; you must not go on deck yet. You must keep quiet for a little while at least, until you are sure you are quite well," said the stewardess.

"I am sure of it now, Mrs. Blossom. I am not a baby."

"But you have wind on the stomach all the same," laughed she. "But here comes the captain, and you must mind him till you are perfectly well."

Louis assured the commander that he was quite well; he had eaten plenty of the soup, and he felt like a new man. He wanted to see the steamer. What was the use of being a millionaire, and owning a steam-yacht of six hundred tons, if he could not see her?

"You may look the cabins over first; and then if you are all right, I will take you on deck, and introduce the officers to you," replied Captain Ringgold, after taking a careful survey of his young friend. "We are now in the main cabin, and it is sometimes called the state cabin. It is the apartment of the owner. It has four staterooms on each side, two of which have bathrooms attached to them, so that the owner can be as comfortable as at the finest hotel in the city of New York. This cabin is nearly in the centre of the ship, where the motion is the least perceptible."

Louis looked into all the staterooms. The two forward ones on each side were very large, and were as elegantly fitted up as the cabin itself. At the after end of the cabin there was a broad staircase leading to the social hall on deck.

At the stern of the vessel was another cabin, fitted up handsomely, and having a stateroom and four berths on each side, but for which there seemed to be no use at present.

"How do you feel, Mr. Belgrave?" asked the captain, after he had shown the state cabin to his owner.

"Very well indeed, sir," replied Louis. "But why do you call me Mr. Belgrave? You have never been in the habit of mistering me."

"Sparks!" called the captain to the cabin steward. "Go on deck, and ask Mr. Boulong to call as many of the officers as can be spared from their duties to the quarter-deck."

"I may call you Louis when we are alone, but everybody on board must call the owner Mr. Belgrave; for it would be highly improper for any officer or seaman to address him by his first name, or to leave off the handle to the last one," the captain explained.

"Well, I suppose I can stand it if you and the officers can," replied Louis, who felt well enough to laugh by this time.

"I have served my time in the navy, though I was a young man then; but on board ship a certain amount of ceremony is necessary. Even on board merchantmen the mates are called mister."

They commenced the ascent of the grand staircase together.

CHAPTER 32
A FORMAL PRESENTATION

Louis and the captain stopped in the social hall at the head of the stairs, with a door on each side of them. It was provided with divans in every practicable place, and contained quite a library. Passing through one of the doors, they entered what was called the *boudoir*. It was quite a roomy apartment, with an upright piano between the doors, and the after part was a half-circle.

The entire sides and round end were composed of thick plate-glass, so that the *boudoir* had the appearance of a conservatory, and it had a stand of plants in the centre. It was furnished with arm-chairs and *tête-à-têtes*. The captain explained that the windows were provided with shutters, which could be put on the whole or a part of the openings in very stormy weather, though he thought they would seldom be needed.

"You ought to be able to make yourself comfortable in this *boudoir*," said Captain Ringgold, when the owner had examined the room. "It is the finest apartment I ever saw on board of a vessel, not excepting the steam-yacht of the Queen of England."

"I had no idea of such magnificence before," replied Louis with enthusiasm. "I am sure I can make myself a great deal happier here than I was on that sandbank. You mentioned the name of Mr. Boulong while we were below."

"Formerly of the Blanche," answered the commander with a smile. "I found that the Guardian-Mother had a full crew on board, selected with the greatest care by Colonel Singfield himself, with the exception of a captain and first officer, who had accepted other positions rather than wait for the sale of the steamer. I had decided to take the command myself, if my owner did not object."

"Of course your owner would not object," laughed Louis. "You are the gentleman above all others I should have selected if it had been left to me."

"Then I am all right, and I am sure we shall be friends. I shall follow all your directions as though you were an older person than I am; but I suppose you will allow me to advise you when necessary, especially on nautical subjects."

"On all subjects, Captain Ringgold; and I shall be infinitely obliged to you for your counsels," added the owner warmly.

"Squire Scarburn has unlimited confidence in you, Louis, and he did not even instruct me to look out for you."

"But I hope you will do so all the same."

"I don't intend to treat you as though I were your schoolmaster. I called upon Mr. Woolridge yesterday to thank him for the use of the Blanche; and when I mentioned that I was in need of a mate, he at once suggested Mr. Boulong. He had been captain of a steamer; but his wife was very sick, and he had been forced to resign his place. He deserved a better place than mate of a yacht like the Blanche, and he recommended him so warmly that I took him. He is a thorough sailor, and understands his duties as officer; in fact, he is competent to command the Guardian-Mother."

"I like him very much, and I am glad you took him."

The captain opened one of the doors of the *boudoir*, and they passed out to the main deck, where all the officers except the second engineer were assembled. They were all dressed in yacht uniforms, looked very trim and nice, and Louis was disposed to fall in love with them all in a bunch.

"Mr. Belgrave, you are already acquainted with Mr. Boulong; but I have the pleasure of presenting him to you as the first officer of the Guardian-Mother," said Captain Ringgold, as they confronted the mate.

"I am very glad indeed to meet you in that capacity on board of this steamer, Mr. Boulong," added Louis, as he gave his hand to him. "We have been friends in the past, and I am sure we shall be in the future."

"Thank you, Mr. Belgrave; I shall endeavor to do my duty faithfully. Allow me to congratulate you on being the owner of the finest steam-yacht that ever sailed out of New York," replied the chief officer.

"Mr. Belgrave, allow me to introduce Mr. P. Lord Gaskette, the second officer of the steamer, who is not only a gentleman and a scholar, but a full-fledged sailor," continued the commander very pleasantly. "He is a graduate of Columbia College, speaks French, German, Spanish, Greek, Latin, Hebrew, and Dutch like an organ-grinder."

"I am very happy to know you, Mr. Gaskette, and I certainly ought to appreciate your linguistic accomplishments," replied Louis, as he shook hands with the second officer. "I have no doubt your seamanship is equal to your skill in the languages."

"Hardly, Mr. Belgrave, for the captain has overdone himself on the languages," added Mr. Gaskette, as he took the offered hand of the owner. "I was a teacher of languages when my health failed. I have been to sea for twelve years now, three of them as first officer of a ship. I shall be happy to do everything in my power to make your life on board of the Guardian-Mother as agreeable as possible."

"Thank you, Mr. Gaskette; I have no doubt we shall be friends," said Louis in French.

"Mr. Amos Shafter, the chief engineer of the steamer, Mr. Belgrave," continued the captain.

"I am glad to make your acquaintance, Mr. Shafter; and I have no doubt we have the best man afloat in charge of the engine," returned the owner. "I hope the engine is as good as the engineer."

"I thank you for your good opinion, made up in advance, of the engineer; and no better engine was ever put into the hull of a vessel than that of the Guardian-Mother," replied Mr. Shafter, as Louis shook his hand like that of an old friend; and the chief went for the second engineer.

"This is Mr. Sage, the chief steward of the steamer, Mr. Belgrave. He is a wise man, as his name indicates, though it also suggests sage and onions for the stuffing of the goose he will sometimes serve at your table," the captain proceeded.

"I am happy to know you, Mr. Sage; for I know what an important person you are on board of a vessel," replied Louis, taking his hand. "I have been starved on a sandbank for the last three days, and I am sure I shall fully appreciate the service you will render."

"I shall do my best to suit you," replied the chief steward quietly.

"The last I shall introduce at present is here now. Mr. Belgrave, Mr. Sentrick, the second engineer, qualified for any position in his department."

"I am glad to see you, Mr. Sentrick; and I shall sleep without the fear of being blown up when the second is the equal of the first engineer in all except the name."

"Thank you, Mr. Belgrave: you are very kind to speak so handsomely of me, but I am still a pupil of Mr. Shafter, for he can teach me a great deal that I don't know," replied the second engineer modestly.

"Now you know all the officers, Mr. Belgrave; and I have no doubt you will find them all ready and willing to do all in their power in your service," added the commander; and all the officers touched their caps and bowed to the owner and to the captain, as they walked forward. "Now, Mr. Belgrave, we will look the vessel over."

The house on deck extended from the *boudoir* to the forecastle; and the captain showed his owner into all the rooms, beginning with the staterooms of the engineers. Then they visited the engine and fire rooms, where Mr. Shafter did the honors. Forward of the smoke-stack was the galley, as Louis had already learned to call the kitchen. It was fitted up appropriately, and was as neat as a pin in every part.

"Mr. Belgrave, I have the honor to present to you the chief cook of the Guardian-Mother, Monsieur Odervie; and I am sorry I can't say it in French," said the commander, laughing.

"I am very glad to see you, Monsieur Odervie," answered Louis, taking his hand, which the cook wiped diligently on his apron for this part of the ceremony; and the owner spoke his speech in French, which delighted the official of the galley. "Your soup has made a new man of me, after starving for three days on a sandbank; and I know you will be one of my most valued friends."

"Thank you, Monsieur Belgraf. Pardon, *Monsieur le capitaine, mais vous savez bien*"—

"No, I don't *savez* a bit!" exclaimed the captain.

"You have promised me another man. *C'est trop pour cuire pour tout l'équipage.*"

"He says it is too much to cook for the whole crew," interposed Louis.

"He is quite right; but I had not time to look up another cook after I learned that one was wanted," replied the captain.

"So much the better!" exclaimed Louis. "There is Baldy; and I promised to find a place for him if I could."

"Baldy?" added the commander interrogatively.

"Bickling, the cook of the Maud, who came on board with me."

"All right! Come here, Baldy," called the captain.

"Which I am 'ere, sir," replied the cook of the Maud.

"Can you talk French, Baldy?" asked the commander, apparently to make sport of him.

"Which I can a little, sir."

"You can!" exclaimed Louis.

"Which I lived two years in Paris with my master, and I had to pick up some of it," replied Baldy.

Louis and the cook spoke to him in French, and the examination was satisfactory, though the candidate had forgotten some of what he had learned; in fact, Louis suggested that he could speak French better than he did English. But the chief cook could speak English when he was so disposed.

"You are appointed second cook of the Guardian-Mother, Baldy; and you will obey Monsieur Odervie in all things," said the captain.

"Which I will do, sir; and I thank you, captain, with all my 'eart," replied Baldy, taking off his hat and bowing very low. "Which I thank you, too, Mr. Belgrave, which you are the owner of the finest steam-yacht that ever floated on the ocean."

Forward of the galley was the ice-house, and then the smoking-room, for which the present owner had no use. The adjoining rooms, with the foremast between them, were the staterooms of the first and second officers; and Louis declared that either of them was good enough for him.

"This is my room, Mr. Belgrave," said the commander, as he led the way into the next room.

"I thought you would take one of the staterooms in the cabin," suggested Louis.

"I don't intend to be an ornamental captain merely, and I desire to be near my work. For the present, while you are alone, I will take my meals with you, if you invite me to do so," replied the commander.

These apartments consisted of two rooms, one of which appeared to be the captain's office, for it was provided with a desk, and several bookcases; and the other was his sleeping-apartment. A door opened from the former into the pilot-house, which was quite a large room. The wheel, the binnacles, and everything else, were of the most approved modern type. The vessel was steered by steam, and a uniformed quartermaster was at the wheel.

"Spokes, this is Mr. Belgrave, our owner," said the captain; and the man saluted him without any speech.

They passed out to the forecastle, where sixteen men and the boatswain were assembled. The commander presented the owner: they all touched their caps, and gave three hearty cheers. This finished the ceremonies; and every man on board, except the firemen, knew "Mr. Belgrave." The young million-aire was then conducted to the captain's room.

CHAPTER 33
ON BOARD THE GUARDIAN-MOTHER

LOUIS WAS TIRED ENOUGH to enjoy the arm-chair the captain gave him in his room, for he had begun to feel that he needed another plate of soup, and he said as much to his friend. The touch of a button connected with the electric bells brought Sparks to the apartment, and the soup was ordered. It came in a few minutes, neatly arranged with biscuits on a tray, and the owner enjoyed it.

"I have gone through all the formalities, Louis," said Captain Ringgold, when the refreshment was disposed of. "I have not yet learned how you happened to be left alone on that sand-spit, for I was in a hurry to make you at home on the Guardian-Mother."

Louis felt quite at home; and he related all the details of his residence on the sandbank, including the adventure with Flounder, the burning of the Phantom, and the escape of the Maud.

"Brisbane left you on that sand-spit!" exclaimed the commander, springing out of his chair. "It was his own fault that his steamer was burned, for he let his crew go to sleep, when he ought to have kept part of them awake."

"I thought of paying him for the loss of the Phantom," added Louis.

"Not a red cent! That man is under obligations to me, and he deserted you on a sand-spit, leaving you hardly food enough to keep you from starving!"

"He did not expect that I should have to remain there so long, as I did not myself," replied Louis.

"Didn't you tell me he said he might have to stay there a week, and that was his reason for abandoning you?" demanded the captain sharply.

"He was not entirely consistent."

"I told Brisbane all it was necessary for him to know, and charged him to see that no harm came to you. I will never trust him with a mud-scow again."

Captain Ringgold then explained that he had been obliged to pay the full sum he had named for the steam-yacht, which was many thousand dollars less than she had cost. He had used all the haste he could in getting her ready to sail, but various matters had delayed him.

"The Maud has gone to Bermuda beyond a doubt," he continued, "and your mother is still on board of her. I don't believe any harm will come to her; but we want her on board of the Guardian-Mother."

"I do, at any rate," added Louis.

"And so do I, my boy; and I think she will be happy on board."

"But I do not quite see how we can reclaim her," suggested the owner.

"We will find a way. I am glad you put a bullet in that beggar who burned the Phantom; and it is a pity you did not put it in another place."

"I am glad the wound was no worse. I knew he was a reckless fellow, and when he pointed his revolver at my head, I fired because I was afraid he would do so," pleaded Louis.

"You did quite right, my boy; if you had not fired when you did, you might not have been here to tell the story," added Captain Ringgold. "But you have not told me, Louis, how you like the Guardian-Mother."

"How would it be possible not to like her? She is magnificent beyond any conception I had of a steamer. In fact, I am so bewildered that I cannot express myself in regard to her," replied Louis with enthusiasm. "Taking her cost and the expense of running her into consideration, I cannot help feeling that it is a very extravagant outlay for a boy like me, only sixteen years old."

"But you are abundantly able to own such a vessel, and to pay the expense of keeping her in commission all the year round, Louis," said the captain very seriously, as he took from his desk a paper on which he had estimated the probable cost of running the vessel. "If she should cost you fifty thousand dollars a year, she will leave you a large margin of your income."

"I am sure I should not have thought of such a thing as buying her if it had not been for the service she is to render me in recovering my poor dear mother," continued Louis, as the tears started in his eyes. "That villain might have led me all over the world in a sailing yacht; and I can truly say that I asked for the purchase of the steamer solely on account of my mother. I should not have dared to ask for such a craft for my own pleasure."

"And yet you might well have done so. With an income of seventy thousand dollars a year, you can afford such a luxury. But I do not look upon the vessel as a plaything for your pleasure and amusement. I think Uncle Moses told me you had fitted for college. Now, Louis, you must make the Guardian-Mother your university. You ought to have on board such instructors as you need, though one may be enough, and pursue your studies just as though you were a regular student in Columbia College."

"This is a new idea," replied Louis.

"But it is a good one. I do not believe you ought to give all your time to your own amusement, even though it may consist of so reasonable a recreation as sight-seeing in the various countries of the world. You can have your mother on board with you, and live as well as you please. I grant it will be a very expensive education; and I certainly should not recommend it if you were not abundantly able to pay the cost. I talked with Uncle Moses about this idea, and he was pleased with it. He even thought he should like to go with you; but he was not sure that you would like to have him on board."

"He ought to have been sure on that point, captain. I should be delighted to have him with me," added Louis warmly.

"I think you understand my idea now, my boy; and I must go on deck, for perhaps you do not realize that we are engaged in a lively chase," said Captain Ringgold, as he rose from his arm-chair.

Louis followed him to the deck. The wind was very light from the west, and the steamer pitched slightly on the long rollers of the ocean; but Louis thought it was exceedingly pleasant sailing. If his mother had been with him, he felt that he should be supremely happy. He walked about the deck to examine the magnificent craft by himself while the captain was attending to his duties, which consisted just then of an examination of the log-slate in the pilot-house.

The Guardian-Mother was rigged as a topsail schooner. Captain Singfield had built her for a voyage around the world, on which he intended to be absent four years; and with an idea of saving expense, for he was hardly as rich as the millionaire at sixteen, she was abundantly supplied with canvas, so that she could make very fair progress under sail alone, as proved on one of her trial trips.

He seated himself in the *boudoir* after he had looked the vessel over, and gave himself up to the reflections of the hour. He could hardly believe that he was the sole owner of such an elegant and powerful steamer, and he was delighted with the programme which the commander had laid out for his education and recreation. But before all, the steamer was to be used to reclaim his mother from the possession of Scoble, and he could not think of anything else seriously until this duty had been fully discharged.

Captain Ringgold came into the *boudoir* just as the cabin steward rang a bell in the companion-way. It was half an hour before dinner, at six o'clock, and the owner thought he was hardly in condition to go to the table, for he had put on his every-day clothes for the work in which he had been engaged. His valise had been put in his stateroom, and he considered it incumbent upon him to dress in a style becoming the owner of such a steam-yacht.

"We are making sixteen and a half knots just now, Louis, which is half a knot better than her former owner claimed for her," said the captain, as he seated himself opposite Louis.

"But when shall we catch up with the Maud? That is the one question of interest to me now," asked Louis.

"The Guardian-Mother will hardly overhaul her for forty-eight hours, for she had a fair and fresh wind for about two days," replied Captain Ringgold. "Don't be impatient, Louis, for I think that within three days we shall have your mother on board."

"Don't forget to bring off Felix McGavonty with her, for he is to be the companion of my voyages as well as my mother."

"You may be sure that I will not forget him, my boy; besides, I am inclined to think you will have a hand in the final work of the present expedition."

"I certainly shall if I am permitted to do so. But it is time for me to dress for dinner, for I am hardly in condition to show myself at the table," added Louis, as he rose from his chair and went below.

His stateroom was the forward one on the starboard side, while the one on the opposite side was reserved for Mrs. Belgrave. Before he opened his valise, he had to look the room over. Its comforts and conveniences, as well as its elegance, filled him with delight. He could not banish his mother from his mind, and he thought how amazed and enraptured she would be when she took possession of the corresponding apartments on the port side. In the bath room he found hot and cold water at the bowl. He had hardly entered it before the electric lights flashed a flood of brilliancy into both rooms.

He dressed himself in his best clothes, and at the sound of the bell went out into the main cabin, where dinner awaited him. The captain was not there, neither was Mrs. Blossom, who was nominally a stewardess.

"Sparks, where is the captain?" asked Louis with all the *sang froid* he could command.

"On deck, I think, sir," replied the steward.

"Find him; present my compliments to him, and say that I desire the pleasure of his company at dinner," added Louis; and Sparks hastened to obey the order.

He returned with the message that the commander would join him in a few minutes. He then directed the steward to deliver the same invitation to Mrs. Blossom. She appeared at once, and thanked the owner for his consideration.

"I do not expect to take my meals at the cabin table with the owner, for, as you know, I am only the stewardess," said the lady very pleasantly, as the captain came below.

"I wish to give my first order, Captain Ringgold," Louis proceeded, as the trio stood near the table. "From this moment Mrs. Blossom ceases to be stewardess, and is to be regarded as the companion, not the servant, of my mother. I expect and desire that you and she will take your meals at my table."

"I had no authority to engage a companion for your mother; and I heartily approve your order, Mr. Belgrave," replied the captain.

"Now, Captain Ringgold, you will oblige me by taking the head of the table," continued Louis. "I will sit at your right, and Mrs. Blossom at your left."

The commander objected; the owner insisted, and the latter had his own way after many pleasantries. The dinner was equal to a Delmonico affair, and Monsieur Odervie was generously praised. A full hour was passed at the table, but most of the time was consumed in conversation.

Louis spent his evening in the *boudoir*, brilliantly illuminated by electric lights, with Mrs. Blossom. He was tired enough to retire early. The dinner had banished the last remnants of his malady, caused by what he called starvation, though this was an exaggeration. He related to his pleasant companion the history of the cruise he had made in the Maud, and the chase after the schooner in the Phantom.

The next two days passed as agreeably to the young millionaire as the absence of his mother would permit. The weather had changed, and the wind was blowing more than half a gale from the north-west. At daylight the next morning Captain Ringgold roused the owner, and informed him that the Maud was in sight.

CHAPTER 34
A WRECK ON THE BERMUDA REEF

LOUIS BELGRAVE HAD BECOME sufficiently accustomed to the motion of the steamer, even in a rough sea, to feel quite at home on deck or in the cabin. The Guardian-Mother had crossed the Gulf Stream while a northerly wind was blowing, and even Captain Ringgold called it "decidedly lumpy." The young millionaire's experience in the Maud, and before that in the Blanche, had very nearly made a sailor of him, so far as his ability to handle himself on shipboard was concerned, and he had made some progress in the details of practical seamanship.

The information given him by the captain that the Maud was in sight was like a bolt of electricity shot into the being of Louis. His mother was actually near him again, and his bosom bounded with the violent emotions which agitated him. The commander only made his announcement at the door of the stateroom, and was gone in a moment. The young man was filled with hope that he should soon be in his mother's arms, and he did not stop to consider the many difficulties that were still in the way.

He dressed himself very hurriedly in his common suit, for he knew not what his next mission in the object of his existence might prove to be. As he had been since the abduction of his mother, he was ready for anything that might come. There were sixteen picked seamen on the forecastle, besides the officers, engineers, and quartermasters. Every person on board comprehended the mission of the Guardian-Mother, for nothing else had been talked about since the young owner came on board of the steamer. All hands were interested in the story told of him and his mother, and there was not a single one of them who was not anxious to assist in the recovery of the lady.

Louis put on his overcoat, and made sure that his revolver was in condition for immediate use, though he hoped there would be no occasion for such a weapon. He hastened on deck as soon as he had made his hurried preparations. The motion of the vessel was more violent than it had been the night before when he left the deck. The air was heavy with moisture, which felt like fog, though he could see none. The wind was directly ahead, and the steamer was pitching smartly in the heavy sea. The wind had gone around to the opposite quarter, and Louis thought it was blowing more than half a gale, as the captain measured it the day before.

"You are getting it rough this morning, Captain Ringgold," said the owner, as he entered the pilot-house.

"Good-morning, Mr. Belgrave; but I hope you don't call this very rough," replied the commander, peering out at the ocean ahead of the vessel.

"Rougher than I have seen it before on this trip," added Louis. "But I don't see the Maud."

"You must have a pair of good nautical eyes to see her under present circumstances; but I have made her out, and I am certain that she is not far ahead of us," said the commander, levelling his spy-glass at the open window. "I can't make her out now, for the air is full of streaks of fog, which may settle down upon us, and bury us out of sight."

"That would be unfortunate," suggested the owner.

"Perhaps not; it may be a good thing for us. But I am confident that Scoble is heading too far to the westward," said Captain Ringgold anxiously, though he did not communicate his fears to his owner.

Half a dozen times in the next two hours the fog-banks settled and rose again, but the Maud could be distinctly seen when she was not wreathed in a mantle of vapor. The relative position of the two vessels was now changed, for the commander had headed the steamer farther to the eastward, and the leadsman was sounding all the time, though his response was still "no bottom." The occasional lift of the fog had revealed the breakers on the reef, twenty-four miles in extent, and about eight north-west of the Bermuda Islands.

"I suppose you know where you are, Captain Ringgold," said Louis, laughing.

"I do, very well indeed; and I wish that fellow in charge of the Maud knew where he was," replied the commander, looking more anxious than ever, for the fog had just settled down again on the chase. "We must have passed him by this time, for if he kept his course, he must be two miles to leeward of us."

"By the mark, fifteen!" shouted the leadsman in a vigorous tone, as though he had important news to tell.

"All right; that settles it, and I know where I am to a hair," added the commander, as he directed the quartermaster at the wheel to head the steamer to the westward.

From this moment two leads were going all the time, and the reports came rapidly. The water was shoaling all the time, and the engine was reduced to half speed. While it looked as though the fog was lifting again, those in the pilot-house were startled by the boom of a small cannon directly ahead.

"What does that mean, captain?" inquired Louis very anxiously, as he tried to penetrate the fog-bank ahead with his vision.

"It means trouble for some one," replied the commander, looking quite as anxious as his owner. "Some vessel has evidently gone on the reef."

"But what vessel?" demanded Louis, almost overcome with an agony of suspense.

"Of course I don't know; but I am very much afraid it is the Maud," added Captain Ringgold, his brow wrinkled and his lips compressed.

"Then my poor mother will be lost!" exclaimed Louis, unable to avoid giving way to his emotions.

"That does not follow at all, Mr. Belgrave. If it is the Maud that is in trouble, she cannot be more than a mile from us, and we have a good chance to save all on board of her. But it may be some other vessel, for a great many wrecks occur on these reefs Don't give up to it, my lad."

Louis braced himself up to the duty of commanding himself as well as he could; but it was the most difficult task he was ever called upon to perform. Captain Ringgold was very active, and the reports of the leadsmen assisted him a little, as they assured the commander that the steamer was rapidly approaching the perilous reef.

"On deck!" shouted Mr. Gaskette, the second officer, who had been sent aloft on the foremast to report any appearance ahead. "Wreck in sight, sir!"

"What is it?" hailed the captain, who had gone out upon the deck.

"A schooner, hard and fast on the reef, with her foremast gone by the board!" shouted the second officer.

"How does she bear?"

"Dead ahead! She is a topsail schooner, with her foremast alongside."

"Steady, Spokes. Twist, go out on the forecastle, and fire two guns," said the captain.

"On deck, sir! The fog is lifting," added Mr. Gaskette.

"And a half twelve!" cried one of the leadsmen, and the other presently repeated it.

The commander rang one of the engine bells, and spoke through the trumpet to the engineer, directing him to reduce the speed still further. Briggs, the boatswain, was ordered to have two of the life-boats in readiness to lower into the water.

"The fog is lifting again!" shouted Louis, who stood at the open window in the pilot-house. "I can see the vessel, though she don't look much like the Maud;" and for the moment he dared to hope that it was not she.

"I can see her distinctly now, and I have no doubt she is the Maud," replied the captain, who was giving his whole attention to the sounding. "You can see her foremast with the yards on it, hanging over the side. She must have ground out the step of her foremast when she went on the rocks. It is all up with her, for she can never get out of that scrape."

"But my poor mother," groaned Louis.

"Don't be alarmed yet, Mr. Belgrave. You can see her people on the deck, and they are all safe so far, I have no doubt whatever. The steamer is not more than half a mile from her, and we can take off her crew and passengers without any difficulty," replied the commander in assuring tones, which greatly strengthened the owner.

The weather was clearer than at any time before during the morning, and Louis directed the glass in the pilot-house to the wreck. He had no trouble in making out every person on the wreck. His mother, supported by Felix McGavonty, was holding on at the lee side. The hull had evidently twisted around so that she was broadside to the fresh gale, for she could not have gone on the reef in the direction she was now headed. The sea was making a clean breach over her, and she seemed to be smothered in the torrents of white spray that swept across her.

"By the mark, ten!" shouted the leadsmen one after the other.

At this report the captain rang the great gong bell in the engine-room, and the engineer promptly stopped the screw. The wind seemed to be increasing in force, and the sea was very heavy. As soon as the steamer lost her headway, she began to roll violently. The captain started the engine again, brought the ship about, heading her into the wind, and gave her headway enough to keep her up to the sea. Her position became much easier at once.

"Mr. Boulong, you will take charge of the first cutter, and Mr. Gaskette of the second," continued the captain. "It is low tide, but you must feel your way over the reef. You will find water enough for the boats, and get on the lee side of the wreck. How to get the people into the boats I must leave to your own good judgment, and I will not embarrass you with orders which may not be practicable."

"In which boat shall I go, Captain Ringgold?" asked the owner earnestly, as the boatswain swung out the davits of the first cutter.

"I can't advise you to go in either, Mr. Belgrave," replied the commander seriously.

"I must go, sir!" protested Louis. "Shall I keep away from my mother when she is in peril of her life? I could not do it, captain!"

"I shall send two officers and eight men in the boats, and that will be abundantly sufficient to save every one on the wreck," argued the captain. "You are not a sailor, and this is a dangerous enterprise, as you can see for yourself."

"Is it any more dangerous for me than it is for my mother?"

"But it is needless for you to expose yourself, and you can do no good by going in the boat."

"Where my mother is I must be, Captain Ringgold, and I shall go to her if I have to swim to the wreck," Louis insisted with all the earnestness of his nature.

"This is your steamer, and these are your boats; and if you are determined to go, I shall say nothing more," added the commander, when he saw that it was useless to argue the point.

"If it were not my mother in question I would obey you like a child."

"I do not command you, Mr. Belgrave," said the captain with a smile. "Mr. Boulong, Mr. Belgrave will go in the first cutter with you, and I need hardly tell you to look out for his safety as well as his mother's."

It was not boys' play to lower the boats into the water, and the second cutter was nearly stove against the side of the ship. Under the immediate direction of the captain the first cutter, with Louis, the first officer and four men, was safely lowered into the water, and shoved off, clear of the side. The boat was like a feather on the bounding billows, and the owner found it necessary to hold on with both hands in the stern sheets, where Mr. Boulong steered the cutter.

The second cutter had more difficulty in getting off, but succeeded in the end, when Mr. Boulong was half-way to the wreck. The boat went over the shoal water, and the bowman caught the rope that was thrown from the Maud. Louis saw that his mother was on her knees in prayer.

CHAPTER 35
THE RETURN TO THE GUARDIAN-MOTHER

JOHN SCOBLE COULD HAVE not the slightest suspicion that the magnificent steamer in the offing, which had come to the relief of his ship's company and passengers, was the property of Mrs. Belgrave's son, or even that Louis was within a thousand miles of him. Doubtless the captain of the Maud believed that he had accomplished all that he had attempted, and that not even the accident of his shipwreck could deprive him of the fruits of his victory over Louis and his friends.

He had obtained full possession of the lady he still insisted upon calling his wife; and it could not have occurred to him that the son was able, or would ever be able, to wrest her from his grasp, either by force or by strategy. The beautiful steamer, less than half a mile distant, whose boats had come to his assistance, was bound to Bermuda, or at least would land his party at St. George or Hamilton. He was perfectly confident that he was the master of the situation.

As he had learned from the various exciting interviews with Scoble, Louis was aware that the persecutor of his mother did not know that the missing million had been discovered, and certainly not that the purchase-money of the elegant steamer off the reef had been paid from this resource. The young millionaire had not deemed it advisable to give him this information, for Scoble would not believe him if he did so. The treasure was still his coveted object.

The blinding spray that broke entirely over the wreck did not permit any one on the deck to examine the faces of those in the first cutter when the rope thrown by the mate was made fast in the fore-sheets. The hull of the schooner had careened over to leeward till the mainmast, the only remaining spar, extended out over the water at an angle of about forty-five degrees; and the cutter had brought up directly under it, as Mr. Boulong intended, in order to carry out a plan he had formed as soon as he understood the position of the wreck.

Under the lee of the Maud's hull the water was not so violently agitated as in every other situation. Still, it was impossible to go alongside the wreck without the peril of dashing the boat to pieces. The wreck itself, the bottom of which was by this time ground out of her on the sharp rocks, had a dangerous motion; and it was only a question of minutes when it would be torn in pieces. There was certainly no time to lose; and the mate, with his plan all ready, proceeded to execute it without a moment's delay.

"Bangs and Williams, I have some sharp work for you," said Mr. Boulong with energy. "Are you ready to run some risk? If not, say so."

"All ready, sir!" shouted both of the bow oarsmen together. "Not a man in this ship's company will go back on his duty!" added Bangs.

"Not one, sir!" roared Williams.

The mate took a purchase from the bottom of the boat rigged with a strong line, and passed it to the men in the bow.

"Now, Bangs, board the wreck with this line," continued Mr. Boulong in a very loud tone, which the noisy sea and the grinding hull rendered necessary. "You will follow him, Williams. Make fast the purchase about twenty feet up the main rigging! Rig a sling for the lady, and lower her into the boat!"

"Ay, ay, sir!" responded the two men.

With the rope fastened around his body, Bangs began the ascent of the fast which held the boat. The mate ordered the two men who were to remain in the boat to back water with their oars with all their might, in order to keep the rope as stiff as possible. But it was a perilous enterprise; and more than once Bangs was swept under water by the slackening of the line. If he had not been a bold, brave fellow, he would have given up the attempt in despair. He struggled with the waves that ingulfed him frequently; and, after a desperate battle with the elements, he reached the wreck, where he was assisted over the bulwark by the two seamen of the schooner.

Louis had taken one of the spare oars, and was pulling with all his strength to keep the cutter at its distance from the wreck. The mate took the remaining oar and joined in the work, while Williams, with the block of the purchase tied to his belt, began to climb the fast. Either because there was a momentary lull in the gale, or because the additional oars kept the cutter steadier, the bold seaman made his way to the deck of the Maud with comparatively little difficulty.

The purchase was hauled on board from the boat; and Bangs, without the loss of an instant, ran up the main rigging with the block in his hand. Williams followed him as soon as he could catch his breath,—for he had been under water several times in his passage up the line,—with the purchase-rope tied around him. The mast swayed badly under the pressure of the heavy seas; but the work was speedily accomplished. The mate had rigged the slings in the cutter, and they had been hauled to the deck.

Suddenly there was a violent commotion in the forward part of the wreck, and the grinding and snapping of planks and timbers could be heard. The stump of the bowsprit, which had been broken off when the foremast went, by the board, dropped into the boiling sea. The forecastle was lifted up as though a charge of dynamite had wrenched it from its position; the whole forward part of the hull crumbled away, and these portions of the wreck were tossed in every direction by the savage waves.

"She is going to pieces!" cried Louis, as he witnessed the destruction of this part of the wreck.

"Not yet!" shouted Mr. Boulong. "The forward part is broken off where the step of the foremast was ground out of her. She may hold on some time yet."

"My mother is still on board of her," groaned Louis, as he sprang to the fore-sheets of the cutter.

He had thrown off his coat and hat when he began to row, and, without announcing his intention, he threw himself upon the fast which held the boat, and began to climb up as the two seamen had done. He had not made six feet before he was submerged by the loosing of the rope. The mate saw his peril, and the three men pulled with all their might till the young millionaire rose from the water and renewed his effort.

"Come back, Mr. Belgrave! For Heaven's sake come back!" yelled Mr. Boulong in an agony of suspense; for he knew that the young man was not a sailor, and he fully expected to see him drop exhausted into the sea.

The mate and his two men made their oars bend with their earnestness to keep the cutter at her distance. Louis did not heed the call of Mr. Boulong, but struggled on his way to the deck of the wreck. His mother was in peril there, in deadly peril, as her son understood it, after the whole bow of the vessel had been carried away. He would have believed that he was a coward if he had retreated from the holiest duty on earth.

There were moments when the tempest lulled a little, and one of these brief intervals, as well as the tremendous efforts of the mate and his men in the boat, favored him, and he succeeded in reaching the bulwarks of the stranded craft, where Bangs hauled him in, very nearly exhausted by his tremendous exertions. The purchase and slings were all ready for use, and Bangs rushed to the waist, where Mrs. Belgrave and Felix were awaiting their fate or their salvation, which ever it might be.

The strong arm of the seaman encircled her, and conducted her in safety to the mainmast. By this time Louis had partially recovered his breath, and he seized his mother in his arms as the seamen released her to attend to the slings. She was blinded with spray, but she was calmer than any of the crew of the Maud. Her prayers had strengthened her, and prepared her for a grave beneath the wild waves.

"Mother!" exclaimed Louis, as he pressed her to his bosom with a sort of wild rapture. "Not a word, mother! You shall be saved!"

Nothing more was said, for the business of saving her was paramount in his mind. Bangs rigged the sling, and seated her in it, very much as she had sat in a swing when she was a child. Then with some lanyards he tied her to the ropes, so that she could not have fallen out if she had taken no care for her safety.

"Here, you blackguard!" shouted Williams, as he seized one of the seamen of the Maud who was in the act of getting on the rope to make his way to the cutter. "If another mother's son of you attempts to get into that boat, I will fling him overboard! We save the ladies first!"

"Don't be frightened, mother," said Louis, as the two sailors began to heave on the purchase-rope. "You will be put into the boat without any danger."

"I am not frightened, Louis; I am in the hands of the Lord, and I shall be saved if it his will, my son," she replied, as she kissed and embraced him, perhaps thinking it might be the last time in this world.

As the men heaved on the line, Mrs. Belgrave rose in the air, and Louis passed her over the bulwark. The block of the purchase had been rigged directly over the cutter by Bangs, and as soon as the passenger had been raised to the shrouds, the sailors lowered her, Louis attending to the guy rope which had been attached to her. With the oars those in the cutter kept it as steady as possible; Mr. Boulong received her in his strong arms, and in a few moments more she was seated in the stern sheets.

"It is your turn next, Flix," said Louis, who had had no time to do anything more than shake his crony by the hand.

Felix objected, and insisted that Louis should descend next; but the owner directed Bangs to put him in the sling, and he submitted. In a few moments more he was in the boat. The owner of the Guardian-Mother had not so far encountered Scoble, or Frinks his mate; and there were only two seamen on board, besides Kimpton.

"It is your turn now, Mr. Belgrave," said Bangs, as he rigged the sling for a third passenger.

"I am all ready," replied Louis, who had no desire to remain any longer.

At this moment Scoble came on deck from the cabin with his hands full of various articles which he was doubtless anxious to save, for he must have had a considerable sum of money in his possession. He staggered up to the foot of the mainmast where Bangs was rigging the sling for the owner of the steamer, for it was not an easy thing to walk on that uneasy deck, even for a sailor. But he looked as though he had been drinking too much brandy.

"I will be the next one to go in the boat," said he, his speech as thick as though his tongue was double its natural size. "I don't want to be separated from my wife."

"She is no longer your wife!" said Louis in a very earnest tone.

"Louis!" exclaimed Scoble, starting back as though he had seen an apparition. "How came you here?"

But Bangs did not suspend his preparations, and in a moment more Louis was ready for the descent. Very likely the sight of his late stepson roused his anger, assisted by the spirit he had taken, and he insisted that he should go next. When he began to lay violent hands on Louis, Bangs waited for nothing more, but knocked him half-way across the deck with a single blow of his fist. Before he could recover, the owner was swinging in the air, and was presently deposited in the boat.

The second cutter had come up and made fast to the stern of the first. Mr. Boulong had three passengers now, and he decided to take no more, as there were only five more on the wreck. The other boat was hauled up to the fast, and secured to it. Two of the oarsmen were transferred from the second to the first cutter, and the second officer was directed to take off those that remained. It was a very rough passage, but the three persons were safely taken on board of the Guardian-Mother.

CHAPTER 36
A HAPPY REUNION

BY SKILFUL MANAGEMENT ON the part of the commander of the Guardian-Mother, the first cutter, containing the three passengers, was hoisted up to the davits, and the lady was assisted to the deck, where she was warmly welcomed by Captain Ringgold. The mate and the oarsmen assisted Louis and Felix out of the boat, for it was impossible for any of them to stand alone on the deck of the plunging vessel. The young millionaire took the arm of his mother, and conducted her to the *boudoir*, where the nickeled rail nearly surrounding the apartment enabled her to preserve her equilibrium, though with no little difficulty.

The first thing she did was to throw her spare arm around the neck of her son, and draw him to her heart, while she wept tears of joy to find herself once more in his presence. Louis returned the embrace very earnestly, and he could not repress his own tears. For some minutes they remained in each other's arms, speaking not a word, for no words were equal to the expression of their emotions.

"Sit down, my dear mother," said Louis at last, as he supported her to the broad sofa, where he seated her, and then bolstered her on one side with the cushions.

"I thank the good Lord that we are together once more, Louis," she replied, taking the hand not in use in clinging to the rail. "But I am utterly bewildered to find you here, as I was when you came to me on the wreck. I gave myself up for lost before I saw the boats of this steamer coming over the stormy sea."

"But you are safe now, and I hope all your trials and persecutions are over," added her son warmly, as he pressed the hand he held.

"But where is that man—Scoble, I mean?" asked the poor woman, with a timid glance at Louis.

"He and his crew will be brought on board of the steamer by the second cutter."

"This steamer?"

"Certainly; there is no other steamer near us. But you need not see him if you do not wish to do so," suggested Louis. "I hope he has not ill-treated you, mother;" and the teeth of the young man were firmly set together.

"No, my son; but his presence is intensely disagreeable to me. Felix has saved me from a great deal of annoyance."

"Flix, my dear fellow, I had almost forgotten you in finding my mother!" exclaimed Louis, as he grasped the hand of his former crony.

"Faix, ye's moight forget the loikes o' me at the prisent moment," replied Felix. "But it's mighty glad Oi am to see you, Louis, me darlint."

"I am just as glad to see you, old fellow; and I know you have taken good care of my mother; and I should have known it if she had not said so," added Louis, as he touched the button of an electric bell, which presently brought Sparks into his presence. "Ask Mrs. Blossom to come to the *boudoir*, Sparks;" and the steward bowed and retired.

"Mrs. Blossom!" exclaimed Mrs. Belgrave. "Is she on board of this steamer? And Captain Ringgold too?"

"Both of them, mother; and the latter is the commander of the steamer."

Before any explanation could be made of the strange circumstances, as they certainly were to the lady and her companion from the wreck, Mrs. Blossom appeared in the *boudoir*, and gave her old friend and her favorite in the house of Squire Scarburn a cordial greeting.

"Now, mother, Mrs. Blossom will conduct you to your stateroom. You will find all your clothes and toilet articles there; and you must change all your garments, for you must be wet through."

"All my clothes here!" exclaimed the lady.

"They are, mother, for Captain Ringgold and I came down here on purpose for you. But I must go on deck and see what is to be done with Scoble, for he shall not annoy you here."

"I was never more astonished in all my life than I am at this moment," said Mrs. Belgrave, as Mrs. Blossom assisted her down the stairs to the state cabin, where her room was opposite that of her son.

"You need make no explanations, Mrs. Blossom," added Louis. "Now, Flix, you must have a wet jacket. Sparks, you will take this young gentleman to the stateroom next to mine, which he is to occupy. Fit him out with dry clothing from my valise, and take the best of care of him."

"Thin it is a gintleman Oi am?" chuckled Felix.

"As you always were, Flix. But Sparks is not a professor of modern languages, and I recommend you to speak English at him."

"I shall certainly do so, Louis; and Mr. Sparks shall have no occasion to find fault with me. But what is the meaning of all this masquerade? I do not understand it any more than I do the black art," replied Felix.

"You shall understand it all in due time, my dear fellow. In the mean time, Sparks and Mrs. Blossom will answer no questions; but as soon as the ship's company of the Maud are disposed of, we will have a meeting here, and talk it all over," said Louis, as he went out on the deck, while Felix followed Sparks below.

The passengers were bewildered and delighted with the elegance of the cabin; but their exclamations were not reported. The owner found the captain and most of the crew of the ship engaged in getting the second cutter up to the davits. All who came in the boat were drenched with the spray, more especially those from the wrecked schooner. But all of them were sailors, and they made their way to the deck without assistance. The climate of this region, even in mid-winter, is very mild and soft, and no one could suffer on account of his drenched clothing.

"Captain Ringgold!" exclaimed Scoble, as he confronted the commander when he leaped from the cutter. "I am extremely happy to see you, sir."

"Happier perhaps than I am to see you," replied the captain bluffly. "I have had the honor to be kidnapped by you, and that is not the way one gentleman treats another."

"But the force of circumstances compelled"—

"I don't care a straw for the force of circumstances, for I know all about them; and the force of circumstances only increased the force of your rascality. As a shipwrecked mariner, it was my duty to save you and your ship's company, and I have done so; but the duty was made pleasant by the fact that the fate of others whom I respect and revere was involved with yours."

"Then, captain, you would have permitted me to perish on the wreck which has just gone to pieces, if my wife and that pettifogger's cub had not been with me?" demanded Scoble with a sneer.

"I did not say that, or mean it," replied the captain with dignity.

"We need not quarrel, Captain Ringgold, for I am indebted to you for saving me and my companions," continued Scoble, smothering his ill-feeling. "I need not say that I am astonished to find you here in command of a fine steamer; but I suppose you are here in the interest of that unlicked whelp of my wife."

"I will not tolerate such language on board of my ship!" said the captain sternly, as Louis stepped from the *boudoir*, where he had remained to observe the scene.

"Oh, so you are here too!" ejaculated Scoble, when he saw his former step-son for the first time.

"I am here, John Scoble, and I would have followed you all over the world to redeem my mother from your poison fangs!" responded the young man, indignant at the invective of Scoble.

"You will have a chance to do it yet, perhaps," replied the late captain of the Maud, now no more. "I wish to be reasonable, Captain Ringgold, and I appeal to your sense of honor and justice. This boy, this young scapegrace, has contrived to rob me of my wife, and has done so by force and violence."

"If you apply another offensive epithet to that young gentlemen, Captain Scoble, I will lock you up in a stateroom!" interposed the commander, with energy. "Mr. Belgrave must be treated with respect by all on board of this steamer. If you cannot learn to do so, my men will show you to your state-room."

"*Mister* Belgrave seems to be in clover here. A young gentleman is he?" sneered Scoble. "Is this a passenger steamer, one of the line to the Bermudas?"

"No, sir! This is a private steam-yacht, and she is owned by Mr. Louis Belgrave," added the captain.

"Owned by him!" exclaimed the captain of the Maud.

"You do not seem to have learned the latest news in New York, and especially in Von Blonk Park," continued the commander with quiet dignity. "You know something about a missing million; and, through the mother of Mr. Belgrave, you intended and expected to obtain possession of it, even at the sacrifice of the young gentleman's life."

"You wrong me, Captain Ringgold; I never had any such intention or expectation," protested Scoble.

"Your conduct can be explained in no other manner. You deceived the lady you call your wife, for you represented yourself as an honest man, of good family, and an honorable gentleman; and you are none of these. The marriage was fraudulent, and in due time will be so declared by the courts."

"I claim to be an honest and honorable man," added Scoble rather tamely.

"After stealing sixty or seventy thousand dollars from those who trusted you?" demanded the captain indignantly.

"I had no intention to steal that money; my stepson robbed me of the whole of it, or I should have restored it to the owners."

"It was restored without your assistance. There are warrants out for your arrest now. But I will not argue this question. I wish only to tell you the news you have not heard, in the hope that it will save Mrs. Belgrave from any further persecution on your part. The missing million, or rather nearly double this amount, was found by Mr. Belgrave himself, and it is all securely invested by his trustee at the present moment; and this steam-yacht was purchased out of his fortune, mainly to recover possession of his mother, and then to make a voyage around the world for the young gentleman's instruction and amusement."

"Do you say that the missing million has been found, Captain Ringgold?"

"That is the fact; and it is well known in Von Blonk Park and in New York."

The expression on the face of Scoble fully revealed the effect upon him of this intelligence. He gazed down upon the deck in silence for a few moments; but he was not willing to receive this declaration, though he could not doubt its truth, as a death-blow to his hopes. His brow began to wrinkle into frowns that betrayed his wrath, and he clinched his fists, as though he had no intention to give up the battle.

"In regard to the missing million, as you call it, I have no interest in it, and it does not concern me. You slander me when you say that I have been struggling to obtain it, either by fair or foul means. Let that rest where it is. My quarrel with—with Louis Belgrave is because he has falsely and wickedly prejudiced his mother, my wife, against me; has caused her to repudiate me. I have been gentle with her from the moment she came on board of the Maud, trying by kindness to win her back. Now hear me, both of you! Maud Belgrave, as she was when we were united, is my wife! I will follow her and her son all over the world, if need be, to reclaim her. I tell you I will have her! If Louis Belgrave comes between her and me, I will strike him down like a dog, as any man in my situation would be fully justified in doing! Louis, beware! Your million shall not save you from the wrath of a wronged husband! I have nothing more to say, except to be shown into the presence of my wife."

"You cannot go into her presence on board of this steamer!" interposed Louis.

"Bangs, conduct this man and the mate of the schooner to the after cabin," added Captain Ringgold. "If he or the other makes any trouble, lock them into the two staterooms. Williams will go with you, and both of you will remain on watch in the cabin. If either of them is turbulent, report it to me."

The two seamen who had proved themselves to be brave fellows in the first cutter obeyed the order, and neither Scoble nor Frinks deemed it prudent to resist it, especially as the captain of the schooner had already been knocked down by Bangs. The two seamen and Kimpton were taken to the forecastle and treated with the utmost kindness by the officers and sailors.

"That is a very obstinate and wicked man, Mr. Belgrave," said the captain.

"I have no doubt he will make it hot for me if he gets a chance. But I must go down into the cabin to see my mother. I wish you could come with me, captain," said Louis, when Scoble had disappeared at the gangway of the after cabin.

"It is not prudent to attempt to get into the port of St. George with the weather as it is now, and we may not get in before to-morrow. I have given the order to stand to the eastward and southward," answered the captain. "This is not a very heavy gale; and, though it is lumpy, we are all right, and I will join you in the cabin in a few minutes."

CHAPTER 37
JOHN SCOBLE'S ANTECEDENTS

WHEN LOUIS WENT INTO the cabin, he found his mother, Mrs. Blossom, and Felix seated on a divan which surrounded the mainmast. Mrs. Belgrave extended her hand and drew her son to a place by her side, embracing him again as she had when she first saw him. Her first question was in regard to Scoble, and she was informed that he was on board of the steamer.

"Sparks," called the owner; and when the steward appeared, he inquired if the door leading from the main to the after cabin had a lock and key.

"There is a lock, but there is no key in the door, sir," replied the steward.

"But I have the key to the lock, Mr. Belgrave," interposed the chief steward, who happened to be within hearing.

"Will you please to lock that door, and keep it locked all the time, Mr. Sage?" added Louis.

"What is that for, my son?" asked Mrs. Belgrave, scenting some danger she could not discern.

"John Scoble and Frinks are in the after cabin, into which that door opens; but they are confined to their staterooms, with two seamen on guard over them. You are in no danger whatever, my dear mother," replied Louis, pressing the hand, he held to reassure her.

"I am not afraid, Louis; I am not as timid as I used to be. But everything here astonishes me, my son. You order these people about as though you were perfectly at home here," continued Mrs. Belgrave.

"I am perfectly at home here, and I wish you to be as much at home on board of this steamer as I am," replied the owner with a cheerful smile; and for the first time in a week the millionaire at sixteen felt perfectly happy, for he had his mother with him on board of the magnificent steam-yacht.

"He ought to be entirely at home, Mrs. Belgrave, for your son is the sole owner of the steamer," interposed Captain Ringgold, who came into the cabin in season to hear the last remarks.

"Louis the owner of the steamer!" exclaimed Mrs. Belgrave. "How can that be possible?"

"When the mate of the Maud played us that trick, and thus got rid of us, he had won the fight for which he crossed the Atlantic, and had you in his possession," the captain explained. "I need not try to tell you how terribly alarmed Louis was when he realized that Scoble had sailed away with you on board of his vessel. Mr. Woolridge's yacht, the Blanche, happened to be at the port where we landed, and Captain Alcorn kindly got under way to assist us in finding you. We cruised all night, but accomplished nothing."

"I was not aware that you or Louis had done anything to find me," added Mrs. Belgrave.

"You did not suppose that I could keep quiet while that man was carrying you off, did you, mother?" asked her son.

"I did not suppose you could do anything."

Louis related all the incidents of the trip on the Phantom, the burning of this steamer, and the escape of Kimptom to the Maud, which had made her way out of the inlet while he was unable to lift a finger to prevent her departure. Captain Ringgold gave the history of the steam-yacht, and explained the theory which induced him to urge upon Uncle Moses the purchase of the vessel.

"But the one thing in my mind was to chase the Maud all over the world if necessary, to get you away from Scoble," said Louis.

"I suppose you have noticed the name of this steamer, Mrs. Belgrave?" added the commander.

"I have neither seen nor heard it," she replied.

"The Guardian-Mother; and I need hardly add that she is named after you, madam."

"I could not call her the Maud after that schooner had had the name;" and Louis explained in what manner he had fallen upon the rather singular name. "You have always been my guardian-mother, and I have always looked up to you as such."

The motion of the steamer was too violent to permit the lady to look over the vessel. The captain had to go on deck, and for another hour Louis talked about the name, and what it meant to him. Then he rehearsed the theory of the commander that the steamer was to be used in promoting his education.

"I suppose Scoble's plans are broken up by the loss of his vessel; but he has doubtless saved all the money he had on board of the schooner."

"He told me that he had a brother in the Bermudas who was very rich, but who had recently been in ill health," said Mrs. Belgrave. "Now you have told him that the missing million has been recovered, he will no longer have any reason for pursuing me."

"I am not so sure of that, guardian-mother. The money has come into my possession in accordance with my father's will; but suppose I should have the measles, be swallowed by a big shark, or be accidentally drowned by falling overboard, to whom would my fortune, including the Guardian-Mother, fall to, as provided by the will?"

"You suggest something horrible, Louis," said his mother with a shudder.

"Scoble has two men in his employ at this moment, Brinks and Kimpton, who would not scruple to commit any crime; and for three years I have believed that Scoble was about as bad as a man could be. Frinks is a rascal, and Kimpton burned the Phantom to enable the Maud to get out of that inlet."

"You frighten me, Louis."

"But we must look these things square in the face."

"Where are these men now, my son?"

"Scoble and Frinks are in the after cabin under guard, and the other men went forward. I suppose Kimpton is one of them, though I have not looked them over."

At Louis's request Mrs. Belgrave and Felix McGavonty related the incidents of the voyage of the Maud, till the time she was wrecked. As she had stated before, Scoble had treated her with great kindness and consideration as a rule, for his object was to win her back to him. In the morning she had permitted him to take the money from her room to pay Frinks.

The "fiddles" had to be put on the tables for lunch, and when it was ready the captain was called. It was hard work for the party to keep in their seats, and harder still to prevent the dishes from dancing hornpipes. The captain predicted a change of wind before night which would bring better weather. But the sea was rough all the rest of the day, and everybody retired early.

The next morning, as the commander had predicted, the wind came from the west, and it had knocked down the sea. When Louis went on deck he found the Guardian-Mother approaching the cluster of islands that form the Bermudas. A pilot was coming off, and he was soon in charge of the steamer. When breakfast was ready the vessel was at anchor off St. George, as Captain Ringgold had decided not to go to the anchorage at Hamilton, for it was necessary to consider the situation very carefully before a decision in regard to the future could be reached. Louis had recovered his mother. The battle had been fought and won for her.

"You are safe, Mrs. Belgrave; but the chess-board, with all the men on it, is still spread out before us; and in advance of making any move, it is necessary to ascertain what complications beset us," said the commander as he rose from the table.

"What possible trouble can we have now?" asked Louis, more from curiosity than from fear.

"We are now in a foreign port. If Scoble should claim his wife, and resort to legal measures to obtain her, he could give us a great deal of trouble," replied the captain. "I am not a lawyer, and I don't know what he might do. Of course you all wish to see these beautiful islands; but this is not the right season to visit them."

"Then I am in favor of going back to New York, and coming again at a more suitable time," replied Louis. "We have had no chance to enjoy this magnificent steam-yacht, and I should rather be sailing in her than wandering about on shore, even in the beautiful regions we can see from the deck."

"We will leave that an open question for the present. I will go on deck now, and attend to the landing of the shipwrecked party," added the commander as he ascended the grand staircase, followed by the owner.

The second cutter had already been lowered into the water, and the gangway had been rigged on the quarter. Scoble, Frinks, and the three men forward were sent for. The captain and mate of the Maud were escorted to the deck by Bangs and Williams.

"I intend to land you and your men at the nearest shore, Captain Scoble," said the commander.

"Do you intend to land my wife with me, Captain Ringgold?" demanded the late captain of the Maud.

"I do not."

"Then I shall soon be on English soil, and I will ascertain whether or not a man's wife can be taken from him by force," growled Scoble.

"That is simply absurd; no force whatever has been used. If Mrs. Belgrave wishes to land here with you, no one will prevent her from doing so; but she absolutely refuses even to see you, much more to go with you. You propose to resort to legal measures?"

"Certainly I do. I have been hunted and hounded by that boy, who has prejudiced his mother against me, and I shall pursue him to the ends of the earth!" stormed Scoble, with fury in his looks as well as in his tones.

Defeated and overwhelmed in his purpose, the late captain of the Maud went over the side, carrying with him the heavy package he had brought from the wreck, which probably contained all his money and other valuables. He was followed by all his men. Kimpton was still lame in his wounded arm, and he had kept out of sight as much as possible since he came on board of the Guardian-Mother. He acted as though he feared that vengeance might be in store for him for his treachery at "Dolphin Bay;" but Louis did not even speak to him.

The second cutter had gone but a short distance before it was hailed by a boat from the shore, with a man in uniform in the stern sheets. He was a Custom-House official, and having satisfied himself that the cutter contained no merchandise, he permitted it to proceed to the shore. The official then came on board of the steamer, where he was received by Captain Ringgold, who explained that no goods or passengers would be landed from the present anchorage, as the ship had come in principally to land the wrecked party he had seen in the cutter. The official declared that he was obliged to remain on board as long as the steamer was at the islands.

"I shall be very happy to have your company, Mr.———"

"Stockling is my name, captain," prompted the official.

"Captain Ringgold is mine. I hope you will make yourself at home on board," added the commander, as he offered his cigar-case to the officer.

The captain directed Sparks to bring a couple of arm-chairs on deck, and had them placed where all that happened on board could be observed. Then he went to the galley, where he found Bickling at his usual duties.

"Cook, I think you told me that Captain Scoble had a brother in the Bermudas."

"Which it is true I did; and his brother's name which it is 'Enery Scoble, and he kept an 'otel in St. George's."

"Henry Scoble, is it?"

"Which it is, sir."

The commander returned to the shady side of the quarter-deck where he had seated Stockling, and took the other arm-chair placed there. He was very polite to his official guest, who praised the cigar he was smoking. The captain told him about the shipwreck of the Maud, and talked about St. George's, the port where the officer resided.

"Do you know a gentleman in St. George's by the name of Henry Scoble?" asked Captain Ringgold.

"I did know him, sir, for my chum, George Hastings, and I had lodgings at his hotel for a few months; but he is no longer in the land of the living," replied Stockling.

"Then he is dead?"

"Died only about a month ago. He kept a hotel in St. George's, but that was not his chief business," answered the official.

"What was his chief business?"

"It would be hard to tell in full; but he was a dealer in spirits and wines, and was a smuggler and a speculator, as well as a wrecker."

"Then he made money?" suggested the captain.

"Loads of money; and his estate is valued at over a hundred thousand pounds, which he gave by his will to his only brother, taking out five thousand pounds for his only sister. But his brother is a bad man, worse even than Henry; and everybody here is sorry that the money goes to him."

"Why do you say that he is a bad man?"

"In the first place because he abused his wife, and then abandoned her to take care of herself."

"Indeed!" exclaimed the captain, but very quietly.

"Then he enlisted in the army and deserted. He was in the States; but suddenly his letters stopped coming two years ago, and for a year and more Henry has been trying to find out what had become of him."

"You say that John Scoble abandoned his wife in England. Are you sure of your facts in this matter, Mr. Stockling?"

"Am I sure of them? Isn't my chum, George Hastings, the own cousin of Mrs. John Scoble? He told me all about it; and we went to Henry's hotel in order to induce him to do something for the deserted wife."

"Is John Scoble's wife still living?"

"She was living six months ago at Nassau, where she went out as the nurse of a family; but about four months ago George had an answer to a letter of inquiry about her, informing him that she had left the island, and no one knew where she had gone."

"What was the lady's maiden name?" asked the captain indifferently.

"Ruth Hastings. Scoble thought she was rich; but when he found that she had only five hundred pounds he abused her, and then abandoned her."

"That's the whole story, is it?"

"That's the whole of it. Henry Scoble was a widower. He would not help the wife, or do anything to bring his brother to a sense of duty," said the official in conclusion.

Mr. Stockling lunched in the cabin with the party, and was treated as well as the governor of the island would have been. Captain Ringgold decided not to say a word about the important information he had obtained to Louis or his mother. If the facts were as stated, the marriage of Mrs. Belgrave was doubly invalid from the beginning. But it was necessary to prove the facts, and the commander felt that he needed the services of Squire Scarburn. Mrs. Belgrave was alarmed at the idea of legal proceedings in a foreign land, and she insisted upon sailing for New York at once, in which she was warmly seconded by her son.

The pilot had been retained on board; a boat came off for Stockling at a signal, and in the middle of the afternoon the Guardian-Mother went to sea. The principal object of the voyage had been fully accomplished, and perhaps something more, though the commander did not feel full confidence in the statements made to him. The steamer made a quick and smooth passage, and Louis and his mother were supremely happy, quite as much so as though they had been in the new house. Louis was hugged by Uncle Moses when he went into the office, and Mrs. Belgrave and Mrs. Blossom were warmly welcomed.

As soon as an opportunity presented, Captain Ringgold privately stated the important information he had obtained in Bermuda to Uncle Moses. The squire was astounded at the revelation, for it seemed to solve the problem that vexed him and the mother of his ward. Was the information reliable?

"The first thing to be done is to make a thorough investigation of the statements," said he, looking very serious for him.

"Where?" asked the captain.

"In Bermuda first, then in Nassau, and wherever the facts we learn may take us, if it should be around the world," said the squire with enthusiasm.

"Louis insists that you go with us, Squire Scarburn, on our next cruise," added Captain Ringgold, who proceeded to relate all that had been said on this subject, both by the owner and his mother.

"Something has been said before about my going with you, and there was nothing I should have liked better. Now I have a good excuse for doing so. Since you went away, I have agreed to take a partner, an old friend, who is an honest man and a sound lawyer. It will take me a month at least to complete my arrangements; but I will go then," replied the squire, who appeared to be as delighted as a child at the prospect of such a voyage.

It was all arranged, and about the first of December the Guardian-Mother sailed for Bermuda a second time, fitted out for a long cruise, which might extend around the world. Louis Belgrave was still "A Millionaire at Sixteen." The cruise of the Guardian-Mother had been successfully finished in the restoration of the mother of the young millionaire; but those who are inclined to attend him still farther, will renew their acquaintance with him in "A Young Knight-Errant; or, Cruising in the West Indies."

www.ingramcontent.com/pod-product-compliance
Lightning Source LLC
Chambersburg PA
CBHW011444170626
46816CB00008B/2518